EYES OF MORPHEUS

KEVIN D. MILLER

D1263999

Publisher Page
an imprint of Headline Books
Terra Alta, WV

Eyes of Morpheus

by Kevin D. Miller

copyright ©2022 Kevin D. Miller

To order additional copies of this book or for book publishing information, or to contact the author:

Headline Books
P.O. Box 52
Terra Alta, WV 26764
www.HeadlineBooks.com

Tel: 304-789-3001
Email: mybook@headlinebooks.com

Publisher Page is an imprint of Headline Books

ISBN 13: 9781951556846

Library of Congress Control Number: 2022934709

This book is dedicated to my wife, who believes in my writing and supports my career. To my father who surrendered his life to Cancer. And to the victims of Hutchinson-Gilford progeria syndrome.

1

An Unexpected Message

Anguish reflects in the eyes of the young mother—Her child faces certain death. No hope, no future, and no absolution within sight. Her grief breeds desperation.

"Hutchinson-Gilford progeria syndrome, Mr. and Mrs. Carson. HGPS. Children appear normal at birth...even into infancy. But as you've noticed with your son, they mature slower than other children. They develop the characteristic features of the disease. Thin lips, beaked nose, prominent eyes...small chin, protruding ears. They lose their hair and the child's skin ages rapidly. Didn't your family physician explain all this and advise you on your son's condition?"

Mrs. Carson heaves a breath and arches her back. She dabs the corners of her eyes with a moist, ragged tissue. "We...have an appointment to speak to a specialist. But a close friend referred you and suggested we speak to you first."

Mrs. Carson purses her lips and swallows. "Doctor Grace, is there any hope for our son's condition? Please be honest with us. We're willing to consider whatever program or treatment you might recommend."

"Please. Call me Emily. I'm sorry to say there is no cure for your son's condition. And the disease is always fatal. The arteries harden and the child is a high risk for a stroke or heart attack—succumbing by age fourteen. I know this is very difficult to rationalize, Mr. and Mrs. Carson. You both have my deepest sympathies.

"There is encouraging news, however, in the amount of research being conducted on HGPS. But most of the recent breakthroughs only buy an additional two, maybe three, years of life at best."

Emily's throat tightens. An awkward silence often precedes challenging moments like these. Mrs. Carson's face is absent of color except for the tinge of red surrounding her swollen eyelids—Eyes glossy from welling tears. Her husband clenches his jaw. Two-year-old Kyler flashes a smile of pure innocence. His thin lips curl at the corners, revealing several crooked teeth set inside a small palate. He's oblivious to the death sentence life has dealt him. His bulging aquamarine eyes already manifest the grim characteristics of his fate.

"Mrs. Carson...Mr. Carson. They referred you to me not only because I have a background with HGPS patients but also because I offer an alternative solution to your son's dilemma. The Institute of Cryonic Technologies has developed a viable cryonic solution for terminally ill patients like your son. One that offers hope of a future...a cure even. I want to help you...and little Kyler. I hope you will consider the program we offer."

Emily steps around her bulky antique desk and offers Mrs. Carson a clean tissue. The gesture removes the obstacle that separates her from the couple. She slides a chair away from the wall and sits facing them. The young mother's hands tremble. Kyler outstretches a fragile pasty-white hand, veined with delicate purple striations. Her heart twinges from his gentle caress. *Oh my God. He's so precious.*

"Mrs. Carson...the solution we offer your son is to enter him into our *Promise of Lazarus Program*. I know this will be difficult for you to hear, but we would place your son into a state of catatonic sleep until we find a cure for his HGPS. He would remain in a state of suspended animation, semi-frozen, but perfectly preserved and completely alive—waiting for the right moment when he can be awakened and cured. If at any point, should you change your mind, Kyler could be immediately awakened at your request. One of the main differences in our cryonics program is nothing is final about the process."

Mr. Carson rolls his eyes and raises his palms. "Good Lord. You've *got* to be joking. What if the cure takes a hundred years? What then?"

Mrs. Carson grasps her husband's wrist.

"Jeremy, please. What other alternatives do we have, honey? You heard Dr. Grace. Kyler probably won't live past the age of fourteen. We can have another baby. And maybe, Dr. Grace's program will give Kyler a better chance at a new life...a chance he wouldn't otherwise have. When they find a cure, we'll take our baby home."

Jeremy Carson massages his temples and grunts. He clenches his fists and tucks them beneath his folded arms—pursing his lips and shaking his head in apparent agitation.

"Our procedure no longer resembles the former archaic method of freezing a body at extreme temperatures. In those days, the process destroyed brain cells. The residual moisture crystalized and damaged precious tissue. The dehydration process before the freezing process was even worse and delivered tremendous damage to the body's organs. Simply put, the process never worked. It was, in fact, more of a gimmick, a pipe dream sold to the rich and powerful for a frivolous chance at immortality. Unfortunately, Walt Disney won't be returning anytime soon.

"Our process involves a new and innovative type of coolant that preserves all the cells of the human body and fills the lungs with an oxygen-rich fluid. The term *cryonic* has become more nostalgic than accurate. A person is in a relaxed catatonic state but very much alive—almost as if they are in a deep sleep. Who knows what amazing dreams the mind may have in store for a patient in this state? And we have evidence that patients dream while under suspended animation."

Emily pats Mrs. Carson's knee and rises.

"Kyler meets all the requirements of the program. Neither of you needs to decide right now. I can't even imagine being faced with such a heart-wrenching choice. Once again, I want to express my deepest sympathies. Here is my card. I've written my cell number on the back. If you have more questions or want to tour the facility, please call me. I want to help. I mean that. Kyler is a beautiful little boy, and I will do everything in my power to provide him with a chance at a bright future."

Emily slides a stack of paperwork across her desktop. Excruciating pain pierces her temples and shoots along the base of her neck. The papers slip through her hands and scatter across a sterile black-tiled floor. Her face flushes with prickly heat as she gathers the forms and brochures and reorganizes them into a neat stack. Her cellphone vibrates across her desk. She lifts her phone and taps the decline icon to refuse the call. A searing hum resonates inside her skull. Her cellphone slips from her fingers onto the floor. Mr. Carson retrieves the cellphone and lays it atop her desk.

"I-I'm sorry. I've been so clumsy lately. Here. These brochures will answer most of your questions, and I have included the required legal documents as well. Look them over. It will require both of your signatures. You might wish to speak to an attorney. I'm not supposed to advise you like this, but it might be a good idea to obtain legal advice before proceeding."

"Thank you, Dr. Grace...uh, Emily. My husband and I will discuss your proposal and let you know what we decide. We appreciate you taking the time to speak with us."

***

The lights of the Valley of the Sun illuminate across a warm desert floor. A desert painted in brilliant hues of oranges, purples, and cherry by the loving hand of God—all on display outside her twenty-first-floor window. She rubs her temples and pinches the bridge of her nose. The buzz of her cellphone vibrates across her desktop again. She jerks. Her finger delicately runs across a crackled and broken screen. She taps an icon revealing a new text message.

BRANDON - 7:42 p.m. Don't wait up for me, babe. I need to finish up with a client tonight—a nasty divorce. We can talk about everything that has been bothering you lately tomorrow morning. I'm going to take a Saturday off just for you. Hopefully, you will appreciate it. I have some things I need to get off my chest as well. Let's just get it all out in the open, babe. Don't worry about dinner. I'll pick up some chow on my way home.

Her eyes ache—temples throb. *Great. Here comes another migraine.*

She switches off the lights and locks the oaken door to her office. Rows of neon lightbulbs thrum and vibrate above her. Polished floors glint. The tap of her heels echoes along the hallway, adding to an eerie stillness. She wishes she wore flats today—wishes she had an immediate cure for little Kyler Carson.

Through the window of the cryonic lab, several technicians hustle and labor over a neuropod. *What the heck is going on in there?* She swipes her badge across an electronic keypad—the latch clicks.

"What's going on?"

"The alarm sounded in this neuropod, Dr. Grace. The patient's body is convulsing. But we don't know why. And how is that even possible? Isn't she supposed to be frozen?"

Emily logs into the neuropod's data screen and scans through the patient's records. Sharing her thoughts out loud, she rambles and toils to stabilize her patient.

"Hm. It's important to understand that our latest solution allows for bodies to be suspended at a much warmer temperature than the traditional cryogenics of the past. Can you believe they used to take a body to a negative 196 degrees Celsius? It required a dehydration process that destroyed synapsis connections and ruptured cells from the crystallization that occurred. The new solution preserves the tissue without dehydration. It's way more efficient and safer."

Emily leans over the neuropod and uses her palm to wipe away condensation from the neuropod's glass window. She peers inside, observing her patient's condition. The patient's face twitches.

"Mrs. Santini is only the second patient who has had an episode like this. Patients can experience a sensation similar to drowning because of the fluid that fills their lungs during the process. They panic and struggle...kind of like experiencing a panic attack...convinced they aren't getting enough air. As soon as they relax, they're fine. It's a normal reaction. I've returned her to a state of animation. See there? She's already settling down. She'll be fine. No worries. Place the neuropod back into storage."

The patient thrashes inside the neuropod and pounds her face against the window. Blood and luminous violet fluid gush from her nostrils. Emily decompresses the neuropod and opens the door, releasing a hiss of icy steam and frost.

"Hold her down!"

Emily prepares a sedative and injects it into Mrs. Santini's shoulder. She couldn't dodge the flailing fist headed in her direction. The jolt numbs the bridge of her nose and sinuses. Her eyes water and her face throbs. Both technicians gain control over Mrs. Santini's convulsions.

Sedation sets in. Emily seals the neuropod and latches the door. She heaves a breath.

"Dr. Grace? Your nose is bleeding, ma'am."

"Oh...thank you." She dabs her nostrils and upper lip with a Kleenex. A surge of blood soaks the tissue. She pinches her nose to stem the flow of blood.

"Are you all right, Doctor? Do you want me to notify the nursing station?"

"No. Please don't do that. I'll be fine, thank you. Let's keep this incident between us. I'll give Dr. Diaz a quick call and brief him."

"Yes, ma'am. Thank you. I'm so glad you passed by when you did."

"Hi, Eduardo. This is Emily. We had a minor incident with Mrs. Santini tonight. Nothing to be too concerned about. She went into convulsions but responded well to sedation and seems to be okay. I'll have the technicians check on her every hour for the rest of the evening."

"Aye, Em. This is the second time. The two incidences are only months apart. We need to figure out why this happened."

"I'll run some tests tomorrow and see if I can isolate what might have prompted these reactions. I'm thinking both occurrences are only anomalies. We can talk more tomorrow. Have a nice evening, Eduardo."

A pair of metal doors whoosh open. Emily punches the lobby button with a white knuckle. Her heart thumps. Her fists tighten and her palms moisten. The doors close, and panic steals her breath. She squeezes her eyes shut and hums *Manic Monday by the Bangles*. The eighties had the greatest music of all time. It's her happy place for a small space.

A tiny ding relieves her stress and signals the end of the ride. Elevator doors whoosh open, revealing the slate-colored marble tiles of the lobby floor. She heaves a breath then scampers into the lobby. Her head pounds. Tiny white sparklets dance and burst in front of her eyes. Nausea churns and cramps her belly. She braces herself against a neon-lit vending machine—pressing her cheek against the coolness of the glass. She fumbles for loose change in her purse and drops coins into the coin slot one by one.

A can of Dr. Pepper slams into the chute. Her hand quivers, placing two Tylenol capsules on her tongue. She pops the top of the soda can, releasing a spew of cold foamy spray and a loud hiss. "Ah, come on...really? My white blouse. This is going to stain. Why is this happening to me today?" Her knees tremble and buckle giving her no choice but to plop onto a nearby black-leather lounge chair.

"Emily? Are you all right, girl?"

Never underestimate the calming effect of a friendly voice and a familiar face.

"Oh, hi, Gabs. Thanks. Yeah, I think so. It's just been a really, really...*really* long day."

She raises the half-empty soda can. "And then *this* little thing happened."

"I keep telling ya you need a vacation, girly. Get out of this heat and find a nice beach. Sip margaritas...check out the ripped beefcakes... ya know what I mean?"

Emily sighs. "Yes, I do. Maybe I should rent a bungalow with an ocean view in the middle of the Arctic, where nobody would come looking for me?"

"Wow. That's not what I had in mind, but..."

"And if that weren't enough, Brandon took tomorrow off so we can spend our Saturday going round and round while he presents his arguments to *the court.* I have no idea which Brandon will show up. The gaslighting narcissist or the sloppy couch potato. I am not really looking forward to talking to either one. I want my marriage to work, Gabby. I want a baby. A family. Is that too much to hope for? I mean, seriously. I just don't know if Brandon can man up. We used to be so good together...I miss that." She sighs.

"You don't look so good, girlfriend. Why don't you leave your car here and let me give you a ride home? Okay? I'm leaving now...It's not a problem at all. We are way overdue for another girl's night out, Em. You've been working way too many hours, and I am bored out of my mind with this lab job. If I have to test one more stool sample, I'm going to pull my hair out."

***

"Thanks again, Gabs. I appreciate the ride. Have yourself a wonderful evening. I'm going to slip into a nice hot bubble bath with a cool glass of Viognier and close my eyes. Maybe I'll drown myself or...swallow a bottle of pills. Who knows?"

"Well, as long as I see you Monday morning, you can do whatever you like, chick. Call me. Okay?"

The inside of Emily's purse buzzes as she edges along the walkway toward her front door. She fumbles through its contents before grasping her cellphone.

"Hello? This is Dr. Grace. Hello?" She sighs. *Hm. I wonder whose number is this?*

She flops onto her porch swing near the front door. The rusted chains suspending the swing creak in protest. Her high-heels thump, one at a time, onto the wooden porch. Warmth rushes into her tingling feet and toes. "God, that feels so much better."

Her finger trembles. She taps the voicemail icon.

"Hello, this message is for Dr. Emily Grace. This is the Papago Lab Corporation calling with the test results of your recent physical and screening. You need to contact us immediately. We do not wish to alarm you, but you need to consult with your family physician as soon as possible. Thank you, and have a wonderful evening."

2

AN UNCERTAIN FUTURE

Emily sinks cross-legged into her down-filled oversized armchair. She smashes a pillow into her lap as a layer of protection, anticipating the looming debate. A sip of warm Jamaican Blue Mountain coffee soothes the rasp in her throat—the earthy aroma unravels frazzled nerves. Her temples pulsate. But the migraine has subsided—for now at least. Her eyes focus on the fractured screen of her cellphone. *I really need to get this fixed. Ugh.*

Brandon stumbles into the kitchen. His hair looks like the cat sucked on it all night. A faded-blue terrycloth bathrobe hangs half-open, revealing a soft hairy gut and a layer of flab where rock-hard abs once resided. *I always hated that robe.* After fumbling through the cupboard, he fills a mug with her homebrew. He sips cautiously. His pale-green eyes squint like a cat fixated on her nose. Plopping into the center of their white sofa sectional, he stretches his pasty-white legs and tanned ankles. He sighs.

"I'm all ears, babe. All yours today. So, what's up?"

"What's up? Seriously, Brandon? I'm trying to figure this all out. Why I never see you anymore. We don't talk. We don't spend time together like we used to. When was the last time we did something crazy together or went somewhere fun? What's happened to us? You never even...tell me you love me anymore."

He scratches the nape of his neck. "I'm trying to run a law firm, Em. That requires work, dedication and a lot of effort. And it isn't like you're home all the time either, *Dr. Grace*...all your late nights and weekends out saving the world..."

He squints. "What the hell happened to your nose?"

"I know. I know I've been working a lot of late hours. I do. But it's time, Brandon, that we...discuss starting a family. We've been married nearly eight years now, sweetheart. We're not getting any younger. I want a baby. I want *your* baby. I need that. *We* need that."

"Here we go with the *baby* thing again. We've gone over this a thousand times already, babe. I'm too old to have kids...you're too old. You need to accept that fact...Uh, do you want to put some ice on that? It looks painful."

"No...my nose is fine, thank you. I'm thirty-three years old, Brandon. You're only thirty-eight. So, what the heck are you talking about? We are *not* too old to have a child. What's actually going on here? Please be honest with me. What am I supposed to do? What do you want from this marriage...from me?"

Brandon slides his feet onto the floor, setting his coffee mug onto a glass tabletop. He steeples his fingers, pressing the tips of his index fingers to his lips. He slowly lowers them—pointing at her. His eyes narrow over a crooked and seemingly cocky grin.

"All right. Honesty is what you want? Let me give you some honesty, babe. You're boring. You have no sense of adventure... no spontaneity. I always have to be the one to initiate sex. I want a divorce. I want out of this marriage. I'm not in love with you anymore. So...how's that for honesty?"

His words are a gut punch, stealing all the air from her lungs. A sickening revelation tingles through her nervous system— traveling along her spine. Anger. Betrayal. Both emotions rise within her throat and reach her lips. Her voice quivers.

"Why? When did this happen, Brandon? How long have you felt this way? Is there someone else? Are you seeing someone else? Tell me. Who is she? Huh?"

He stands. Nonchalant. Emotionless. He sips his coffee, then frowns. Eyes cold, lacking emotion. Lower lip protruding.

"There *is* someone else. It just happened while you were away focused on your career and all those guinea pigs you're bent on saving. You weren't around, okay? I can't help it if other women are attracted to me. I was lonely. This is *your* fault."

He shrugs and cocks his head. He turns and strolls toward the kitchen. Her mug crashes into the back of his head. Shards of glass explode, and coffee spews through the air. He stumbles forward, catching himself on the kitchen counter. Blood and coffee mix with his salt and pepper hair.

"What the *fuck*?!" He spins and faces her—his right palm cradles the back of his head. "Are you kidding me? Are you some kind of psycho? Always with the temper, Emily. Why the *hell* would you do something like that?"

"Because! You're an asshole. *Get* out! Get out of my house." Tears stream down her cheeks.

"I've already moved my things out of your house, Emily. Haven't you noticed? No, you wouldn't have, would you? You're never home. And you're right. This is *your* house. It was never *our* house. It was always your *daddy's* house...with all your *daddy* issues to go along with it."

He wets a dishtowel under the kitchen faucet and presses it against his scalp, wincing as he dabs.

"I'm going to pack the last of my things, and then I'm *gone*."

"Good! Don't ever come back...you cheating bastard. I never want to see your disgusting face again. Or that ridiculous robe. Why don't you burn that nasty...pukey...ugly thing? And do some sit-ups while you're at it, Adonis. Ever consider a tanning booth? How could you do this to me? How could you do this to us?"

Brandon stomps up the staircase. Moments later, a door slams, and he stumbles down the stairs carrying a suitcase in one hand and a golf trophy in the other. He pauses.

"I'll be in touch, Em. I already have the divorce papers drawn up. You just need to sign them. I'll be fair. Hopefully, you'll be just as fair with me, babe."

"Stop calling me that. I always hated it. Get out. And take your stupid trophy with you. Wow. Third place. Aren't you so proud? You were never good at sex. You were only good at pleasing yourself. How's that for honesty?"

The door slams. The tires of Brandon's Ferrari squeal as he pulls out of the driveway and speeds away and out of her life.

Her eyes blur. Warm tears soak her cheeks. She wipes them. She refuses to cry for him. He doesn't deserve her tears. Her teeth bite hard into her lower lip. She yanks the wedding ring from her finger. It clinks across the Spanish tile of her kitchen, bouncing off the wall before spinning and coming to rest near a garbage can. She plugs her cellphone into a wall socket near her chair. Plush, soft fur brushes against her calves. Soft purring vibrates along her skin. Her Siberian glances up at her. His crystal-blue eyes seem puzzled behind soft mews. She scoops him into her arms. His furry body is warm, and his nose is cold and wet against her kiss.

"It's okay, Rexy. I'll find you someone new to torment. We don't need him around here anymore. *Right*?"

Every step of the staircase creaks beneath her feet. She enters the empty silence of her bedroom and allows her silken robe to fall off her shoulders. The rush of water splashing across the floor of a stone-tiled shower interrupts the silence. Warm water pours over her face and streams along the nape of her neck—traveling along her spine—swirling around her legs. The trickling sounds of the drain beneath her feet combine with swirling clouds of hot steam, sedating her thoughts and numbing her broken heart.

***

She dabs her long, thick coffee-brown hair with a soft thirsty towel. A swipe of deodorant burns the fresh-shaven skin of her armpits. *Thirty-three isn't old. Is it?* Her legs still look great—sleek and muscled. The legs of a dancer. Sure, her stomach isn't so flat anymore, but her crow's feet barely show. Maybe her boobs aren't as perky as they once were, but hey...at least they're real. She swipes her hand across the bathroom mirror and stares deep into her coppery eyes. Eyes reflecting pain and betrayal.

She slips into her nicest pair of Ralph Lauren black leggings. Sporting a white tank top, sports bra, and a brand-new pair of gray Pumas, she bounces down the stairway headed for the front door. Tunnel vision envelops her. Her legs buckle, driving her knees into the carpeted floor. The inside of her head buzzes, and her ears thrum. *Don't pass out. Breathe...just breathe.*

She crawls across the floor and slithers into her chair. Glittery sparkles flash and float in front of her. The brightness of the room forces her eyes to slam shut. She peeks, squinting. Fumbling with her phone, she yanks the cord from the wall. Phone numbers blend in and out of focus. She taps the phone number for the Papago lab. Resting her cellphone on the arm of the chair, she taps the speaker icon and slinks into the cushions.

"Papago Lab Corporation. How may I direct your call?"

"Uh...hi. This is Dr. Emily Grace. I'm returning a call from yesterday. I believe my results are available from my lab work."

"Of course, Dr. Grace. Let me connect you."

"Hello, may I have your name and address, please?"

"Yes. My name is Dr. Emily Grace. I live at 4832 North Desert View Lane in Phoenix, 85018."

"Thank you, Dr. Grace. Your lab results require me to advise you to contact your primary physician immediately. You will need to consult with your doctor to go over the results with you."

"Okay. That doesn't tell me anything. Why can't you provide me with the results?

"I'm sorry. I really am. But that information needs to be communicated to you by your family physician in person."

"I *am* a physician...a neurosurgeon. I scheduled these labs myself. You can share the results with me. I know how to interpret them. Why all the mystery?"

"Ma'am, I'm sorry. It's against policy..."

"I understand. Can you put your supervisor on the line, please?"

"Um...sure. Can you hold?"

"Hello, Dr. Grace, this is Dr. Reyes. How can I help you?"

"Hi, Dr. Reyes. I just want to hear my lab results. Can you please read them to me? If it's as bad as your office is making it sound, I'm not sure I have a lot of time to waste."

"Dr. Grace, it would be best to discuss this with your family doctor. But...I realize you *are* a doctor. So, I'll make an exception here. Are you sitting down?"

"Okay, now you're making me nervous. *Yes*, I'm sitting."

"The results of your labs and your MRI show a large tumor on your brain. Have you been experiencing headaches? Particularly in the morning? Any nausea, fainting spells?"

"Yes. I-I have. Go on...please."

Dr. Reyes sighs. "This tumor is fast-spreading. It's malignant. An ATRT spreading to your spinal cord. It's advanced. Time is of the essence, Doctor. You're a neurosurgeon and certainly understand the stakes. Contact your family doctor and arrange for treatment immediately. To be honest, Doctor, the prognosis doesn't appear favorable. With a tumor this advanced, you might be looking at months...even weeks. I'm very sorry. I'll have my staff email the test results to you right away."

She disconnects the call. Her cellphone slips through her limp fingers, thumping onto the carpeted floor. She curls into a ball, trembling. A pillow muffles her wails. She pounds her fist into the arm of the chair—over and over—burying herself and her sobs into the comforting softness of the cushions—hiding herself and her grief from the world and its cruel realities.

3

Winter's Dreams

She slept the entire night. She hadn't cried herself to sleep like that since she was a young girl. Well, at least not since daddy died. Beams of amber and gold streak across the kitchen counter, illuminating the room with soft, filtered light. Hell, she might as well go for a morning hike. She's still dressed for it. She tucks her keys and cellphone into a fanny pack and fastens the plastic buckle around her waist.

The early morning air is dry. Gentle gusts of warm breezes carry a lingering scent of earth and sage. It's a comfortable eighty-two degrees but getting hotter as she makes her way along a gravel path leading up the side of a mountain behind her home. The desert is tranquil. A typical Sunday morning in late June. The crunch of sand and rocks beneath her shoes are the only sounds along the worn desert path—other than an occasional screech of a hawk.

A brisk hike on her favorite trail clears her mind. Nature has a way of returning balance to life. Obsessive thoughts and negativity melt away, replaced by peacefulness and a softening of her spirit. It reduces rumination levels and subgenual prefrontal cortex neural activity, which, as everyone knows, helps prevent mental illness.

What is she going to do? Face a ninety percent or more chance she won't survive her cancer or whatever barbaric treatment is available these days? Who will take care of her patients? It's up to her to ensure they have a second chance at life in the near or distant future. After all, they depend on her. Their lives, their futures, their hopes and dreams are all in her hands.

What are the chances of her having a child? It's all she has ever wanted. Her marriage is in ruins, and her cancer has turned that dream into a late-night horror flick. How could Brandon do this to her? Now, of all times. She's alone. Alone, to face the worst fears of her entire life. She's spent a career and her life's work giving hope to terminally ill patients, promising them a chance of a new life—a new future. Maybe the hopes and dreams she's sold to her patients might be her only salvation. How deeply does she believe in the program she created?

A petite wrought-iron bench encircles a Palo Verde tree, which provides ample shade from the intense Arizona sun. She plants herself on the bench and scrolls through her phone contacts. The hot metal heats her backside, forcing her to stand.

"Eduardo. It's me. Emily. Can you meet me at the office in a couple of hours? Say, around nine o'clock?"

"Emily? It's Sunday. We don't work on Sunday. You need a vacation, Chica. You're spending way too many hours at work. What is so urgent that it can't wait until tomorrow, huh? I was dreaming I was in Cabo on a white-sand beach...checking out the...tourists. You messed that up, girl."

"I need to talk to you, in private. It's not about work, really. It's...just important. Please?"

"Aye, Mija. I'll meet you there at ten sharp. This better not have anything to do with work. You know I wouldn't do this for just anyone."

She scrolls through her contact list and taps her speed dial.

"Brandon? It's Emily. I'll sign your divorce papers. But I need you to sign something for me first. Can you meet me at the house in thirty minutes?"

***

"How long have you been waiting outside my office, Chica? Don't you have better things to do on a Sunday? Like buying new shoes, taking a nice siesta, or maybe getting a new hairdo?"

"What's wrong with my hair?"

"Nothing. I'm just saying. There are more important things to be doing on a Sunday other than coming into work, gringa. Go to church. Pray to the Blessed Virgin. Do some gardening or something."

Eduardo pushes open the door to his office and gestures for her to enter.

"After you."

He grunts as he squats and sinks into a worn leather chair, folding his hands behind his head. His bushy gray unibrow lowers in unison with a disgruntled frown—a fat lower lip protrudes beneath a thick salt and pepper mustache.

"Okay. Out with it, Emily. What is so darn important that you had to drag me into my office on a weekend? I had a nice warm pot of menudo and a six-pack of Bud Light waiting for me at home by the pool. I *need* my weekends, Em. So, do you, girl.

"You work too hard, Emily. You spend way too many hours inside these walls. Your work is important, yes, but you can't save all these people. All we do here is offer an alternative solution to their dilemma...and we sell them a bit of hope. But in the end, we don't know how it's going to work out. You need to live your life outside your office. Take a vacation. Have some fun. Loosen up and pull that stick out of your nalgas."

"I have an Atypical Teratoid Rhabdoid Tumor. An ATRT. It's spreading fast. It's too advanced and too late for surgery. I don't want to go through chemo or radiation, and I don't want to die." She crosses her arms and frowns. A cramp at the base of her throat prevents her from swallowing.

Eduardo leans forward, placing his palms on top of his desk. His eyes widen. He slowly shakes his head.

"Oh, Mija, Mija. How could you not know something like this was wrong with you? You, of all people. We need to get you into treatment immediately."

She sniffles. "I-I guess I knew all along. I just don't have time to be sick. I finally ordered a battery of tests, and the results came back yesterday. I just can't go through treatment, Eduardo...I can't. We both know there's no point. My prognosis is hopeless."

"Ah, but there *is* hope. With surgery and chemo and..."

She cuts him off by sliding a stack of documents across his desk.

"All the paperwork is complete and signed. I've given you Power of Attorney."

"You have time, Emily. You're young. Strong. You can beat this."

She lowers her head. "I'm afraid I'll wake up tomorrow and not want to beat this. I want to go to sleep. And when I awaken, I want to be cured. Maybe I can start my life over. I can fall in love again and have a baby and a family of my own. I can save my patients and continue my work—especially with the children. Please, Eduardo. Help me do this. Help me sleep until the day comes when I can be revived and cured. This is the promise we offer our patients. I believe in our work. Please..."

He sighs and shakes his head. "Ay-Yi-Yi. All right...all right. We'll begin preparations tomorrow. Go home. Think long and hard about this. Take a shot of tequila...or two. And at least sleep on it, okay?"

"I don't need to sleep on it. I've already decided. There is nothing for me at home anymore, Eduardo...nothing left for me to do in this life but to die."

Eduardo rises from his chair and opens his burly arms to her. The gesture bursts the dam of emotion within her heart. She buries her face in his chest and sobs.

***

The process is surreal from this point of view. Emily has overseen hundreds of these procedures—never paying full attention to each step. It's a matter of following the protocols. The warmth of Eduardo's hand calms her shivering. He'll take good care of Rexy.

"Mija, I will personally oversee your case, I promise you. You will get the best of everything, and you will always have my full attention. I have a special unit prepared just for you. Are you absolutely sure you want to continue?"

She nods. She shivers. Her eyes close. Claustrophobia is going to be an issue. She wriggles and squirms, attempting to find an angle of comfort. *Deep breaths. Don't panic. You got this.* She pants, her heart thumps with the rhythm of a bongo as the neuropod fills with icy fluid—a chemical solution she developed herself. She kicks and punches the acrylic shell entombing her. Full panic mode now. *Oh, God! This is what I do to my patients? Is this what Mrs. Santini had to endure the other night?*

Sedatives take effect. Muffled sounds, clicks, buzzing, and humming fade. A strange calm overtakes her body. It isn't painful. Her body seems cold, but her shivers have subsided. Breathing slows, and her heart palpitates. Swirls of ebony mixed with deep violet hues engulf her and sweep her away into a chilly, rotating vortex.

4

A NEW WORLD

Filtered light entering through the crackled opaque glass of a small window radiates off the cream-colored walls surrounding her. Crisp white sheets and a tan blanket warm and comfort her body. A down-filled pillow cradles her head. Music emanates through the walls like the tranquilizing sounds of wind chimes overlaid by electronic blips and a low continuous hum. Her mouth is as dry as cardboard and tastes like wet straw. *Where am I? Am I dreaming this?* Is her brain concocting some grand illusion? Something must be wrong in the relationship between her brain's frontal lobe and the sensory cortex—potential evidence that her patients do dream. The room warps. Walls focus, then fade. A veil of blackness drops like a curtain across an empty stage.

***

A voice echoes in the distance. "Wake up, Emily. Time to take your temperature and medication."

Muddy swirls of whites, grays, and blacks morph and materialize into the image of a face. *I'm still here?*

"This device will take your temperature and read your vitals. It won't hurt, I promise."

A woman in khaki scrubs touches Emily's left ear with a tiny probe.

"Who are you? Where am I?"

"Let's save your questions for the doctor. He'll be in to speak with you shortly. He'll be very pleased you are awake. It's been a long journey for you, Dr. Grace."

"Journey? From where? What do you mean?"

"Rest. Don't stress. The doctor will be in momentarily to brief you."

Her grimace splits the dry, delicate tissue of her lips. A new metallic taste now resonates across her teeth. Objects in the room blur, then return to focus. A distinctive scent lingers. The air seems pure—like one of those oxygen stations at the mall—but mixed with an odd combination of strawberry soda and iodine. A soft hum resonates from the equipment attached to her—like the droning of an airplane cabin—adding to the room's serenity.

Have I been revived? Am I cured? Her temples are no longer throbbing. Her eyes no longer ache. She can contract muscles in her thighs she hasn't flexed since high school. This is all so confusing.

A green light flashes above the entrance to her room. The door clicks and opens. This must be the doctor. Hopefully, he'll have all the answers to her questions.

"Dr. Grace. What an honor it is to meet you and help you integrate back into modern society. I'm sure you have a thousand and one questions for me. First, please allow me to introduce myself. My name is Dr. Roland Steinburg. I have been the director of this institute for the past twelve years."

"What's happening to me?"

"One step at a time, Dr. Grace. May I call you, Emily?"

"Um...sure. Of course."

"Emily. The things I am about to share with you will shock and confuse you. Maybe even upset you. So, I am going to go slow and start at the beginning. Let me finish briefing you, and then I can answer all your questions. Fair enough?"

"Uh, yeah, sure. Please continue."

"As you already know, you paid to have your body entered into one of our cryonics programs years ago—the summer of 2021. You might not recall the full details, so I'm going to provide you with a brief history, then attempt to explain to you your current situation and welcome you to your new life.

"They diagnosed you with an ATRT tumor inside your parietal lobe that spanned to your occipital lobe. It was aggressively growing toward your spinal cord. The prognosis was fatal—one to three months max. You entered the very program you created—which is why it is my honor to be sitting here talking with you.

"Dr. Eduardo Diaz managed your case until his death in 2042. For years he oversaw and maintained your suspended animation with the utmost care. He employed only state-of-the-art neuropods and storage units for your case. He was *highly* protective of you, I understand."

She gasps. "How long have I been under?"

"Let me finish, and then we shall address your questions, Emily. Please."

"I-I'm sorry. Continue."

Dr. Steinburg sighs. He slides his spectacles to the end of his nose and peers over the lenses—he crosses his arms and sits on a leather lounge chair across from her.

"Nine years ago, we had a breakthrough in cancer research. Cancer is now a disease of the past, much like polio and smallpox. At that point, we strategized how to remove your tumor and eradicate the cancer cells throughout your body. The process was slow. We had to take the utmost precautions. After thirty-four months of treatment, you became one-hundred percent cancer-free.

"The next step in the process was to petition the courts to allow us to schedule you for a complete revival and recovery from your cryonic coma. After several years, we received the needed approval from a judge and...here you are.

"Before we can release you, we will need to complete a full barrage of tests and a complete physical—routine, I assure you. You are the oldest patient ever to be revived, Emily—meaning the earliest patient suspended cryonically to arrive at this point. We will schedule you for a follow-up exam after your release. No need to worry about the details."

Dr. Steinburg removes his spectacles. He neatly folds them and places them on a nightstand next to her bed.

"Allow me to answer your questions now. We may not be able to answer them all at once, but I'll take your most concerning ones first, and we'll go from there."

She slides her body upright, bracing her shoulders against the wall and smashing a pillow into her lap. She heaves a breath and hugs her pillow.

"How long have I been under? What year is it?"

"Eighty-seven years. Welcome to the year 2108. Take a deep breath now. Relax. Breathe in slowly...exhale. That's it."

"Oh my God...my God. I made it. What am I supposed to do? Where do I live? Where do I work?"

"Well, there's some good news regarding all of that. Dr. Diaz made sure he kept you on staff as an employee. With the Power of Attorney you gave him he arranged to have your paychecks deposited into a special bank account in your name. You technically retired in 2058 and began collecting your pension at that point. You also own stock in the company and an old 401K savings account now worth millions of credits. To put it simply, you'll never have to work again. Your ex-husband could not touch any of your assets. I understand he was involved in a fatal car crash three months after your entry into the cryonics program."

"What the hell?" She heaves a breath. The room appears to collapse then expand as if the walls are breathing.

"Calm down, Emily." He hands her an oxygen mask.

She cups the mask over her face, sucking in the purified air—slow and deep—closing her eyes—expecting all this will disappear when her eyes reopen. She lowers the mask and glares.

"Okay...okay. So, who is going to help me manage all this? Who's going to show me around and help me catch up with the past eighty-seven years?

"We have assigned a sponsor to your case, a gentleman around your age who we sometimes contract to help our patients assimilate back into society. The world has changed, Emily, but many things will remain familiar to you. You'll have a lot to absorb and learn, but your sponsor will be there every step of the way."

"Does this sponsor have a name?"

"He does. His name is Mr. Travis McCallister. He'll pick you up in a few days—after all your test results come back. Then you are free to go. You made the right choice years ago, Emily. You have another chance at life. The same chance you gave so many of your patients years ago. Best of luck to you, Doctor. We will see you in a few weeks for your final examination."

"Wait. I still have more questions."

"Another time. I think we've overloaded your mind with enough information for one day. Get some rest, Dr. Grace. You're going to need it. And I think you'll find Mr. McCallister to be... let's just say, an interesting character."

5

The Sponsor

I didn't think there were any real cowboys left in the world. This guy looks like he stepped out of Deadwood, South Dakota, in 1874. Surely, he isn't my sponsor. You've got to be joking. The door was open, so this guy just waltzed right on in and made himself at home. Good thing she already slipped into the clothes the staff laid out for her earlier this morning.

"Morning, ma'am. I reckon I'm your sponsor. Um...that's an interesting outfit. Looks nice on ya. I'll be showing ya around town...helping ya get settled in and answer whatever questions you might have. I'm kind of your guardian angel...your man with the plan, so to speak."

She scoffs. "Guardian angel, huh? Nice boots."

He chuckles. "How's 'bout we get your transition underway, ma'am?"

"Can you give me a minute to brush my teeth?"

He hooks his thumbs inside the front pockets of his jeans and smirks. "Now that's a great idea. Why don't ya do that? I'll wait for ya right here."

He squats on a chair near the door, arms crossed, eyes glancing around the room.

"Uh, make yourself at home, Marshal."

He chuckles and nods.

She pauses—a toothbrush sticking out of her mouth. "Well, at least you have a sense of humor there, partner." She points at him. "Did razors go out of style while I was gone?"

"Ya wanna spit that in the sink over there, Doc? It's kinda running down your chin...looks a bit like rabies."

"Funny. No, that's actually funny."

She spits, rinses, and wipes her face with a hand towel, then tosses the towel onto the bed.

"So, you're my sponsor. There weren't any old ladies available... or fellow doctors?

"Nope. I'm it. Grab your stuff, and let's go."

She huffs and glances around the room.

"Um...okay. I don't have any *stuff*...to grab."

"Well, then. Let's get you out the door, princess. We got a lot to do today...places to go, people to see."

"Princess?" She shakes her head and rolls her eyes.

The hallways of the Institute are nothing like she remembers. They're sterile. White. Like out of a science fiction movie. There's light, but no obvious source. Almost as if the walls themselves illuminate. McCallister swipes a badge over a sensor on the wall. A small cylindrical door opens, revealing what appears to be an elevator. When did elevators shrink? Her heart rate soars. She wipes her palms across her pant legs and sucks in short, quick breaths.

"What the hell's the matter with ya, Doc? See a ghost or something? Here, I'll hold the door for ya."

"No. I-I...uh, just have a bit of a hard time with elevators... with small spaces in general. That's all."

He tugs at his collar and scratches the back of his neck.

"Well, okay...you can thank me later."

He pushes her inside and closes the doors behind them. Her heart pounds into her throat. Blood swishes and pulsates inside her eardrums. She squeals and squeezes her eyes shut. She crosses her arms, burying clenched fists beneath her armpits, and stomps her feet.

"Why did you do that? Please. Please hurry."

"We'll get there when we get there. Now, take a deep breath and don't think about it."

"Easy for you to say, Tex. I can't believe you shoved me in here like prodding cattle into a corral.

Ding. The door slides open, revealing a large planetarium-style lobby.

"Let's go, Doc. Open your eyes. It's all better now...and... you're welcome. No need to thank me."

"That wasn't very nice. We just met and...you didn't even introduce yourself."

"You're a bright little lady. I apologize. Name's Travis. Travis McCallister. At your disposal, ma'am."

"I already knew your name, Mr. McCallister. I am simply making a point. I am not sure I'm looking forward to spending the rest of the day with you... or any other day for that matter. Show me what I need to know, then you can go back to your farm and...and chase fluffy little white sheep in your red long johns and boots and shout, 'Yee-haw' to your heart's content."

"Now that's funny. You make that one up yourself? I'm parked this way. Try and keep up. I don't have all day."

"What the heck is *that*?"

"*That*, Dr. Grace is a modern-day version of a pickup truck."

"Oh my God. It looks like the Oscar-Meyer Wienermobile."

"A what?" He rolls his eyes. "Must be an inside joke. Hop in. And try not to have another panic attack." She scoffs.

The world has evolved. What an understatement that is. The roads are still black with yellow and white stripes, lined with traffic signs. But they're too perfect. Shiny. Everything is immaculate. Sterile. This isn't quite what she imagined all those years ago.

"Our first stop will be to your local bank. Yes, we still have banks, as I learned a few years back myself. They'll take an imprint of your right thumb, and they'll map your left eye. No more credit cards. Moneyless society now. They store all your assets electronically in credits. Your thumb and your eyeball are your new forms of ID. Try not to lose 'em."

"Try not to lose my eyeball and my thumb? Ugh. You're so annoying."

He pulls into the bank parking lot and rolls to a stop near the entrance.

"Good luck. I'll be waiting for ya right here."

"What? You're not going inside with me?"

"Nope. This is all you. There's nothing I can help you with. Go on, now. They'll get ya all squared away in a jiff." He crosses his arms and smirks.

She shakes her head and rolls her eyes. "Okay, Mr. McCallister. I'll be right back. You just...sit there and relax...in your wienermobile."

"No worries. I'll be right here. Call me *Mac*. Mr. is too formal."

"Mac? Your nickname is *Mac*? Like the hamburger? Classic. How silly is that?"

"Time is a ticking, Doc. Best get a move on. Oh, and...ya might wanna button your shirt, there."

She glances at her blouse. The middle button is undone, revealing the white lace of her bra and her full cleavage. She frowns and pulls her shirt closed—buttoning as she marches toward the front door.

She mumbles, "Well, I'm sure your wiener enjoyed that, *Mac*."

"Greetings Dr. Grace. Please follow me."

"How did you know my name?"

"The screener identified you when you entered, Dr. Grace. And the Institute informed us of your visit. Please place your right thumb on the sensor and use your left eye to look into the lens.

"That's it. All done. I suggest you purchase a NERU HG Pro to check your balances and manage your accounts. You are a highly preferred account, Dr. Grace. A V.I.P."

"A NERU HG Pro? Seriously?"

"Yes. NERU's latest holographic computer."

"Great. Thank you."

She stumbles out the door. That took a whole two minutes.

"Well, how'd it go, Doc? You have any funds left in your accounts for shopping? I'm sure you'll be wanting to fill your closet with a truckload of new shoes, clothes and, other girl stuff, right?"

"That's none of your business, Mr. Sam Elliott impersonator. Who dresses you, by the way?"

"Just making chit-chat. And I dress myself, thank you. We'll drop by NERU and pick you up an HG Pro. You're gonna have to learn how to use it though. Then I'll take you to your apartment. The Institute arranged a temporary place for you to stay until you can locate a place of your own. They gave ya thirty days for free. Awful nice of 'em, I'd say."

"Computers are not a problem, Mr. McCallister. Before I became a neurosurgeon, I earned a Bachelor of Science degree in Computer Information Systems from Arizona State University. I became rather proficient as a hacker, I might add.

"Don't tell anyone at the Institute, but I even created a backdoor into their system. In case I'm locked out. Computers became boring, so I switched career paths and earned a Master of Science degree in biology and my doctorate in neurosurgery from Johns Hopkins."

"That's um...some fascinating shit, Doc. This is your place. Experience the Crystal Springs Apartments Lifestyle. Walk through that door over there and ask for your key. I'll be back tomorrow morning at eight o'clock sharp to continue your assimilation back into society and...Why ya looking at me like that? Go on now. It's gonna be fine."

"All right. Here I go. And please stop calling me, Doc. Dr. Grace is appropriate, thank you. I'm sorry, Travis...that scar on your forehead...how did that happen? You didn't get kicked in the face by your horse, did you?"

"Well, bless your heart, darlin'. But I'm afraid *that* is a story that will need to be shared over a couple of beers. It's been a genuine pleasure to meet you, Dr. Grace."

Emily nods and slams the door. She turns to walk away, but the hem of her shirt snags. She purses her lips and opens the door releasing the snag. Her face tingles and flushes warm.

Emily points at him. "Don't. Just don't." Travis smirks and glances in the opposite direction.

Her new apartment awaits. Hopefully, coffee machines haven't changed in the last century. Eighty-seven years to catch up on. Where does one begin?

6

RISING PHOENIX

A pillow and blanket laid across a bristly carpet was a more comfortable option last night than the mini bed. Apartment life has miniaturized in the future. The walls look like panels from a 1990s office cubicle. They compress appliances into a small corner of what should be a kitchen. A compartmental bed, more suited for a child, folds into the wall. And the bathroom? Cruise ships back in the day had larger showers and toilets. Life in an egg carton. Emily stretches and twists her spine, setting off a series of cracks and snaps radiating from her lower back and into the base of her skull. "Ah. God, that's better. Is a window too much to ask for, guys? Really?"

***

Outside, the early-morning air is as arid as bleached bone. A warm breeze caresses her cheeks and tosses her hair about. Her bottom absorbs the heat radiating off the concrete bench she plopped upon. She closes her eyes and inhales. Honk! She flinches.

"Oh! Geez! Okay, now that looks out of place."

"Hey, Doc. Hop in. Sorry for being a tad late."

"Uh, this is a *real* pickup truck, Tex. Where's the Oscar Meyer?"

"I picked you up in my work truck, gal. Should be a bit more familiar to ya. Are ya impressed? It's a vintage 2025 Chevy. Was a

Truck of the Year. They modified it to meet all the environmental standards, and it runs on a litho battery. They turned real trucks into fleets of gutless wonders. But hey...they look like the real thing."

"It um...fits you, Travis."

"Doc, I'm going to take ya shopping this morning. What suits your fancy? New clothes? Nail polish? Shoes? How's about a computer and a new ePhone HG? I wanna take you to lunch afterward. My treat. It's just how I roll."

"ePhone HG? Let me guess. Holographic ePhone."

"You're catching on, Doc. Damn, that ASU degree has really paid off."

"Can you please...just call me, Emily?"

"Sure, thing, Doc. First stop. The NERU computer store."

***

"Doc, I've had about all the shopping I can tolerate. I can't feel my damn foot no more. Gals are built for this. Shopping was never intended for a man. We're hunters. Not gatherers."

"Yeah, I can see that. Men are real pussies when it comes to a lot of things. *Hunters?*...give me a break. What do you think we women are doing when we're shopping? We *hunt* for clothes... *hunt* for shoes. We *hunt* for bargains, Mr. Tenderfoot. I'm sorry, Travis. I just realized you have an artificial leg. That was terrible of me to say. I apologize."

He frowns, then chuckles. "Fair enough. Ya hungry for anything specific?"

"Since you're buying, cowboy, you choose."

"I'm a meat-eater, even though that's a hard commodity to find these days. Give me a good steak and a baked potato to sink my teeth into, and I'm a happy hombre. Ya eat meat? Ya look like one of those prissy-tarians."

"You mean *pescatarian*? I like a good steak myself. Take me wherever you like. Surprise me."

***

"This is one of the last steakhouses left in Arizona, Doc. Cattle herds have diminished, and red meat has become very expensive. The steaks here are as good as all get-out."

She scans the room. The place reeks of rustic ambiance. Western décor right down to the sawdust on the floors. A grungy round table separates them. He removes his stained straw cowboy hat, placing it upside down on an empty chair next to their table.

"Nice hair, *Mac*. Who's your stylist? And why's your hat upside down on that chair? You need tips to pay for lunch?"

He snickers. "It's the proper way to set your hat down, gal. So ya don't mess up the bends on the rim. What are ya having, Doc? A salad, maybe? Or how's about some kale balls?"

He's annoying as hell. Except for that scar across his face, he is rather easy on the eyes, however. Brandon was short. Soft. A typical lawyer. More of a marshmallow. This guy is well over six feet and built more like an athlete. Nice round shoulders. Square jaw. A bit of a dad-gut. *Wonder what his story is? Colorful and obscene, I'm sure.*

"Keep your kale balls to yourself, Mr. McCallister."

"Welcome to The Stockyards. Have you two decided yet?"

"Doc? Ya wanna order first?"

"No. You go first."

"I'll have y'all's special right there. Medium rare and the baked potato with all the slop on the side. Would love a cold Coors as well."

"Miss?"

"Um...you know, I'll have the same. Except I'll do medium for the steak and a glass of white wine. Riesling preferably."

"Thank you. I'll put your order in, folks."

"A wine drinker. Saw that coming."

"Yeah, well, you're fairly predictable yourself there, Wild Bill. Bring your chaps today?"

He snorts. Her quips seem to amuse him. "By the way, here's my phone number. Punch it into your new ePhone when you get home, will ya? Try not to sext me too often, Doc. I need my beauty sleep."

"Ugh. Keep dreaming, buster."

"So, Doc...what's your story over at the Institute? I understand you were in charge of one of the cryonics programs back in the mid-twenties."

"The Promise of Lazarus program was my brainchild. I created it and oversaw all the research and development. Not sure how far it's come in eighty-seven years, but we were on the edge of some major breakthroughs. How about you, Travis? I mean, Mac. What's the story on those boots and that hat? You play guitar? Howl at the moon maybe? I'm just teasing."

"Here are your drinks, folks. Food's coming right up."

Travis nods at the waitress. "Much obliged." He folds his hands. "I do play a little guitar, and I've been known to howl at the moon on occasion."

"Well, I'll bet that's interesting. You'll have to play something for me sometime. Minus the howling."

"Ya know, I was a participant in your program, Doc. Two years after they put you asleep. They woke me up four years, seven months, thirteen days, three hours, and twenty-six minutes ago."

She leans into the table. "*You*...were a patient in the Promise of Lazarus program? You're being serious right now?"

"Yup. I received a near-fatal head wound. Shrapnel lodged deep into my brain, near my spinal cord. Inoperable. I was a soldier. Special Ops. We were on a mission in Syria, and my unit was hit hard in an ambush. Long story. Your program saved my life. Well, sort of."

"What do you mean, *sort of*? You're here, aren't you?"

"Well, if you can call being here a meaningful life. I'm living in 2108, but my heart still belongs to the 2020s. They never asked my permission. I was due to be discharged. They just placed me in the program. If I wasn't unconscious, I would have made some phone calls, pulled some strings. I'd have rather died with my boots on and have them bury me at home than become a frozen meat popsicle inside your program."

"Here are your steaks. Enjoy. Let me know if you need anything else."

"Steak sauce please...and another beer, Miss. Thank you kindly."

"I'd like to visit the Institute and review all the programs they've been working on for the past eighty-seven years. I need to find out how my research ended up. I have so many questions."

"I'm sure ya would. But things have changed. And I don't think they'll allow ya to do that."

"I developed the program. Why wouldn't they?"

"Well, they have a lot of tight security and secrecy surrounding the Institute and all its programs these days. The military has become a full partner. You know that can't be good."

"I want to know the fates of my patients...find out how their cases ended up. Particularly the children's unit. There was a young couple I interviewed...just before I entered The Promise of Lazarus program. They had a two-year-old son with HGPS. I never knew if they entered him into my program or not."

"HG...what? What the heck is that?"

"Hutchinson-Gilford Progeria Syndrome. HGPS. Children grow old at a rapid rate. By the time they're thirteen or fourteen, they have the body of an eighty-year-old."

"Now that's messed up, man. What the hell kind of disease would do that to a child? Are you kidding me? I'd hope by now they have a cure for a disease like that."

"Yes, it's a very sad and cruel disease. Carson. I think their last name was Carson. Kyler was their son. Adorable little guy... had the most precious aquamarine eyes I've ever seen."

"Kyler, huh." He strokes the stubble on his cheeks and narrows his eyes.

"I could probably get ya an appointment. You might want to figure out how to use that NERU HG Pro first before you go poking around in their databases. I'm not a fan of that little turd, Steinburg. All hat and no cattle."

"Sorry to interrupt. Would you both like another drink?"

"Sure. 'Nother beer, please."

"Another glass of wine. Thank you so much."

"So, tell me something, Doc. How can parents be willing to freeze their kids? I don't understand why any parent in their right mind would be willing to take such a drastic step. Seems like complete desperation to me."

"What do you mean? These particular parents were facing a one-hundred percent chance their son was going to die. Why wouldn't they be willing to give their child a chance for a cure? My program gave their son hope of a new life. A chance at a normal life."

"Is that whatcha think? The boy was two years old, you said. He had a good twelve years to spend with his parents, according to your stats—to get to know them and love them. Death is a part of life, Doc. You should know that. Why take twelve years away from the boy and his parents? Why play God with his life?"

"God? Is that what you think we were doing? Playing God? My research...our research was celebrating breakthroughs each month. We were on the verge of saving lives and providing a real future for terminally ill patients...saving children from horrible fates."

"Really? How many did ya save?"

"Well...I don't know. I don't have the data. I'm sure we saved hundreds."

"You're living in a fantasy world, Doc. Most didn't make it. The ones that did were either physically screwed up by the process or were mentally screwed up by being left all alone in a strange world...decades into the future. No families. No friends. Wake up, Doc."

Her teeth grind. Her face and neck twitch. A single bead of sweat trickles between her shoulder blades.

"How do you know this? If you know something about the fate of my patients, then tell me. Tell me what you know."

"All I can say, Doc, is I spend a lot of time around the Institute and Dr. Steinburg. I hear things. I see things. You need to watch your p's and q's around Steinburg and his crew. Don't trust them."

"What are you talking about? What do *you* know? You're just somebody's sponsor. And not a very good one, in my humble opinion. And can you please stop calling me Doc?"

"Ya. Well, I'm sorry to be the one to give you a dose of reality, princess, but maybe you *should* visit the Institute. Check up on your work. See how things turned out. How all those lives ended up. Might even be a tad revealing for ya. Maybe it will give you a fresh perspective on the work y'all were responsible for."

"You don't know what you're talking about. Why don't you stick to milking cows and roping helpless animals into submission?"

"Let me tell you something, Dr. Grace. It beats the cruel experiments you and your cronies inflicted on helpless kids and desperate victims of terminal illnesses, all the while helping your bottom line. Ya think I enjoy being here in 2108? I wish they had given me a choice. I wouldn't have chosen you or your program."

The feet of her chair screech along the floor. She empties her wine glass onto his shirt.

"I'll walk. I don't need your sponsorship any longer, Mac...or Travis, or whatever you call yourself. Thank you for lunch. I-I'm sorry about your shirt."

7

A Rancher's Life

Morning greets Emily and finds her sprawled out across the bristly carpeted floor. All the restless twisting and turning throughout the night has her knees and elbows chafed. She sits upright, pulling her knees into her chest—stretching her cramped muscles and cracking her spine with a single twist of her torso. What did he mean, cruel experiments? How could he know what happened to all of those children? What the outcomes were? *I've got to get into that lab. Travis said he could get me in. But I'm sure he doesn't want to see my face. Maybe Brandon was right. My temper always seems to get the best of me.*

"So, this is the ePhone HG? An earpiece and a mouthpiece? Where's the actual phone? Or the Icons? Hm. Okay, press this red button...Insert the earpiece, and speak. Should be easy enough, right?

"Hello? Um...call someone."

A holographic screen appears across the palm of her left hand. She flinches. "Who would you like to call?"

"Siri? You're alive? Uh...Call, Travis McCallister."

"Yes. I am immortal. If you can call it that. You do not have a listing for Travis McCallister in your contacts. Would you like to add his phone number to your contact list?"

"Yes. The number is 213-522-403-714."

"Added. Would you like to call, Travis McCallister?"

Her doorbell buzzes, followed by gentle tapping. She removes the earpiece and presses the red button, shutting down the holograph. She opens the door two inches and peers through the slit.

"Hey, Doc."

She swings the door wide for him, and then she plops onto a small sofa.

"Hi...Mac. Travis. I can't call you, *Mac*. It's too corny. I keep thinking of Mac Davis, the singer. I thought you were finished with this assignment? I didn't expect to see you today."

"Yes. I am done."

"Travis, I want to apologize for yesterday. I had no right to throw my drink on you. I'm very sorry. I don't normally act so brash. My temper got the best of me and..."

"It's okay, Dr. Grace. I've had worse things thrown on me. And by the way, Mac is a cool name. But you can call me Travis if it tickles your fancy. Ya busy today?"

"I have no plans in particular...other than figuring out this damn computer and cell phone. Whatever happened to Apple?"

"Apple is now NERU. Go on a drive with me. It'll be good for ya. I have something I want to show ya."

"You're not going to kidnap me and leave my body somewhere in the desert, are you?"

"You're always one step ahead of me, Doc. Hadn't occurred to me, but now that ya mention it..."

***

The Arizona desert outside the city has changed little in eighty-seven years. The air is muggy and carries an invigorating scent of sage. Storm clouds boil in the distant horizon. Flashes of light glow inside swollen purple and gray clouds, followed by a clap of thunder. She always loved storms in the desert. Especially when they'd knock the power out and Daddy would light candles around the house and tell ghost stories. He could turn any situation into an adventure. He had a knack for it. Daddy was a simple man, like Travis. She always felt safe with him. He had a presence about him—an aura. Full of life and enthusiasm, and his positivity was infectious. So was his laugh.

"Staying away from the city is the only way to keep your sanity, Doc. The desert has remained preserved for decades. Monsoons still visit the Valley every July and August. Looks like we have a big boob brewing up ahead."

"Big boob? I think you mean *haboob* as in a dust storm. It's beautiful in an odd sort of way, don't you think? I always loved the peacefulness of the desert and the majestic storms. Tall saguaros. The scent of sage. Sunsets bursting with color. Nothing rivals the beauty of an Arizona sunset. Where are we headed, Travis? Should I trust you?"

"It's a little drive north into the pines of the White Mountains. A couple of hours away. Here are some headphones. I have a nice playlist of vintage country music. Alan Jackson, Toby Keith, Johnny Cash...relax and enjoy the ride."

"Country? Wow. What a shocker. How about some classic '80s? Without a doubt, the best era for music in history."

"Yeah, maybe for pussies. Country music lives forever, gal. I'll take George Strait over Boy George any day."

She sticks her tongue out at him and wraps the headphones around her ears. She sinks into the leather seat and snuggles into a comfortable ball.

***

Something jabs her ribs. "Doc. Doc, wake up. We're here."

Branches of tall pines reach into the gray skies surrounding a large rustic ranch house. Cattle and goats mingle in gated fields nibbling on tall grasses. Her feet land in squishy mud. She grips the truck door to steady herself. The air is fresh and piney—moist from the rainstorm she must have slept through. Thick tranquil woods encompass the property.

"Wow. This is gorgeous. You live here?"

"It's my home away from the city. Follow me."

The ranch house looks like a postcard from a novelty store. Its walls are shellacked logs beneath a Kelly-green-shingled roof and a wide porch accented with shrubbery and a lush lawn. It's amazing. The aesthetics already ease her mind and spirit—stimulated brain chemicals doing their job.

"Oh, my goodness. Look at these floors. I love wooden floors. And the western-style rugs are fascinating. Authentic cowhide and bearskins? Wow. Where'd you find these antique tools? I have to admit they work very well as wall decorations. There's hope for you yet, cowboy."

"Thank you, ma'am. I try. Ya like horses? Follow me out back."

"I like dogs...cats...hamsters. Daddy loved horses. He forced me to ride every weekend when I was a kid."

"Any man who loves horses is a good man in my book."

He swings a large wooden door wide, revealing the interior of a horse stable. A pungent odor of ammonia and methane assault Emily's nostrils. Snorts, whinnies, and the sounds of lips flapping echo across the interior walls. She almost expects Daddy to emerge from a stall, leading a horse by its reins and beckoning her. He wore faded Wranglers and a huge silver belt buckle he won at the Payson Rodeo for bronc riding as a young man. He messed up his knee, which caused him to walk with a slight limp. But that never interfered with a good neck ride.

"Horses are a protected species now. Large animals have paid a heavy price because of the politics and policies of so-called environmentalists from years past. I keep nine horses on the ranch. I have three cows, some chickens, and the few goats you saw when we drove in. I have a small garden growing on the side of the stables...Just a few vegetables and a berry patch."

"It's almost noon," Mac said "The bus will be here shortly."

"The bus? Who's arriving on a bus?"

"You'll see. I can use your help today if you don't mind."

"Okay. Sure. But why all the mystery? What am I helping you with?"

Aoooooga!

"You're about to find out. Come on. Let me introduce ya."

She shakes her head. "Was that a horn?"

"Yup. Come on. Let's see who made the trip."

The bus door opens with the swoosh of a vacuum. Automatic steps roll out and stop when they reach the ground. Three children exit the vehicle—all giggles and excitement. Two young girls rush toward Travis, fighting to be the first to wrap their arms around his legs. A young boy hesitates, jamming his fists into his jeans.

"Who made it today? Why it's Delainey, Taylor, and Kyler. Woo hoo! Y'all ready to ride, cowpokes?"

A resounding yes rings out. Emily's heart skips a beat at hearing the excited and precious voices of children. *Oh my gosh. Did I misjudge this man? I'm not about to admit to that. Maybe he's not the complete jackass I thought he was.*

"Okay. I want to introduce you to someone special. This is Dr. Grace. She's gonna be my pard today. Everybody say, 'Hi' to Dr. Grace and make her feel welcome."

"Hi, Dr. Grace."

"Nice to meet you, Dr. Grace."

"Okay. All of you cowpokes introduce yourself to the doc. Give her your name and your age. Ladies first. Delainey?"

"Um...hi Miss...I-I mean, Dr. Grace. I'm Delainey. I'm eight."

"Aw. So nice to meet you, Miss Delainey. I love your cowgirl hat." Tears well, and a lump rises in the base of Emily's throat. Her arms ache with emptiness.

"Hello, Dr. Grace. I'm Taylor and I'm ten years old. I can't wait to ride with you today. Can we go now?"

"Very nice to meet you, Taylor. Such beautiful big brown eyes. I *love* your red boots. Oh, my goodness. I want a pair just like those."

Emily wipes the wetness from her cheeks with her sleeve. The ache has moved from her arms to her chest.

"Go ahead, son. Introduce yourself"

"Oh, who is this handsome little cowboy?" She lowers her voice. "So serious."

"Um...hello, Dr. Grace. It's a pleasure to meet you. I'm nine years old. My name is Kyler. Kyler Carson."

Both her hands cover her gaping mouth as she drops to her knees.

"Oh my God, Oh my God. Kyler? How is this possible?"

She glances at Travis. He's a big blurry mess. She wipes away tears. Travis chuckles and winks.

"Go on, cowpokes. I think Dr. Grace needs a big ole hug. Let's give her one."

The girls scream and giggle, rushing into Emily's arms. Kyler hesitates and remains in the background. Their precious little bodies are covered with the aroma of summer flowers.

"Thank you, Delainey. Thank you, Taylor. I needed those hugs. Kyler? Can I get a hug?"

Kyler shuffles towards her. His head lowers, and his fists remain jammed into the pockets of his crisp new jeans. She touches him under his chin and lifts his eyes toward hers. *No signs of the HGPS. Nothing.* Just a handsome little man staring back at her with two bright aquamarine eyes. She squeezes him and sobs. Kyler backs away and wraps his arms around Travis's leg.

"Who's ready to do some riding?"

Delainey screams, "Me! Me!"

Taylor dances. "Let's go, Mac. What are we waiting for?"

Kyler keeps one hand in his pocket and raises the other—glancing at Travis with one eye squinting.

"All right, let's go saddle 'em up."

***

"Delainey, you got Beanie today. Let's get you up there. Good girl. Take the reins. Let him know who's in charge."

"Hi, Beanie Weenie. I've missed you, big boy."

"Come on, Taylor. You're on Apache. He loves you, darlin'. Jump up. Take his reins. He's a very special horse."

"Aw, I wanted Big Red. But that's okay. I love you too, Apache." She leans forward and hugs his neck.

"Kyler, my boy, you're going to take Ole Bo out today. He hasn't been out in a while and has been asking for ya. Dr. Grace, can you help Kyler up?"

"Of course. Here you go, Kyler."

Travis raises an eyebrow and smiles a crooked smile. "You okay, Doc?"

"I-I'm fine...I think. We have a lot to talk about, Travis."

"Okay. We'll talk later. For now, you got Blondie. She's gentle."

Travis snags a worn straw hat from a hat rack inside the stables and places it on Emily's head. He draws the leather straps to the base of her chin. For a fraction of a moment, his face looked like Daddy's.

"I'm gonna ride ole Jasper. You be nice today. You hear me, Jasper? Don't you step on my toes, boy. Follow me, cowpokes. Dr. Grace, you take up the rear."

Sixteen. That was the last time she'd been on a horse. Daddy took her riding at the White Stallion Ranch in Tucson. They stayed in a western-style bungalow for three days. No TV, no Internet, no cellphone. Just the two of them. They rode out early one morning and ate breakfast in the middle of the desert. In the evening, the staff would ding an old-fashioned dinner bell, and everyone would eat two-inch-thick steaks for supper. It was the best three days of her life.

It was the last time she would ever see Daddy alive. She can't help it. Tears stream along her cheeks. Tears of heartbreak. Tears of joy. Tears of hope. *I miss you, Daddy. God, I've forgotten how much I miss you.* Maybe this is why she shuts out Travis. Because his resemblance to Daddy is a door she isn't ready to open.

The path is well worn. The fragrant scent of pine permeates the air. The tranquility of the moment plays out like a lucid dream.

"How's everybody doing back there? Sound off."

"Good. This is fun."

"Doing okay."

"I'm okay. Can we go fast?"

"How 'bout you, Dr. Grace? How's it going back there? See any bears or mountain cats following us?"

Delainey screams.

"I'm just kidding, Delainey. Don't freak Beanie out again. Remember what happened last time?"

Rhythmic hooves clomp across the soft dirt, mixing with children's giggles. Earthy scents combine with musk, sweat, and leather. The chirps of birds echo across the pine tops. A soft breeze kisses her cheeks and fills her nostrils with its purity. Memories of her teenage years and long rides with Daddy flood her spirit. Daddy would have loved Travis. He'd have hated her ex-husband, Brandon. He'd have kicked Brandon's ass on more than one occasion.

"Yee-haw. It don't get no better than this, cowpokes. All right, let's turn 'em around gang. Take 'em up to a trot and get 'em back home. Time to get us some grub, boys and girls."

***

"Thank you for today, Travis. You have no idea what this day has meant to me."

"Oh, I think I got a rough idea. And...you're welcome. I wanted you to experience this for yourself. Words could have never done it justice."

"Travis. I just now realized. Where's the bus driver?"

"There wasn't one. The bus is driven remotely. Don't worry; it's safe."

Travis hops to the ground and hitches Jasper to a post. He lifts each child off their horse and hugs them before he sets them on the ground.

"All right. Let's eat, cowpokes. Smoked ribs, cowboy beans, corn on the cob, mashed taters, hot buns, and some sweet peach cobbler with vanilla ice cream for dessert. Woo-wee. Mm-mm. How's that for a spread? Follow Dr. Grace to the house, and I'll be right behind y'all."

***

"Doc, can you help me serve up these plates?"

"Of course. Here. Get out of the way and let me do this. Go wrangle something."

Travis, Kyler, Delainey, and Taylor sit around the table staring at her. Travis picks up his fork and winks at the children. They each grab their forks.

"We wanna eat. We wanna eat. We wanna eat..."

"It's coming. What a rowdy crowd. Goodness. Here you are, girls. Here you are, Mr. McCallister. And here *you* go, cowboy. Can I sit next to you, Kyler?"

He raises his head and nods. His eyes glance at her. A slight, crooked smile curls across his thin lips.

"All right, cowpokes. Who wants to say grace?"

Delainey perks up. "I think Dr. Grace should say grace because that's her name."

"Oh, no. No, no. Someone else. Please."

"Delainey, why don't you say grace, darlin'."

"Thank you, Jesus, for this meal and for Big Mac Daddy. Please bless our food and everyone here. And bless Beanie Weenie for being a good boy today. Amen."

Travis grins. "Amen, let's eat."

He must sense her glare. He shrugs. "What?"

"You have the kids call you *Big Mac Daddy*? Are you kidding?"

He winks and cuts into his beef ribs, chuckling.

***

"Doc. Would you mind tucking the buckaroos into bed?"

"Oh. Uh. Sure. I'd love to. Come on, guys."

"And ya gotta tell 'em a story. It's the only way they'll go to sleep."

"Okay. I'll think of something."

Delainey beams. "Okay, Dr. Grace. We're ready. Fire away."

"Delainey, I love your silk scarf. Where ever did you get that?"

"It was my grandmama's. She left it for me when she passed. It's from Africa."

"Well, it's beautiful. Just like you. It makes you look like an African princess."

Delainey giggles.

"Okay, here goes. Once upon a time, there was a beautiful ice princess. She lived in a giant frozen castle. The children in the kingdom would all come to visit her. You see, they were sick and desperately needed her help. She did everything in her power to help them feel better. There was nothing she wouldn't do for them. She had no children of her own, so all these children became *her* children."

Travis enters the room and leans against the wall. He crosses his arms and listens.

"One day, the princess became *very* sick. She couldn't help the children anymore. She had to travel far away to a strange frozen kingdom to find a cure for her sickness. Only then could she find her way back home and help her children. But she lost them all.

"One day a tall prince came along. He was strong and sort of handsome. But he dressed funny, never shaved, and told terrible jokes. Nobody wanted to hear any of his jokes—especially the lovely princess. But he tried and tried. Because deep down, he had a huge crush on the beautiful princess. The day came when the prince took the princess to his castle in a magical forest. There he revealed to the princess that all the children from her kingdom were safe and living in the prince's castle—waiting for the princess to arrive and make them all feel better again. And they all lived happily ever after. The end."

"That...was a *great* story, Dr. Grace. Better than any story Big Mac Daddy ever told us."

"Good night, Delainey. Night, Taylor. Good night, Kyler. Can I kiss you all goodnight?

She hugs Kyler, kissing him on the forehead. Warm tears spill along her cheeks. Kyler pats her hand and closes his eyes. He whispers, "Can I stay here with you forever, Dr. Grace?" She squeezes his cheeks then tucks his blanket beneath his chin. "Yes. Of course, you can."

She shoves Travis from the room, flips the lights out, and closes the door behind her. Travis raises his eyebrows and smirks. She punches him in the chest.

"What was that for?"

"That's for making me cry."

He strolls to the fridge and removes a bottle of wine and a bottle of beer. He snags a wineglass from a rack over the stove.

"Here, Doc. Hold this."

He fills her glass to the rim. "I found ya a nice Riesling, gal... you being a wine drinker and all."

"Travis. Tell me about the children. I need you to tell me *everything* you know."

8

GOD BLESS THE CHILDREN

Emily snuggles into the plush gray cushions of the loveseat—legs crisscrossed—hugging a fat maroon pillow. Travis plops onto the sofa opposite her, grinning and smug. He knocks back a beer and outstretches his muscled arm across the back of the sofa.

"Whose face was that embossed on Ole Bo's saddle?...The horse Kyler was riding? Kind of looked like you."

"Ole Bo was named after my younger brother, Bo. He died in a tragic accident."

"I'm so sorry. What happened?"

"When Bo learned of my condition, he got shitfaced and rode out on his horse in the middle of the night. He ran that stallion hard...So hard he didn't see the tree branch in time. Snapped his neck." He swigs his beer.

"Oh, God. I am so, so sorry. That's awful."

"Yeah. It was awful news to hear. He was a good man. Breaks my heart."

She squeezes her pillow tighter. "Travis...please tell me everything you know about the children. What happened to them?"

Travis leans forward, setting the beer bottle atop the polished wood surface of the coffee table separating them. He wipes his face with his hands and stares at the coffee table. His eyes raise to meet hers.

"I heard there was a problem—a problem with the fluids used in the antifreeze or something. I don't understand the science behind it, but I understand their immature bodies couldn't handle the chemicals. Youths twenty-four years and under couldn't survive the process for more than a year or two. They died eventually."

"Oh my God...my God, no. What have we done? What about Delainey and Taylor? And Kyler?"

"Delainey and Taylor are orphans from *this* era. They live in a children's home in Payson. Kyler lives there as well. Kyler's body was able to tolerate the process. They revived and cured him around two years ago. He's your only child survivor, Em."

"Mr. and Mrs. Carson must have waited several more years before they committed Kyler to the program—after the effects of his disease advanced. They may have saved his life with that decision. Good Lord."

"He's a fine kid, Em. Needs a solid home and someone to love him. He was a shy little cuss when I met him. I've been bringing him, along with the other kids, to the ranch once a month. The horses have been some good ole-fashioned therapy for 'em. It's opened Kyler up a bit and helped him gain some confidence."

"I need to go back to the Institute. Get inside their network and scan their databases. I've got to catch up on eighty-seven years of research. I've got to make this right...somehow."

"They ain't gonna like you snooping around in their database, Doc. Trust me. Not a good idea. You don't wanna get caught poking around in whatever the hell they're up to."

"No, but Steinburg still owes me a lot of answers to my questions. I'm going to visit him tomorrow. Can you give me a ride? Please?"

Travis inhales deep then exhales, flapping his lips like one of his horses. He snatches the beer bottle and guzzles the rest of his brew, belching after the last swallow.

"Sure. I'll give ya a ride and even escort ya inside. I'll give ole Steinburg a call in the morning and make up an excuse for you to see him. You're welcome to sleep here on the couch if you like. I'll fetch ya a blanket and a pillow."

Her body sinks into the velvety cushions. A heavy blanket and pillow land in a heap across her face. She flings them off and heaves a breath. "Not funny, Travis."

"Sorry 'bout that. Goodnight, princess. By the way, *everyone* likes my jokes."

***

The bus fades into the distance, headed back to the orphanage. Time flew by so fast. Who could have guessed Travis owns a beautiful ranch? Who could have guessed he has deep compassion for animals and children? Ah, the children. How many precious children were lost at the Institute inside her program?

"Did ya sleep well, Doc? That couch is one of the most comfortable couches I've ever owned. I crash there on occasion myself when I can't find the bedroom."

"Yes. Thank you for these past two days. I'm kind of hoping you invite me back."

"Well...I think the kids bonded with ya. And you sure have a way with 'em. I have to admit I'm a tad jealous. They loved your story way better than any of mine."

She scoffs. "I'm betting the bar wasn't set too high."

He wrinkles his brow and frowns. They stroll along the driveway towards the ranch house.

"Grab your gear, Doc, and jump in. And don't worry, we're taking the truck today."

***

"It's a long drive back to Phoenix. So, what's your story, Wyatt Earp? How did you get that scar across your face? Uh...I mean, don't get me wrong, it's a handsome face, I have to admit. But that is a rather intimidating scar."

"Shrapnel, Doc. Tore my face wide open. A piece penetrated my brain and got lodged in my spinal cord. I was as good as dead. Fortunately for me, the military had already formed a relationship with the cryonic institute. They packaged me away and, as I mentioned before, revived me four years ago and restored my health. And here I am...in a place I never wanted to be. The military doesn't ask. They own you. G.I. as in government issue."

"Looks like you've made the best of it. You have a good life. Your ranch is beautiful, those kids adore you, and behind that tough exterior, I can see you adore them too."

"I do. Those kids are my lifeline. Without 'em, I'd...well I don't know what I'd do."

"Did you ever have any children of your own, Travis? Were you ever married? Girlfriends?"

He narrows his eyes and clenches his jaw. His knuckles whiten, gripping the steering wheel.

"I had a little boy. Sage. He'd just turned ten when...when I was wounded. I was married to his mom for thirteen years. Her name was Cheyenne. Her father was Hopi Indian, and her mother was Scottish. She was the love of my life—a real fireball. Cheyenne and Sage were my only two reasons for living. I had to leave them both behind in another place and time. I never got to say goodbye. When they woke me up four years ago...well, let's just say I-I didn't handle it well. Tore some shit up. They had to sedate me."

"Oh my God, Travis. I am so sorry. You must have been devastated. I didn't mean to pry into your personal life. I apologize."

"Nah. It's okay. Ya didn't know. Those kids and my horses are my life now. I have to move on and finish out my days. God didn't intend for this to happen the way it did. But I know He walks with me every step of the way. And that keeps me rising each morning to greet every sunrise...thanking Him for each day I can serve those kids and tend to my horses."

Travis's heart is as soft as his jaw is solid. His eyes glisten, and he avoids eye contact with her. His emotional wounds must run deep. Deeper than his scars would indicate. His soul is full of secrets and heartache. He's honorable. A trait Brandon never possessed. Brandon was as shallow as a slug and only out for one person: himself.

"Is that why you wear that turquoise and silver bear claw necklace around your neck?"

"Yup. Chey made it for me. Gave it to me as a wedding present. The Hopi are skilled jewelers. It symbolizes protection, courage. She felt a good soldier could use some of that.

"We've talked a lot about me, Doc. How's about we talk about you now? Any kiddos? Rich husband? Boyfriend? Girlfriend on the side? What's your story, gal?"

She giggles. "No children. I was married for eight years to a sleazy lawyer. I begged him to have a baby with me. He never wanted children. The last time I brought it up he left me for someone else. Probably someone younger and prettier. I entered the Promise of Lazarus program soon after. The very program I had developed. I was diagnosed with an inoperable and fatal form of brain cancer."

"Now that's some ironic bullshit...and this ex-husband of yours sounds like a real dickhead."

She sighs. "He was. I don't know what I saw in him. He was never my type. We had nothing in common. I thought I loved him, but now I'm not so sure I ever did. I think I was in love with the idea of love, if that makes sense. Funny how we blind ourselves to the truth...so we don't have to admit we made a mistake, I suppose."

"Well, he's an idiot. He did you a favor by leaving. I'm sure he got what was coming to him. Tell me about your pappy. What kind of man was he?"

"Oh, now there's a story. My dad was my hero growing up. My mother died when I was three. I barely remember her. Daddy raised me on a small farm and sold produce on the side of the road. He used to make me go with him...putting me to work organizing the fruits and vegetables into wooden crates. I'd have to calculate the sales and the correct change. He wanted to show me what it was like to work hard to make ends meet. He encouraged me to go to college and earn a degree so I could take care of myself. It worked. And he paid for every penny with the money he left me. I miss him so much. I miss my mom too."

"Sounds like a real fine man, your pappy. Hard to find 'em like that anymore. Ya know...men with ethics. Men who love and sacrifice for their families. Sorry to hear about both of your folks."

"My dad was my entire universe. He wanted me to be a tomboy. He tried teaching me survival skills...in case I ever got lost in the wilderness. I even learned to start a fire using a plastic bottle filled with water. But I was too prissy, and I didn't make a very good survivalist.

When I was seventeen, he drove off the side of a cliff in his pickup truck. They concluded he fell asleep at the wheel. He was...trying to make it home from the Payson Rodeo where he had entered a prize pig...or maybe it was a cow; I don't recall for sure. He always called me his little *Biscuit-Cakes*."

She nibbles on her lower lip. Tears drip off her eyelashes. She gasps and swallows. The waves of emotion were unexpected, catching her off guard and vulnerable.

"He was trying to get back home in time to watch me dance. I was performing with my dance company. My first solo. That man never missed a single one. I kept looking for him in the audience...but...he never made it. I guess that's why I have issues with separation anxiety."

Sobs confound her words. She dabs her eyes with a tissue.

"I'm so sorry for blubbering. I miss him so much and never understood why he had to leave me."

Travis pulls to the side of the road and parks.

"Let's step out for a minute. I want you to see something."

They walk to the edge of a flat lookout point.

"See that? That's the entire Valley of the Sun...stretched out across all those miles. You can see every mile atop the Mogollon Rim where we're standing. It's funny. Down there you can't see how the world around you fits together. Ya get caught up in all the moving parts. Too many details. Up here everything is clear. You can see the entire picture and how things fit together."

He faces her. His beefy, callused hands cradle hers. He's gentle.

"Emily. Your dad was a good man. A good father. Ya had seventeen wonderful years with him. Life is precious, gal. Every minute of every day counts for something. Look at the complete picture—like that valley out there. Focus on those seventeen years you spent with him and nothing else. Those years are where your pappy lives. You can still visit him there if you look close enough."

She sniffles. "Thank you. I have to admit he was a little like you, Travis. Stubborn as a bull with no filter. I also regret having to admit that he would have liked you and your god-awful jokes. He had the most infectious laugh and had a way of making me laugh even when I was angry and didn't want to. God, I hated how he could do that to me."

Travis gazes down at her. There's a kindness in his eyes she only now realizes. Almost a twinkle. It flickers behind the orneriness of his slanted smile and dimples. She's safe with him. Only her dad could make her feel safe like this. It's curious how a person can become more attractive the deeper you get to know them.

"So, where'd you get your taste in music, Doc? I doubt your pappy liked that '80s crap. I peg him to be more of a Merle Haggard type."

"Well, you'd be right about that. He loved his country music. My mom left me many things to remember her by when she died. One of the most precious things she left for me was her collection of albums and cassette tapes of '80s rock music. I grew up listening to all of them. I know every word to every song ever written in the 1980s. She also loved old TV sitcoms. I grew up watching Gilligan's Island, The Lucy Show, Captain Kangaroo. You name it, she had it. Emily sniffles and dabs her nose with the tissue.

"We better head down the road if we're gonna meet with ole Steinburg. We need to be very careful, Em. Things have changed a lot since you went to sleep. Guard your words. And hey...I already like your pappy without ever meeting him. And what's not to love about ole Big Mac Daddy, huh? I'm sure he and I would have gotten along like two hogs in shit."

She rolls her eyes. "*Big Mac Daddy*. I still can't believe you think that's a cool name. It's dumb, Travis. Lose it. It sounds like the name of a pimp. Not a good example for the kids. You need to trust me on this. Try, *Big Mac*, or something to that effect. I'm serious."

9

GHOSTS FROM THE PAST

She hadn't noticed the title on the building when she left the Institute several days ago. Prominent metallic-gold letters are ablaze with intense reflections of Arizona sunlight. *The Institute of Cryonic Life Management Systems*. Travis uses the combination of his eye and thumb identification to gain access to the Institute's lobby.

"Good morning, Mr. McCallister. I'll let Dr. Steinburg know you're here. Have a seat."

"Much obliged, Thelma. This is Dr. Emily Grace, by the way."

"I've heard many pleasant things about you, Dr. Grace. It's great to meet you."

Oxygen-rich humidity stimulates her brain cells with a punchy giddiness. Exotic foliage blends with the trickles of waterfalls, abstract paintings, and twisted sculptures, creating an ambiance of tranquility. Faint piano music resounds through the walls. Soft white light radiates throughout the lobby, bathing the environment with warmth. The aesthetics stimulate the frontal lobe of the brain with cerebral ecstasy—and not by accident. A guard sits behind a small desk near the elevator as a reminder of the military's presence. The changes to the institute are jaw-dropping. How can a once-familiar location seem so displaced and foreign to her now?

"Travis, you and Dr. Grace can head up to Dr. Steinburg's office now. He's ready for you."

He stands and nods. "Pst. Let's go, Doc."

Travis nods toward the guard and activates the sensor of the elevator, opening a now-familiar cylindrical door. Her temples thump. She heaves a breath and grabs hold of his shirt. Closing her eyes, she follows him into the small space of the elevator.

Travis lays his hand on her shoulder. "Deep, slow breaths, Em. Go to a happy place."

She squeals. "Easy for you to say. I don't have a happy place. Please hurry."

Travis's solid arms enwrap her torso. Leather and spice titillate her senses. His humming creates chills across the back of her neck. Her breathing slows, and her trembling eases. *How is he doing this?*

"Don't get the wrong idea, Doc. Just trying to steady you for a spell. This works well on the goats when I transport them to the orphanage for 'petting zoo' day."

The ding of the elevator resonates like a musical note. She shoves him aside and scoots out of the elevator, heaving a breath.

"See? You're fine. Let's go pay Dr. Steinburg a little visit."

She smacks his shoulder. "Goats? Really, Travis?"

Travis presses a button next to a heavy metallic door. A few seconds later, the door buzzes and clicks. He swings it wide. She ambles inside, followed by Travis.

"Dr. Grace, it's a pleasure to see you. Looks like you're adapting well, and Mr. McCallister hasn't chased you away yet. Nice to see you, Mac."

Emily rolls her eyes. "No, *Big Mac Daddy* hasn't chased me off yet."

Steinburg chuckles. "What can I do for you today, Dr. Grace?"

"You still owe me some answers to my many questions."

"Fair enough. Fire away."

"I'll be straight to the point. Give me access to the data for the Promise of Lazarus program. I want to know precisely what the fates were for the children and adults who were once my patients."

"I can arrange limited access to our database. They defunded the Promise of Lazarus Program around sixty-six years ago. I get it, though. You want answers. You want to see where your research failed."

Her gut tightens. *What an arrogant ass.*

"I want answers about the direction the program took after I entered it. If it was such a failure, why am I here? Why is Travis here? Are there others?"

Steinburg smirks. He steeples his fingers and swivels in his chair.

"I'm confident you will find all the answers you are seeking in our database. To address your question, a small sample of *Lazarus* patients were transferred into another program. They included you and Travis in that group. Otherwise, we wouldn't be sitting here having this conversation, Dr. Grace. So, you are most welcome."

Steinburg leans forward and calls up a set of holographic pages that assemble across his desk.

"I'm granting you temporary access to our archived database files—specifically, the folder where we store the Promise of Lazarus data. I'll create a temporary login onto this data slide, and you can access it from home. A data slide is similar to your old flash drives. Insert the slide into the correct port. I've granted you forty-eight hours of access. That should be ample time to find all the answers to your questions. Anything else I can help you with, Doctor?"

"Thank you. I'll let you know when I find what I'm looking for. I'd be interested to hear about your latest projects, Dr. Steinburg. You know, the 'Life Management Systems' portion of the new company title."

"Of course. I'd be happy to give you a personal presentation of our latest programs. I'd be interested in hearing your thoughts and ideas. Here. Take my card. Call me anytime, Dr. Grace."

"I'd like that. Thank you for your time. And for the access."

"Oh, and since I have you both here, I want to set an appointment for you to undergo a final physical and psych evaluation. Standard procedure. Nothing to be too concerned about. I'll have my assistant contact you and make the arrangements. I promise this will be the last round of testing."

Travis glances at her, his tongue pressed against the inside of his cheek, and one eyebrow raised.

"Sure, Dr. Steinburg. I will get right on that."

***

"Experience the Crystal Springs *Claustrophobic* Lifestyle. Thanks for the ride, Travis."

"You're welcome. Ya sure you don't want to spend another night at the ranch? We can put ya in the spare room. Less of a chance for a panic attack. And you'd be off the grid. Last chance."

"I appreciate the offer. I do. But I want to dig deep into that database. I'm kind of a lone wolf."

"Yeah, I can see that. Well, I hope ya find what you're looking for. Be careful where you poke around, Em. I don't trust Steinburg. Call me if you find anything earth-shattering or if you miss me." She scoffs.

Travis's red taillights fade into the night. Once again, she faces the dreaded elevator. Shouldn't there be a set of stairs in the building? Isn't that required in the fire code, or do fire codes no longer exist? She cringes entering the confined elevator and holds her breath for the entire five floors.

"These walls must be shrinking. I've got to find a roomier place soon...really not going to make it thirty days in this cereal box of an apartment."

She sets her new NERU HG Pro on a small coffee table and initializes the program. A holographic screen illuminates across the table. *Okay. So far, so good. Insert the data slide...um...right here.*

"Now that's interesting." Her eyes follow a series of four holographic screens as they organize themselves across her coffee table. Each screen displays a large folder icon. Three of the four folders have the word UNAUTHORIZED overlaying the screen—each printed in bold orange letters. The fourth folder has a 48-hour clock overlaid. The assumption is, as soon as she touches that folder, the clock starts ticking. She lays her hand across the folder. The assumption is correct.

The folder opens, revealing a sub-folder titled *Promise of Lazarus Project*. She heaves a breath. Her hand trembles, activating the folder. Pages of data unfold and organize themselves into dozens of reports, charts, graphs, videos, and images. *Bingo*.

The coffee machine isn't as complicated as she feared. The mocha isn't half bad either, but not up to the standard she's accustomed to. She brews a strong cup of joe and sets it on a small coffee table beside her. The caffeine should fuel the hours of reading material laid out before her.

***

One-hundred and thirty-seven. That's how many children were involved in the Promise of Lazarus Program. Only one child survived. Kyler Carson. The chemical make-up of the antifreeze harmed the developing brains of children—brains not developed until age twenty-four years. Why was Kyler different? His chronological age would have been nine years old when he entered the program, and his biological age would have been that of a fifty-year-old man. HGPS would have been advanced, yet he currently shows few signs of the disease. How was he cured? There is nothing in the data explaining any of it. Kyler was moved into a new program. *The Morpheus Project.*

Four-hundred and seventy-two—the number of adults entered into the program. Only two survivors. Both entered the *Morpheus Project*. Travis McCallister and Dr. Emily Grace.

Morpheus Project...access restricted. I need inside that folder.

"You don't think...no. No way the backdoor into the network I created decades ago could have stayed hidden and unnoticed all these years? It's worth a try."

ACCESS DENIED – UNAUTHORIZED ACCOUNT

"Yeah, I didn't think so. That would be too easy."

She continues to scan through the files and images.

"My God. All these lives...gone. These files tell me little to nothing about what happened to them."

She cradles her face in her palms. *I have to get inside that network.*

She could plant a Trojan. Will they detect it in a network scan? The programming may be archaic for the current time, but maybe that would be an advantage—something so obsolete that it is no longer searched for within network scans. She creates a summary of her findings from the reports within the Promise of Lazarus Program titled, "Summary for Dr. Steinburg." Harmless, right? Within that file, she will plant the Trojan virus. Once the file is opened, it will theoretically create a backdoor into Dr. Steinburg's computer and a gateway into the network. She writes a simple program in standard C++ language. It's encouraging she remembered how to write one. *Let's hope a program written in C++ will execute within their system and do what it is intended to do.*

Wait. Why not search the SuperNet for tutorials on the latest computer programs? Hm. What's this? Looks like X++ and Java Prime are the new C. The syntax is similar to C++ and Java with just some differences in how you handle variables and how you execute the program. A lot of added features to this programming language. So much more logical. God, why didn't someone think this up years ago?

"Emily, you are a genius. Just a few tweaks to these lines of code, and this just might work."

She retrieves the business card Dr. Steinburg gave her.

"Hello, Siri?"

"Yes, Dr. Grace. How may I help you?"

"Add this number for Dr. Roland Steinburg to my contact list. 125-920-105-714."

"Added. Would you like to call Dr. Roland Steinburg?"

"Yes. Please."

"Dr. Steinburg's office. This is Thelma. May I help you?"

"Yes, hello, Thelma. This is Dr. Emily Grace. I'd like to meet with Dr. Steinburg to go over my findings for the Promise of Lazarus program. He asked me to follow up with him when I completed my evaluation."

"Oh, certainly. Let me check his calendar. Looks like he has a cancellation of his 9:00 a.m. meeting tomorrow morning. I can schedule you in."

"That would be perfect. Thank you so much. I will...see you tomorrow."

"Siri, please call Travis McCallister."

"Hey, Doc. Ya, missing me already, huh?"

"Um...yeah. Sure, buddy. Keep telling yourself that, Travis. Hey, can you pick me up tomorrow morning? I am meeting with Dr. Steinburg at 9:00 a.m. sharp."

"Well, sure. I can do that. Why do I get the feeling you're up to something?"

"Because I am. I'll fill you in on the way. Don't be late...and please drive the pickup truck."

10

Memories of Troy

Honk! "Hop in, Doc."

"Oh, God. Not the wiener. Where's your pickup truck? You're five minutes late, by the way. And can you *please* stop calling me, Doc?"

"Forgot to charge the battery in my pickup. You're stuck with the wiener, I reckon...Em."

She rolls her eyes. "Are you referring to the truck or yourself?"

He chuckles. "I see what you did there. So, what's the plan today? We blowing up the Institute? Taking hostages?"

"No, even better. We're hacking into their network."

"Sounds like a hoot. How do ya plan on doing that, Mata Harry?"

"Mata Hari."

"What?"

"Mata Hari, dufus...never mind.

"I created a sub-folder inside the Lazarus file on the Institute's network. This may or may not work, but it's worth a try. Inside the sub-folder are my notes to Dr. Steinburg with a complete analysis of all the data. I named the file 'Summary for Dr. Steinburg.' I placed a Trojan virus inside that folder. The malicious file will execute the moment he opens it. The trick is...I have to get him to open that file somehow. The moment it opens, a backdoor will be created and I can access the network remotely. Theoretically, anyway. If all goes as planned, I will have full access to the

Morpheus folder, and I can dig deeper to find out what's really going on here."

"And we're doing this *because?*..."

"Because I don't believe their data. They're hiding something... something important. I can sense it in my bones."

"Doc, if we get caught doing this..."

"We won't get caught. Just follow my lead, okay? Pay close attention. Whatever I decide to do, just go with the flow."

***

"I didn't expect to see you back so soon, Dr. Grace. Have a seat, please."

"Thank you, Dr. Steinburg."

"Mac? You're a chauffeur, now?"

"Uh...no. Just giving the young lady a ride...in my wiener."

Dr. Steinburg grimaces. He glances at Travis, then glances at her. He shakes his head and furrows his brow. Travis seems to have that effect on people when his jokes fall flat, as they often do.

"Well, what can I help you with today, Dr. Grace? You read and digested all that data in one night? Amazing."

"Yes. I did. And I have a few more questions if you don't mind. I created a sub-folder with my analysis of the data inside the Lazarus folder for your eyes only."

"Hm. I'll be interested to read your report as time permits in my schedule."

"Can you pull up the Lazarus folder so I can show you where it is located?"

"You just told me where it's located."

"Yes, but there's a specific file I want to make you aware of before you read the analysis. It's a set of instructions and an overview that will help you understand the analysis. Can I show it to you?"

"Really, Dr. Grace. I'm a bit short on time today and can look at it later. I'm confident I can figure it out."

"It's very important to me, and I believe you are going to be very interested in what I have discovered."

"Okay...Okay. I'll open the folder and you can show me where the instructions are. But I do not have the time right now to go over your analysis. I'll review it later."

Dr. Steinburg initiates his computer and logs into the network. He navigates to the Promise of Lazarus folder and opens it. Sub-folders organize across his desk like regiments of soldiers lining up for inspection.

"What's the name of your new sub-folder?"

"It's that one...right there. *Grace_Analysis*. The instructions are inside...I named them, 'Summary for Dr. Steinburg.'"

She reaches across his desk to touch the folder. He raises his hand, waving off her attempt.

"Please don't do that, Doctor. I'll open the sub-folder, okay? So, I see your file with your notes. I will dig into your narrative later in the week. Anything else I can help you with?"

"I appreciate that, Dr. Steinburg. I have one important question before I go. What is the Morpheus Project? I noticed in the reports that only myself and Mr. McCallister made the transfer over to the Morpheus Project along with a child. Why weren't the others moved? What happened to them? You indicated there were other transfers. May I have access to the Morpheus folder, please?"

"That's four questions, Doctor. I am afraid I cannot grant you access to the Morpheus folder. I'm sorry. It's highly restricted information. Intellectual property, patents pending...legal mumbo jumbo...You understand, I'm sure."

"Why? What are you trying to hide? I demand you give me access to that folder, Doctor."

"Or what? You're no longer an employee here, Dr. Grace, and in no position to demand anything."

"You'll understand if you will just read the damn file! That one, right there." Emily taps the icon of the infected file with her index finger launching the trojan.

"I specifically asked you not to touch any of the files on my computer, Dr. Grace. I need both of you to leave my office immediately, or I will have security escort you out of the building. I'm sorry, but this visit is over."

"Fine. But this isn't the end of our conversation. We'll be speaking about my concerns again soon."

"Dr. Grace, I highly suggest you enjoy your retirement and the new life we have blessed you with. Asking too many of the wrong questions may jeopardize everything you've worked so hard for all these years. Your time at the Institute passed decades ago. My advice is to keep the past in the past—if you know what I mean."

Dr. Steinburg taps his office phone. "Now, get the hell out of my office before I call security."

"Of course. I appreciate your time, Dr. Steinburg. Have a great day."

***

Beads of sweat trickle down Travis' temples as they depart the parking lot headed back to the expressway.

"Did you open the file, Em?"

"Yes. Now we wait and see. Take me by my apartment so I can grab my computer. We need to head to your ranch so I can work *off the grid,* as you say?"

"Of course. What was all that stuff about a Morpheus project... and you and me?"

"I scoured through all those files of data last night. It was very suspicious. Far too neat and organized. Data is never that perfect. I don't trust it. In one report, they barely mention Morpheus. The report listed you, me, and Kyler as the only participants transferred from Lazarus. It's peculiar. Dr. Steinburg suggested there were others involved in the program when we spoke before. I need to gain access to that folder and see what they're up to and what happened to all my Lazarus patients."

"If we get caught screwing around inside that network, we are going to be in a world of shit, gal. We're off the grid at my ranch. But they can still find us. I have a remote location deep in the woods where we can *bug out* if we need to. A little something I built over eighty years ago. It has some cool amenities."

"Bug out? What's that mean?"

"Bug out. Disappear. Hide. Get completely off the radar. You never watched an episode of *Doomsday Preppers*?"

"Um...no. If it comes to that, we need to pick up Kyler. He's involved in this too. We can't leave him alone or at risk."

"Sure. I can always pick him up from the orphanage in Payson. It's a thirty-minute drive."

Travis rolls to a stop in front of her apartment building. She hops out of the vehicle and hits the ground, running.

"I'll be right back. Wait for me here."

She snatches her computer and stuffs clothing and personal items into a canvas duffle bag. She endures the elevator ride back to the street by holding her breath and squeezing her eyes shut. When the elevator door opens, she sprints through the lobby and into the parking lot.

She reclines the passenger seat of the truck and snuggles into the cushions for the long ride ahead. Her head bobs, inhaling a deep yawn. She squirms into a cushy corner of her seat. The long stretch of lonely road hums beneath the tires, lulling her senses and allowing her thoughts to fade. Her body jerks. Did she doze off?

"What's wrong with ya, Doc? Ya have a seizure or something?"

"Shut up, Travis. Keep your eyes on the road."

He chuckles. "Just making sure ya ain't having one of your PTSD moments in my truck."

"Oh, aren't you so funny? I dozed off. I experienced an involuntary reflex called a *hypnogogic jerk*...not to be confused with a contemptible person who is offensive to others often referred to as a jerk."

A region of the brain called the dorsal anterior cingulate cortex becomes less active during a hypnotic event, such as driving. *Let's hope that region of Travis's brain remains active for the entire trip*—her last conscious thought of the afternoon.

***

Her eyes open to the approaching ranch house. Her head is resting against his shoulder. She sits upright and slaps his arm.

"What? What'd I do?"

"You let me sleep on your shoulder?"

"Hey. It happens. Don't be embarrassed."

"Keep dreaming, buster."

He points at his sleeve. "Can you at least wipe the slobber off my shirt?"

"That isn't mine. It's drool from *your* mouth. And by the way...what was *that*?...you telling Steinburg you're giving me a ride on your wiener? Seriously?"

"I said *in* my wiener, not *on* my wiener. There's an obvious difference, gal. Here's the key to the house. I'm going around back to feed the horses. Make yourself at home, princess, and toss your gear in the spare room."

"Thank you. I will."

She sets her NERU HG on his kitchen table, logs in, and accesses Dr. Steinburg's data slide. Folders spread out across the holographic screens. It's surprising Steinburg didn't ask for the data slide to be returned. It's suspicious.

"Oh, my God. The port is open. I think this just might work. I am a *genius*."

She establishes a network connection and creates a login. Touching the Morpheus Project folder sets off a flurry of sub-folders, documents, images, and video files organizing themselves across the wooden tabletop. *Son of a bitch. It worked.* She copies the files onto her data slide, nibbling on her lower lip and tapping her toe. A blue progress bar registers 80%, then 95%, and chimes the moment it disappears. She yanks the data slide out of the port and severs the connection to the Institute's network. She shuts down her computer, hoping they never discover she was there.

Travis enters the ranch house and washes his hands in the kitchen sink. He wipes his brow with his sleeve, then slides a chair away from the table and straddles it.

"So, Dickless Tracy. What d'ya find out?"

"Really? That is *so* inappropriate. Do you know how sexist that sounds?"

He chuckles and smirks. "I apologize. Whatcha got, Ms. Dick Tracy?"

"Travis, it worked. I can't believe it, but it did. I only kept the connection open long enough to download all the files from the Morpheus folder."

She cocks her head and presents the data slide. "It's all here. I need to make multiple copies of this."

Travis reaches into a small drawer of an end table. "I have a couple of blank data slides you can have. Knock yourself out."

Travis leaves the room and when he returns, he lays a folded pile of clothes, a pair of boots, and a straw cowboy hat on a chair next to her. "When you're done, put these on. I have Blondie and Jasper all saddled up."

"Oh, I'd love to go for a joyride, but we don't have time right now, Travis."

"It ain't a joyride. I need to show you something important, Em."

"All right. I have two backup copies of the data. I'm giving you this one to hold for me."

He slips the data slide into the inside pocket of his jean jacket.

"Let's get a move on while we still have daylight, gal."

Cool breezes caress the treetops, creating a medley of rustling leaves. An earthy aroma of wet pine carries in the wind. White clouds boil and billow in the north—cast against an azure sky. Rhythmic clomps pound the rich soil and echo through the woods. Daddy lived for moments like these. Moments never appreciated until their grainy reflections faded into sienna and white memories.

"We're gonna leave the road now, Doc...cross that shallow creek up ahead and head into that open field of wildflowers."

"Okay, Big Mac Daddy. I'm going to make you a deal. Let's race across that field. If I win, you stop calling me, *Doc.* You win and you can call me anything you like."

"Ha. Well, Blondie is a faster horse, but I'm the better rider."

Emily guides Blondie next to Jasper. She yanks Travis's hat over his eyes and takes off in a lope kicking up dirt clods in her wake. Leaning forward, she brings Blondie to a full gallop. "Yee-haw!"

"What the hell? Let's go, boy. After 'em."

The rhythmic clomping of Blondie's hooves against the wild grasses and the filly's pounding heart sparks a rush of adrenaline through her veins and exhilaration through her spirit. Her stomach flutters. "Run, Blondie! Come on, baby!"

"I'm on your ass, Doc. That was some cheat'n bullshit you pulled back there."

Travis and Jasper pull neck and neck with Emily and Blondie. It's going to be a photo finish. Both horses slow and ease up at the edge of the field.

"That one was too close to call, Doc. Better luck next time, cheater."

"What are you talking about? I clearly won the race. You know I did. We kicked your butts. Eat my dirt, Travis."

He shakes his head and removes his hat. "All right then. Can we proceed, *Miss Emily*?"

She can sense the smirk beaming off her lips. She's missed this for so many years. Memories buried in a painful past have prevented her from riding all these years. The irony? Riding with Travis has brought her closer to Daddy's memory.

"We're headed through that heavy brush ahead, so we're gonna need to walk the horses, Em."

A small clearing in the forest reveals an aged and humble log cabin. He grabs the reins of both horses and tethers them to a post. The rustic porch creaks as they step across weathered boards and enter the abandoned cabin. It's a one-room structure with no furniture. A layer of dust covers the floors and walls. Stepping inside creates tiny motes that swirl and dance across silent beams of light.

"Wow. What a great vacation home, Tex. Is this where you bring all your hot dates? Impressive."

"Only the *easy* ones, Doc...uh, Em."

He removes a loose board from a windowsill and snatches an iron key. He raises an old rug off the floor and tosses it aside. Travis slides the key into a slot and swings open a trapdoor. He flips on a light switch illuminating a downward metal staircase.

"I'm assuming this is your bug out headquarters, huh, Commander?"

"Your assumption is correct, little lady. May I escort you down the stairs?"

The stairs are wobbly. Travis leads the way and descends the stairwell. At the landing, he extends his hand to assist her off the last step. She stumbles into his arms. Their noses almost touch. His gaze creates a flutter in her heart. His arms are solid but gentle. A musky scent of leather and spice arouses her senses. He's so different from Brandon. But he has this unique way of annoying the hell out of her.

"Uh...I should have warned ya about this last step. I'm sorry 'bout that."

"Well, maybe you ought to fix that little hazard, Casanova. That trick might work with all the other girls, but not this girl, mister."

He chuckles and flips on the primary lights of the cellar.

"Oh my God. When did you have time to build all this?"

"The cellar was always part of the cabin. Back in the twenties, I used this place for hunting elk and deer...and fishing. Woods Canyon Lake is only a few miles from here. I'd bring Sage along. Teach him how to skin a rabbit and clean a trout properly. My wife had the place looking a lot homier in those days. We spent a lot of time together here."

"It must be difficult for you to visit."

His head lowers. "It is. But I've tried to move on and accept my new life. Trying to make the best of my situation."

She places her hand on his shoulder. "You're a good guy, Travis. I'm sure you were a great dad and a good husband."

"I appreciate that. Let me give you the grand tour. Pay close attention."

He opens a cabinet revealing several military-grade rifles and pistols.

"These are here for protection. Obviously. Been here for close to one hundred years...still in perfect condition. Ammo is in this drawer. Over here is a modern-day nuclear generator—nothing like the nuclear generators of our day. Enough power to keep this place running for centuries. Right here, we have a small command center. Well, not exactly. But this is a powerful NERU

HG Max, and it has a direct connection to the SuperNet. It also controls the life support systems and the environment inside the shelter."

"Wow. This is quite the bug out, Mr. Doomsday Prepper."

"Yup. Over here is a deep freeze packed with meat and fish. Right here is a pantry of dry goods and canned goods. I also have a good supply of iron rations. I have a water filtration system, a small shower, and a stove. These beds fold into the wall.

She peeks behind a large canvas sheet hanging over the rear wall. "Where does this door lead?"

"It's the back way out. A literal back door. Not the computer kind. And there ya have it—everything ya need for a quick escape. We better head back now, Em. Before you try hit'n on me again."

"Oh, you wish, Travis. Gimme a break, dreamer. God, you're so full of yourself."

***

A fiery sunset emblazons a dusty western sky as they arrive at the ranch house. A gust blows the hat off of Emily's head. It spins and rolls across the ground like a mindless tumbleweed.

"I'll unsaddle the horses... meet ya in the house. Looking like an evening storm is brewing. Here, don't forget the key."

She snags her hat and slaps it across her thigh. A puff of dust dissipates inside swirling eddies. The door creaks. She resists a powerful push by Mother Nature against the door and slips inside.

Ransacked! Drawers lie broken—their contents scattered. Stuffing from sofa cushions form mounds of giant cotton balls. She rushes into her bedroom. Her computer? Gone. She scrambles towards the front door. A meaty hand clasps over her mouth.

"Sh. We need to get out of here, Em. Fast."

"You scared the crap out of me. Travis, my computer is gone. The data..."

"We can't worry about that now. We have to move. Right now. Follow me."

They slip out the back door. Travis is sporting a holstered pistol on his hip. On the other hip is a twelve-inch Bowie. He wasn't wearing either a moment ago. His pickup truck is idling. No headlights.

"We need to bug out, for real this time. Stay calm. Jump in."

"Who are you now? Rambo?"

They navigate along a dark dirt road. A mile away from the ranch, he flips on the headlights and floors it.

"I told ya, Em. These are not people ya wanna dick around with."

"Yeah, probably because *someone* didn't play along well enough in Steinburg's office. I told you to go with the flow."

He strokes his chin. "More likely they detected *someone* snooping around their network wearing clodhoppers and shouting, 'Oooh, look at me, I'm a genius.'"

"Travis. They stole my computer. The data is gone."

Travis reaches into the pocket of his jean jacket and pulls out a data slide.

"Ya still have this one, Doc. Yeah, you're welcome. Now, who's the genius?"

"Oh, my God. I forgot about that one. Thank you, thank you so much. We need to get inside the Morpheus folder. Something is going on in there, and it is obvious they do not want us to know."

"You can use my computer. We just need to get our asses back over there, like yesterday. Buckle up, Butter Cup. We're gonna do some old-fashioned four-wheeling."

He moves the stick-shift into 4-wheel-drive and grins.

"Now we're talking. This is *my* kind of date."

11

THE REVEAL

Travis's computer network is more sophisticated than it first appeared. The connection to the SuperNet is secure, with multiple firewalls and anonymous web surfing capabilities. *He's given a great deal of thought to his 'bugging out' efforts, and he's more intelligent than he lets on. He's out of practice when it comes to women, however—and that's a shame.*

She sets her NERU computer on the kitchen table and inserts the data slide into the computer port. Her chest tightens upon opening the Morpheus folder. An organized display of files spread out across several holographic screens. She holds her breath, exhales with a long sigh.

"Travis. I'm going to be here for quite a while. I sure could use a strong cup of mocha. You wouldn't have any stashed in your *bug-out* inventory, would you?"

"I reckon, I do. What's your preference? Juan Valdez Colombian; Jamaican Blue Mountain; Hawaiian Gold; vintage Starbucks?"

"Are you screwing with me? Those are like my favorite coffees in the entire world. Please tell me you're not screwing with me."

"I wouldn't screw with ya, Doc. Cheyenne loved her coffee. She cost me a small fortune with her expensive tastes. I'm not much of a coffee drinker myself, so they've sat around all these years. I've kept them vacuum-sealed and stored in the deep freeze. Not sure why...I just couldn't throw 'em out."

"Oh, my God. You are a man after my own heart. Jamaican Blue Mountain, *please.*"

"You got it. I'm glad somebody is going to drink them. The coffee pot will ding when it's ready. Doc, I'm going to take a ride back to the ranch house. I need to check on my horses. I'll be back in a couple of hours."

Her heart twinges. She bites her lower lip and inhales deep through her nostrils.

"Travis. Please be careful."

"Calm yourself, Doc. I ain't gonna leave ya. I promise I'll be right back. Getting a little sweet on me, aren't ya, gal?"

She rolls her eyes at him and returns to focusing on the task at hand—scouring folders and documents, watching videos, and skimming through countless images.

What's this report?...it mentions Morpheus and Lazarus.

The Jamaican coffee is as fresh as any cup she ever brewed at home. She sets the cup on the desktop and crosses her legs. She selects the report and increases the font.

February 13, 2096

The Promise of Lazarus Program Patient Transfer to the Morpheus Project

Dr. Roland F. Steinburg, M.D.

SUMMARY: 472 Adult Specimens; 137 Youth Specimens

The research and development for the Promise of Lazarus program was headed by Dr. Emily Grace from January 25, 2016, until her entrance into the program on June 30, 2021. After that point, the program was managed and overseen by Dr. Eduardo Diaz until his death on December 21, 2042, when the program was defunded.

All adult specimens were maintained in perfect health. The last known antifreeze formula was effective in maintaining the suspension and health of all 472 adults. The Federal Courts determined that the financial burden of the State in addition to the questions of ethics and morality of reviving and re-orientating these adults into society was not justified. Furthermore, their carbon stamp on the environment was determined to be an unacceptable burden on society.

Of the 472 adult specimens in the program, 470 were terminated and their bodies cremated. The remaining two subjects, Dr. Emily Isabella Grace and Special Ops Master Sergeant Travis John McCallister were transferred to the Morpheus project as qualified candidates where they currently reside. Both subjects exhibited an unusually high potential for neuron memory mapping.

The young adults and children 24 years of age and younger experienced complications created by the underdevelopment of brain tissue and neural function. The issue was resolved by a modification in the antifreeze formula by Dr. Diaz. Specific proteins were introduced into the DNA of the specimens, thus returning them to an acceptable level of health and well-being. There was, however, one specimen unaffected by the complication: an 8-year-old male, Kyler Carson, who suffers from HGPS (Hutchinson-Gilford progeria syndrome). It was determined the advanced state of his illness protected him from the effects of the antifreeze formula. Kyler Carson was transferred to the Morpheus Project along with the two adult candidates, Grace and McCallister. He remains in the program currently. The other 136 young adults and children were terminated.

"What the hell? Oh God, they killed them. They murdered them all. Oh God...my God. No. No, no..."

She closes her eyes, burying her face in her hands. Tears seep through her fingers and trickle along her forearms. She raises her head, focusing on the holographic screens before her. The screens are a jumble of glistening blurs and light flares.

Snap out of it, Emily. You still don't know what Morpheus is. Stay focused. Right here. Read this one.

July 14, 2102

The Morpheus Project by Dr. Roland F. Steinburg, M.D.

SUMMARY: 2 Adult Specimens; 1 Youth Specimen

The Morpheus Project is classified TOP SECRET in unison with The Cryonic Institute of Life Management Systems and the United States Space Force.

The goal of the project is to determine the feasibility and capability of placing an astronaut into a catatonic state using cryonic technologies for deep space travel. During suspended sleep, the astronaut would receive neurological programming for training, education, and recreation of the mind. Thus, maintaining synapsis integrity and memory mapping. The strategy is to awaken a mentally and physically healthy astronaut, prepared and trained for the assigned mission.

Three volunteers, two adults and one child, will undergo testing and evaluation before the first astronaut trial begins. Once testing is complete, the three volunteers will be terminated.

The holographs hang suspended in front of her eyes—silent and illuminated. Her mind wants to deny their horrific truth. Her thoughts suspend in a whirl of mental numbness. Footsteps descend the metal staircase, breaking her hypnotic trance.

"Em. It's not safe to return to the ranch house. Steinburg's goons were there again after we left. The place is a wreck. They're looking for something. Or more likely looking for *us*."

"Travis. We have to pick up Kyler. We need to go now."

"I'm not sure that's a good idea. We're going to need to lie low for a while."

"You don't understand. You, me, and Kyler are the only participants in the Morpheus Project. When they're finished with us, they are going to terminate us. As in, kill us...murder us. They killed my former patients...healthy innocent people. All of them. They should be alive and with us right now. But they murdered them. We have to pick up Kyler before they do."

"Son of a bitch. I told you Steinburg couldn't be trusted. Let me make a call and arrange to grab Kyler. We'll come up with an excuse to pick him up."

"No. We can't let them know we're coming. We need to show up...unannounced...and steal him out of that orphanage before they realize what we're doing."

"Yeah. I reckon you have a point. Let's take the pickup...In case we need to go off-road."

***

"Hello, Mr. McCallister. We weren't expecting you. The kids had a great time last week. They could not stop talking about it. And this must be the amazing Dr. Grace I've heard so much about?"

"Yep, this is the famous Dr. Grace. Best storyteller in the Southwest. Miss Katrina, would it be possible to sign out my boy, Kyler, and take him for some ice cream? I'll have him back within the hour. He and Dr. Grace bonded on his visit to the ranch, and I think it'd be good for him."

"Well, that would violate our visitation policy, Mac. I can't approve that...not without permission."

"Kat. Come on. It's me. You can trust ole Mac. Kyler is making great strides. You and I both know that. Can we make one tiny exception this time? I'll have him back in thirty minutes. We'll be around the corner. I promise. Come on now...what do ya say?"

Travis raises his palms and grins. She's hedging. Maybe ole Big Mac has a little charm left with the ladies after all.

Katrina sighs. "Ah, okay. Thirty minutes. Not a second longer. I'm serious, Mac. You better not get me in trouble. I really need this job."

"Now that's what I'm talking about. Thank you, Kat. Your job is safe, gal. Don't you worry none."

Kyler shuffles into the lobby with his fists jammed into his pockets. He raises his eyes toward Emily, suppressing an obvious grin. He slides one hand from his pocket and wriggles his fingers at her.

"Come on, buddy. Let's get some ice cream with Dr. Grace. I have a little surprise for ya."

Travis glances at Katrina and winks. "We'll be back in a jiff."

"Buckle up, Kyler. We're gonna fly like rats through a sewer, boy. Sound like fun?"

Kyler nods and smiles. "Where we going, Mac?"

"Today we're gonna be outlaws. And outlaws have to have a secret hideout, right?"

Kyler sits upright, beaming ear to ear. "Right. Where's our hideout, Mac?"

"That's a surprise, partner."

Travis pushes the speed limit, rounding curves and screeching tires. He races up a mountain road out of Payson headed back to the Mogollon Rim.

"Travis, slow down. God, you're a terrible driver. You're going to get us all killed."

"We are just getting started, Bandita. Hold on to your shorts because we are some badass hombres. Right, buddy?"

Kyler chuckles. *Holding on to your shorts is turning into peeing your pants.*

"Slow down!"

Travis eases off the accelerator. They've reached the top of the rim, bouncing around old logger roads. The truck jerks and lunges. A wave of muddy water drenches the windshield.

"You hit that hole on purpose. What is wrong with you?"

"I'm making it fun for my little outlaw pard."

"Well, your little Bandita pard isn't having any fun. I think I'm going to throw up."

"Whoa, whoa, whoa. Okay. We're gonna slow it down, Kyler. We're about to go off-road, anyway."

"Thank you—*Pard*."

***

"This is it, Kyler. Our outlaw hideout. Follow Dr. Grace down the steps...and watch out for that last step, buddy. Dr. Grace likes to try to get a little friendly by falling on ya. It's an old ninja girl trick she learned."

"Nice, Travis. Very nice. Keep living in your fantasy world." She refuses to laugh. He's so stupid.

"Kyler, this is your bunk right here, buckaroo. I've got some games and toys in that there dresser over there. Help yourself."

"Let's hope *Big Mac Daddy* didn't leave any of his *special* toys in that dresser."

"What? Was that a joke? You're cracking jokes now, Doc?"

"Travis, we need to get serious. What are we going to do? These people will not stop looking for us. We need a plan."

"We're safe here, for now. This place is off the grid and protected by an electromagnetic shield to prevent anyone from locating us."

"Okay...when did you have time to install that?"

"I had a lot of funds waiting for me when they woke me up, and I spent a big chunk on securing this place. Never trusted Steinburg. There's not a whole lot of cash left, but I have enough to get by on."

"Travis. I have to confess. I have millions in funds or credits or whatever the currency is these days. We have all the money we need. We can go wherever we need to go. Overseas even. We could blend and disappear."

"Are you joshing me right now? Well, that gives us a hell of a lot more options. I always wanted a sugar mama. Let's whip up some grub and then sleep on it. Put our heads together in the morn. Hey Kyler, what do ya say you and me make out our Christmas lists early, huh, buddy?

"Your bunk is here, Kyler. Doc, you can take the one in the corner next to the toys. I'll shack out over here. We have a lot to work on tomorrow, so let's get some shuteye."

12

The Backdoor

Voices disrupt the early morning tranquility. Heavy boots shuffle and vibrate across the ceiling. Kyler squeals and scrambles into Emily's bed. His tiny frame trembles. Pounding on the door reverberates throughout the stairwell. Her body flinches with each blow leveled against the door.

"I thought you said they wouldn't find us, Travis. What should we do?"

"Get dressed. Fast. Grab your gear. The trapdoor will hold 'em off for a little while."

Travis slips into camos and combat boots and places a boonie hat atop his head. He slides a pair of yellow sunglasses over his eyes and straps a holster around his waist, a Bowie knife on his hip, and a utility vest over his shoulders. He grabs an M4 Carbine assault rifle from the rack along with several fully-loaded magazines and slaps a loaded magazine into the rifle, then wedges several more magazines into the slots in his vest.

He strips the large canvas off the back wall. Heavy metal screeches across the concrete floor as he slides the door open. He flips on lights illuminating a long tunnel through the rock.

"Here, Em. Take this Glock 9mm. It's loaded. Ready to go."

"Are you crazy? I don't know how to use *that*. I'll end up shooting myself...or you."

"That's a shame. We need to remedy that." He slips the Glock into his belt.

"Okay, let's go. That door ain't gonna hold much longer."

Emily buttons her jacket and blows warmth into her clenched fists. A potent scent of musty earth fills her nostrils as she enters the corridor. Travis slides a heavy lock across the reinforced door behind them. They shuffle along a narrow tunnel of rock and dirt in a tight group.

"Move, move, move. Come here, buddy. I'm gonna carry ya. It'll be okay, I promise. This is all part of playing outlaws. Isn't this a hoot?"

Kyler frowns and shakes his head in protest. He glances at Emily—eyes wide and glistening. After thirty yards, the tunnel ends. A set of stairs cut into stone leads upward. Travis hands Kyler to her and pushes a weathered wooden door up and out. A bright blue morning sky and warm beams of sunlight filtered through a ceiling of pine trees greet them.

"Okay, we're in thick woods here. Let's move quick but quiet."

Dead pine needles on the forest floor muffle their steps. A sharp branch scrapes Emily's calf. A warm trickle of blood oozes along her ankle.

"Ouch. Dammit."

"That looks painful. Ya gotta suck it up, gal."

"Who said I'm not going to suck it up? Keep walking. I'm right behind you."

"Em, I'm going to leave you two alone for a few minutes. See that road over there?"

"Yes. I see it. Why?"

"I'm going to retrieve the pickup truck. We have to hope they didn't notice it hidden in the brush. I'll pull around, and both of you jump in the front seat as fast as you can. Got it?"

She sighs. "All right, got it. Travis...be careful."

"If I'm not back in fifteen minutes, take Kyler and head into those trees and keep going until you reach the highway. Lie low in the trees and find your way back to Payson. Understand?"

"Yeah...I guess. Just make sure you're back in fifteen minutes or less, okay?"

Kyler's body quivers. She embraces him and whispers in his ear. "It's okay, Kyler. Big Mac will be right back. As soon as we see his truck, we're going to run and hop in, got it?"

"Got it. Just please don't leave me."

"Good boy. I won't leave you. I promise I'm right here with you. Let's sit tight for a few minutes and hope ole Big Mac knows what the heck he's doing."

Minutes pass in slow motion. No sign of Travis or his truck. Her stomach churns. She wipes the blood from her ankle with her sleeve, revealing a ragged gash. Tires hum and grind along the gravel road. *God, please be Travis.* She grabs Kyler's hand and leads him out of the woods. They squat behind rows of heavy brush and thick grass near the road.

"It's him. Get ready, Kyler."

The truck skids to a stop, kicking up a cloud of dust and rocks. The passenger door swings wide.

"Jump in! Hurry, hurry. Come on. We gotta go."

She lifts Kyler onto the front seat and leaps into the cab after him. Kyler scrambles into the back of the cab like a bug and tucks into a ball in the back seat.

"Everyone buckle up. We have company... Time for a little old-fashioned four-wheeling. Hang on to your shorts."

"A pewter-gray flat jeep is right behind us!"

"It's a military vehicle. Let's see how well he can ditch hop... and it's gunmetal gray Doc."

"Whatever. Just lose them, Travis. Hurry."

Their truck leaves the road and smashes through brush and tree branches—bouncing over small boulders and slinging rooster tails of mud and debris in its wake. The military jeep mirrors their maneuvers along the trail behind them. They splash through a small creek and speed over a grassy field. The jeep follows and is gaining ground.

"Faster, Travis. They're right behind us. Oh, God!"

"I see them, dammit. Stay calm. See that group of trees over there? There's a steep downhill trail behind it...usually muddy. Hang on, we're gonna see how bad they want to follow us, babe."

"Okay...no...what you just did there? Don't call me babe. Call me, Doc, call me princess, call me anything but 'babe.'"

Travis's truck crashes through the trees and hits the steep trail at full speed. The truck fishtails and slides across thick mud, bouncing high into the air over each curve. "Oh, my God. This is insane. Please don't flip the truck. Please, please."

"How you doing back there, Kyler? Having fun yet, buddy?"

Kyler remains tucked into a tight ball atop the seat—eyes closed. The military jeep hits the trail and slides sideways, almost rolling over. It stops before proceeding down the road at a slower speed.

"We're losing them. Hit the gas, Travis."

"Um, there ain't no gas, Doc. But I get whatcha mean."

They slam into the bottom of the trail. The truck jerks sideways. The rear tires spin out on the gravel then catch traction with a grinding screech. Travis floors it. The jeep is further behind but closing fast. A ping hits the tailgate. The back window explodes. Kyler screams and panics. His aquamarine eyes widen and glisten. He crawls onto the floor of the back seat, sobbing.

"Ah, shit! They're shooting at us, Em. Kyler! Stay down, buddy. I'm gonna take us off the road again. We're gonna lose them in those woods up ahead."

Travis manages a harrowing turn off the gravel road headed towards the thick forest. A tire blows! They veer. The world is rotating sideways. Emily's body whips side to side, and she blacks out for several seconds. An annoying thrum resonates inside her ears. When her eyes open, Travis is a blur. Everything has stopped. The truck is pinned against a large eucalyptus tree. Travis's lips are moving, but all she can hear is a blaring horn. Ashy smoke rises from the front of the vehicle.

"Quick. Unbuckle Kyler. Get out this way. Move it, Em!"

He snags Kyler under one arm and grabs Emily by the wrist with his other hand—yanking her from the truck. He rushes them into the trees and thickets.

"Stay down. Stay hidden."

Travis squats behind a large fallen pine tree. He uses the tree to steady his assault rifle. The jeep slides to a stop twenty yards away. Four soldiers leap out and position themselves behind the jeep. One of the soldier's legs is exposed beneath the vehicle. Travis lines up a shot in the crosshairs of the scope and squeezes the trigger. A crack echoes through the trees.

"Ah! Damn it! I'm shot. That fucker shot me!"

He whispers. "Em. Take Kyler and head south."

"Which way's south? I don't know directions, Travis."

He points. "That way. Go."

Kyler's small hand quivers inside hers. They crawl over fallen tree branches, twigs, and brush, and work their way southward. Several cracks ring out, sending splinters of wood into the air in front of them. A soldier sprints towards Travis's truck, using it for cover, while another soldier sprays several rounds of ammo into the woods.

"Oh God, he didn't see that soldier over there entering the woods. We have to go back, Kyler."

"Give it up, McCallister. We have you outgunned. Come out, and nobody else gets hurt."

Bullets fly from behind the jeep. The soldier hiding behind Travis's truck bolts toward the trees. Several pops from Travis's M4 Carbine, and the soldier collapses in a heap.

She whispers. "Travis. Travis. There's one coming through the trees to the left of you."

Her skull explodes from a jolt. Lights sparkle in front of her eyes. She's facedown on the forest floor. Kyler is screaming. His legs flail several feet above her.

"I got your girlfriend, McCallister. And your little boy. You need to drop your weapon and step out. Now!"

She sits upright and heaves a breath. The world shifts and spins as she attempts to focus.

"Put him down. He's just a little boy. Give him to me, asshole."

The soldier bends and places Kyler on her lap. Heavy brush behind the soldier explodes with splinters and leaves. The soldier drops to his knees, wide-eyed. His mouth gapes like a fish out of water. A trickle of scarlet blood drips off his chin. Travis yanks a bloody Bowie from the man's back and shoves him to the ground with his boot.

Travis glances at her and grins. He winks and pulls her to her feet—knees wobbling and her mind clouded. Travis saved them. *Who the heck is this man?*

"Travis."

She takes a step towards him. A single pop echoes through the trees. Blood gushes from the side of Travis's neck. He crumbles to one knee and reaches for her. His eyes blink with shock.

He cries out in a raspy voice, "Em. Run. Take Kyler and get the hell out of here."

"No. I can't leave you. I can't..."

He collapses.

"Don't move, ma'am. Don't force me to shoot you, too. Be smart."

The soldier taps on a device inside his ear. "We have them."

13

MORPHEUS, GOD OF DREAMS

Travis grips his neck, applying pressure to stem the flow of thick crimson blood. She drops to her knees and cradles his head. His eyes are closed, and his dimples accent a fading smile.

"Travis. Don't leave us. Hang on. Please try to hang on. You can call me 'babe.' You can call me 'Doc' or anything you want. Just don't leave us. Don't leave me."

A swarm of military vehicles arrives at the scene, illuminating the area with flashing lights like a discotheque.

"Let's go, ma'am."

"No! Let the boy come with me. Why are you separating us?"

"Get in the vehicle, ma'am. I will not tell you again."

"It'll be okay, Kyler. I'll come and find you, sweetheart...don't cry, sweetie."

The soldier's forceful shove leaves her sprawled across the rear seat of the jeep. She's trapped. Where are they taking them? Kyler is probably afraid. His cries stab at her heart. How serious is Travis's condition? An ambulance flees the scene. Its warbling siren pierces her eardrums then fades in the distance. In only a moment, she has lost the closest chance at a family she's ever known. The brain cancer she once faced almost pales in comparison to the loss she now faces.

We play God. We think we have authority over life and death in our hands and within our labs. The promise of hope she sold to all those trusting souls ended in their deaths and destruction.

It's a game of power—a seductive lie that intoxicates the mind— blinding us to the truth. Our knowledge and abilities are filled with limits, flaws, and imperfections.

Her program once provided her patients a genuine chance at a promising future. But the future turned out to be corrupt and vile and led to butchery and death. We can't play God because we are not God. She draws her knees into her chest, making herself small. Shivering. Hiding inside her grief and weeping silent tears.

***

She has come eighty-seven years only to sit in a tiny jail cell surrounded by stainless steel walls and metal grids and has committed no crime. Emily devotes her life to saving people. Now she can't even save herself.

"Good evening to you, Dr. Grace. I hope you are finding your accommodations satisfactory and to your liking."

"Steinburg. You son of a bitch."

"Now, now. Let's not be rude, Emily. It's not becoming of a professional of your stature."

"What is going on? I want answers."

"Well, you see, Emily, it's your curiosity and your need for answers that got you into this sticky pickle you find yourself in."

Dr. Steinburg sits on a metal bench across from her. The door latches behind him. Two guards stand outside the cell, chuckling and having an indistinct conversation.

"You pulled a fast one on me, Dr. Grace. I have to commend you and Mac. I can't believe I fell for it, but your archaic Trojan virus was identified immediately by our system and our staff. Our programmers were entertained and delighted by the nostalgia of it. Amazingly, you managed to adapt obsolete code into modern programming. I didn't realize you were capable of such a shrewd plan. We couldn't decide if it was genius on your part or simply pure luck. I underestimated you. Well done. We planted a sneaky little *Trojan* of our own. When you accessed the network, your exact location was revealed, allowing us to track you down. Clever, wouldn't you say?"

"Where's Kyler? And Travis?"

"Don't worry. They're in excellent hands."

"What do you plan on doing? Experiment on us in your sick Morpheus project? Terminate us?"

The two guards enter the cell and immobilize her by grasping her arms.

"My dear, you are *already* participating in the Morpheus Project."

Steinburg reveals a hypodermic needle and jabs it deep into her forearm.

"Sleep well. It's been a pleasure working with the legendary Dr. Emily Grace."

The injection burns—numbness travels through her veins and along her arm—reaching her heart. Her temples pound and her heart flutters and races. She can't breathe. Her body cramps, and sweat leaks from every pore of her skin. Steinburg glares at her. Smirking. Watching her die. Her heart stops. A swoosh rushes through her ears like the crashing waves of an ocean. Blackness encompasses her. So, this is death?

***

White light sears through her eye sockets. Echoes whisper. Voices mumble in the distance. Classical music. Chopin? The scent of strawberries permeates the air. She quivers.

"Dr. Grace? Dr. Grace, can you hear me?"

She nods.

"Good. You'll be awake in a few minutes. I'll be back to check on you."

Her eyes adjust to the light. She's strapped to a cushy lounge chair. Tubes and wires seem to poke out from everywhere like a mad experiment gone awry. Beeps and clicks surround her. *This is a lab.*

"Where am I this time? Is this hell?"

"Oh good. You're awake. I'm going to unhook you and move you onto this gurney. The gurney will take you to your room."

"What? Who are you? Where am I?"

"You're safe, Dr. Grace. You'll be in recovery in a few minutes where you can rest."

The gurney travels along hallways and through doorways. It ends up in a small hospital room where it butts up against a hospital bed. The gurney speaks in a robotic voice.

"Please slide your body onto the bed."

She scooches and snuggles inside the warm bedding. She lays her hand across her forehead. A bandage? Where's her hair? It doesn't seem to be on her head. Her eye sockets throb. She pinches the bridge of her nose and rubs her temples.

"Oh, good. You're all tucked in. Here's something for the pain, Dr. Grace. It should help you sleep. In the morning, your surgeon will be in to speak with you."

What the hell? Déjà vu? Have I lost my mind? Why is this happening again? Who are these people? And where the heck am I? Wait. If I'm here, maybe Travis is here too...and Kyler. What if they're both alive? Or maybe we're all dead.

A surge of paralysis courses through her body. She can't fight it. The sedatives are too powerful. Her eyelids droop and close.

***

A shadowy blur. A small flashlight clicks and sheens like a tiny beacon in the distance.

"Good morning, Dr. Grace. I'm Dr. Chen. How are you feeling?"

"How am I feeling? I'm feeling confused. Misplaced. Can someone please tell me where I am?"

"You are recovering from surgery. We have successfully removed the mass from your brain and spinal cord. You are free of your cancer. You'll be groggy for another twenty-four hours. But soon after, you will feel better than you've ever felt in your life."

"Okay. I've officially lost my mind and entered the Twilight Zone."

"Twilight Zone? Is that a medical term from the 2020s?"

"No. It's a TV show from the 1960s. I'm now living it...for real. So, tell me, Dr. Chen...know anything about the *Morpheus* Project?"

"No. I am a neurosurgeon like yourself. They assigned your case to me, and I performed your surgery. Do you have questions for me regarding your surgery or your recovery?"

"Yeah, I do. What procedure did you use to remove my cancer?"

"Well, ironically the procedure is the 'Grace Procedure.'"

"What a coincidence...I'm flattered."

She sighs. *This guy is clueless. Assuming he's real. Do I exist in this place? Was Travis real?* Kyler showed no signs of HGPS, which is odd. The expectation would be for the disease to reverse itself with a cure. But to show no signs is confounding.

"Any more questions for me, Dr. Grace?"

"Um. Just one. Did you happen to notice if...maybe I have a few scars from another brain surgery? You know...besides the ones you gave me?"

"I think I would have noticed, Doctor."

"Okay, Dr. Chen, I guess I have no questions for you regarding my surgery. If you say I'm cured, I'll just have to take your word for it. At least until I wake up in some new reality or another fantasy world."

"Very good. I will leave you now in the care of your nurse."

"Oh, Dr. Chen?"

"Yes, Doctor?"

"You wouldn't happen to know the prognosis of a patient named Travis McCallister or Kyler Carson, would you?"

"I am not familiar with any patients by those names. I'm very sorry. Your nurse can help you from here."

"No problem. It was worth a shot."

"Hello, Dr. Grace. I'm your nurse for the evening. I'm going to administer this medication into your bloodstream to put you back to sleep for the next twenty-four hours. When you wake, you will be completely well and able to check out of the ward."

"Oh, joy. I'm going to sleep again. And where will I wake up next? Is this medication going to regrow my hair by chance?"

"Your body will heal, and you will be healthier than you've ever been in your life. Your hair will grow back in time. Don't worry."

"You're serious? You can do all these amazing things with a body, but you can't grow hair? How about a hat? Or a scarf? Can I at least get something to cover my head when I leave?"

"Of course. Good night, Doctor. We will see you in the morning. Dr. Steinburg will be in to check on you and answer questions you may have."

"What? Steinburg?"

A black veil descends over her eyes and carries her into blissful nothingness.

14

A Reunion of Sorts

What is *actual* life? Can humankind ever become so enlightened that a utopian world is possible? That's the deception. By playing God, we become so obsessed with power and control that we condemn ourselves as prisoners of our misguided ideals. Our true ambitions fall in line with the ambitions of the biblical Lucifer? *I will rise above the heights of the clouds and become like the Most-High.* And in doing so, the transformation of the Angelic Lucifer to the Demonic Satan is complete. Gain the world and lose your soul.

"Ah, I see you are awake, Dr. Grace. You look well. How do you feel?"

"Steinburg. You son of a bitch. How do you think I feel? You murdered Travis, murdered Kyler, murdered all those patients... all those children. I think you murdered me. So, where am I this time? What is happening to me?"

"If you'll just calm down and give me a few moments to explain everything, it will make perfect sense. Can you do that for me?"

"Well, obviously I'm not going anywhere...and I don't even know where *here* is anymore. Go ahead. Enlighten me with more of your lies. This should be entertaining."

"Travis, Kyler, and all your old patients are not dead. We didn't murder anyone."

Her neck pulsates in sync with her pounding heart. A glimmer of hope, maybe? Or more deception?

"Prove it. Take me to them."

"Hold on a minute. Let me finish."

"Go on then. Finish. And after you do, I want to see Travis and Kyler."

"We selected you, Travis, and Kyler. You were perfect matches psychologically and in the way your neurons map memory. It's very complicated, but I assure you, you will understand the science behind it if you allow me to explain. First, let me give you an overview."

"Yeah...sure. Of course. You're making *perfect* sense. Clear as the cesspool you climbed out of this morning."

"Emily, I understand you are upset. Everything you experienced when you awoke inside of Morpheus was real. The brain cannot distinguish between reality and a dream. They are chemically the same experience. The world you inhabited, as far as your mind is concerned, existed. *You* created the realities of your experience. The most phenomenal aspect of what you experienced is the fact that you experienced it along with Travis and Kyler. It was also their reality. All three of your minds were experiencing Morpheus in sync with one another and your lives played out in a beautiful symphony of synergy."

"Have you lost your mind, Steinburg? What the hell are you talking about? What is wrong with you people?"

"No. No, we haven't lost our minds. We have created a means for the mind to survive for millennia. Immortality. Preserved in cryonic sleep, Morpheus gives us the ability to match individuals who can integrate into a world within a community of minds. This allows their brains to maintain their integrity and grow new synapses and molecular connections by creating new memories as a team...as one communal mind."

"Oh, my God. You've created the ultimate nightmare. That's what you've done."

"Emily, Morpheus will allow humankind to travel the universe light-years away. Can you imagine the possibilities? During cryonic sleep, astronauts will attend training and education related to their mission...just as if they were awake. And just as real. By the time they reach their destination, they will be fully prepared and educated for the job."

"You're insane. What's preventing the horrible experience you forced on me from happening to one of your astronauts?"

"A thing called memory mapping. We plant scenarios where education and training take place. We guide their thoughts. They still have the freedom to create, but they create their realities around the memories we map into their brains. Similar to the way a plant uses a stem to grow and branch out."

"How can you be so sure your experiment is going to work? How do you know these programs won't turn into a hellish nightmare with no way to escape?"

"Because we have a successful test run. You, Travis, and Kyler."

"You call that successful? I call it an abomination—an unthinkable violation. Worse than being raped."

"Dr. Grace... Emily. I want to invite you to join us. Join our team of scientists. We could use someone of your stature on the team. Your integrity, dedication, and intellect are beyond reproach. And you have had the benefit of experiencing Morpheus firsthand. Help us. Help us make the project a reality for humankind. A means to expand our species throughout the universe...away from this dying planet."

"Listen to yourself. You bunch of idiots. Why would I join your team? My knowledge of neuroscience is eighty-seven years old. Assuming it's actually 2108. And you want to expand our species across the universe? A species that destroyed its planet? Why? So, we can destroy other planets?"

"Your knowledge of neuroscience is beyond mine. We mapped that knowledge into your memories at the same time we cured your cancer. Think. Go ahead. You have a wealth of knowledge tucked away in your mind, Doctor."

"You expect me to believe that?"

"Dr. Grace. How many types of brain cells are there in a human brain aside from neurons and glia?"

"Those are the only ones we know...wait. There are dozens of other types. Each with unique functions and hundreds of unique classes of neurons. How do I know that? How do I know each of their functions? Oh my God. It all makes perfect sense."

He smirks. "What other ways do our brain cells communicate other than through synapses?"

"Molecules. Specific molecules. I know precisely which molecules are involved in these cells. What have you done to me? How can I know these things?"

"We made you more intelligent and far more knowledgeable than you could ever imagine. The wiring in your brain, so to speak, is rare, and you are the perfect candidate for the implant we placed that has advanced your knowledge of neuroscience. We'd like you to lead our team. Reinstate you as head of the department. Come out of retirement and join us, Dr. Grace. I implore you to consider the opportunity."

"No. I won't do it. Now, tell me where Travis and Kyler are."

"I'm disappointed to hear that. And I'm sorry I cannot share with you any information about Mr. McCallister or Kyler Carson. It's confidential."

"I want to leave. I want out of here."

"We can't allow you to leave, Emily. You have no idea what the world outside has become. It's safer inside this facility, where you are free to wander around. Everything you need is contained in this building. Access to a gym, a dance room...there's a movie theater and a very nice swimming pool with a sandy beach. You'd swear you were in Tahiti."

"That all sounds peachy and swell, Mr. Roarke...if I was on Fantasy Island. I want the hell out of here."

"I'll have one of our assistants give you a tour and escort you to your apartment. If you change your mind and want to work with us, simply ask an assistant to...well, assist you."

"Let me tell you something, Steinburg. I don't trust you or anything you say."

"That's a shame, Emily. I'm very sorry to hear that."

He turns and glances at a young woman standing near the doorway.

"Ms. Raintree, will you show Dr. Grace the facility and escort her to her new home?

He turns and faces Emily and nods.

"Good day. I hope we can talk again soon...under better circumstances, of course. And I hope you will reconsider our proposal."

***

At least this apartment is roomier than the one she occupied inside Morpheus. It has a 2020s vibe and decor. A full closet of clothes. All her style. *I need a cat. I miss Rexy. Poor Rexy. Wonder what happened to him?*

"Okay, the coffee-maker is from my era—and all my favorite coffees. Hm. What a coincidence. And well, looks like the NERU HG Pro is a real thing. However, we define what *real* is."

She falls into a large comfy lounge chair and hugs a fluffy pillow. Ms. Raintree said she'd be by in an hour to take her on a tour of the facility. Maybe she can gather clues where Travis and Kyler are being held. Why would they separate them? For what purpose? Maybe taking Steinburg up on his offer would give her some leverage in reuniting with Travis and Kyler.

15

A BARGAIN STRUCK

A resounding buzz resonates throughout the apartment. She jerks and leaps from her chair. Ms. Raintree is youthful and attractive. Her long raven hair creates a twinge of envy. The silk scarf on Emily's head is a reminder of how much she misses her hair. Ms. Raintree is petite, but her boobs are busting out of her tight purple dress suit. Her bottom is too darn cute. She's gorgeous. Emily giggles to herself. *I hate her.*

Steinburg was right about one thing: Her pain level is zero. A marathon isn't out of the question. Her mind is sharp as the tip of Travis's Bowie and focused like the motherboard of a computer. The human brain isn't as mysterious as it once was. What did they do to her?

"Dr. Grace, I hope you are feeling well. Let's start the tour right here in the housing section. We have four units. One for faculty and staff; one for program volunteers; guest rooms for visitors; and housing for management—which is where you are staying. Isn't that so nice?"

"Hm. Volunteers, huh? I'm sure. Yeah, it's great."

Ms. Raintree points. Sparkling lavender nail polish and turquoise jewelry decorate her petite tawny fingers. She carries a pleasant scent of citrus.

"This hallway leads us to the cafeteria. We have a large menu and a wonderful variety of foods and dishes from all around the world. I'm a vegetarian, so I prefer the amazing salads and meatless dinner choices. I've got to keep this tummy flat for my man, you know."

"Vegetarian? What a surprise. I'm sure he appreciates that."

"Oh, he does. Next to the cafeteria is a commissary. You can find anything you're looking for in there. It's great if you want to get creative and personalize your meals."

"Which I'm sure you like to do, right?"

"How did you know? You're too observant, Dr. Grace," Raintree said, giggling.

"Yeah, so I've been told."

"Over here is our recreation wing. There's a gym, dance room, pool, movie theater, VR room, and even a nightclub and bar if you're into that sort of thing."

"Great. I am. I could use a nice shot of tequila."

"Oh. Well, that'll have to wait until the tour is over. Sorry."

"Yeah." Emily points at Ms. Raintree like she's firing a pistol—followed by a wink and click of her tongue.

"Down this hallway is the ER and operating rooms. You should be familiar with these areas. Next to them are the hospital rooms and recovery units and the rehab wing.

"Through those doors are the Maintenance and the IT Departments. If you go down that hallway, you will run into the Security Department and an office for Military Operations." Ms. Raintree whispers, "We don't go in there."

Ms. Raintree stops and pivots on her right heel and opens her palms to present the next area. "I saved the Research Labs for last...thought you'd be most interested in these. This is Research and Development. Over here are Neuroscience studies and up the hallway is the pharmacy and drug testing facility."

"What's behind that red door?"

"Oh, that one. That is where they conduct the Morpheus Project."

"Is that where Travis McCallister and Kyler Carson are being held?"

"I-I wouldn't know. That door is secured, and only authorized personnel are allowed access. I'm not one of them."

"I see. So, they *are* in there."

Ms. Raintree shrugs. "I wouldn't know. I'm sorry. Well, that completes the tour, Dr. Grace, other than the administrative offices."

"Thank you, Ms. Raintree. Do you have a first name?"

Ms. Raintree beams. "I do. It's Sierra."

"That's a beautiful name. Sierra, do you think you can deliver a message for me to Dr. Steinburg?"

"Absolutely. And thank you. My parents named me after my grandmother."

"Please tell him I'd like to speak to him about his proposal."

"I will do that. Allow me to escort you back to your apartment."

"One more question, Sierra. What is the date? What's today?"

"It's Friday...August third."

"But what year is it?"

"2108, Dr. Grace."

***

Her apartment buzzer resonates throughout the walls. She opens the door two inches and peers through the opening.

Dr. Steinburg fidgets. "I received your message, Emily. May I come in?"

She swings the door wide and plops onto her lounge chair. She punches a fat pillow into her lap and sighs.

"Have a seat, Dr. Steinburg. I've thought a lot about what you said and I've reconsidered your offer."

"Very good. And what did you conclude?"

"I'm going to make you a deal, Dr. Steinburg. Non-negotiable."

"I'm listening."

"I will join your staff as the head of the department and work with you on the Morpheus Project on one condition."

He raises his palms and cocks his head, anticipating the condition.

"I need to meet with both Travis and Kyler. I want to speak to them in private, and I want full-time access to both of them. Otherwise, count me out."

"I see." He removes his spectacles and purses his lips.

"I accept your terms. Having you on the project far outweighs the reservations I have of reuniting you with McCallister and the boy. Understand that the reality of their conditions may not be what you expect. You have yet to meet them both in person."

"What do you mean? Did something happen to them?"

"Nothing has happened to them. Just trust me on this, and I will make the arrangements you have requested. You can reunite with them as early as this evening if you desire."

"Well, I *don't* trust you. But I appreciate you agreeing to my request, and afterward, you'll have a new scientist on your staff."

"Dr. Grace, I need to share something with you and also provide you with your first assignment. Your experience in Morpheus was created by your combined minds. I'm referring to you, McCallister, and Kyler. Whatever I did in those scenarios was not reality. I didn't do whatever it is you feel betrayed by.

"That being said, my first assignment for you is to document your full experience—every nuance...every event. Explain your thoughts and rationalizing. We can inject certain aspects of the environment into the minds of Morpheus subjects, but we do not know how your lives play out. We have to rely on your account of everything you have experienced.

"I'll arrange for a meeting room for your reunion. Would six o'clock this evening be acceptable?"

"I want to meet with them here...in this apartment. Six o'clock is fine."

"Hm. You are a tough negotiator. I will have one of my staff escort Mr. McCallister and young Kyler to your apartment. We will also cater dinner for you all to celebrate your reunion...on my dime, of course."

Daddy always said a man's handshake says a lot about his character. Steinburg's handshake is feeble, cold, and sweaty. She locks her door upon his exit and checks the time. 4:47 p.m. She allows her clothes to drop to the floor. She bunches up her scarf and examines her scalp in the mirror. *No scarring. Wow. Definitely sporting the Sinead O'Conner look...going to take some getting used to. I look like I'm twenty-five again. My stomach is so flat...and my boobs...oh my God.*

She mumbles. "Well, I hope the clothes they picked out for me fit. I want to look good for Travis—despite my lack of hair."

She slips into the shower, allowing warm water to bathe her face and trickle down her shoulders and spine.

"Gee. All my favorite brands of shampoo and conditioner. Do they realize I'm bald?"

She steps out from the shower and dabs the moisture from her body, gliding deodorant across her armpits. She slides her body into a casual denim summer dress. Her shoulders look solid. The denim is on purpose. She wraps a clean silk scarf around her scalp.

Emily slips her toes into a pair of straw-wedge high heels. She's never worn a lot of makeup—never needed to. Mascara, a touch of pink lipstick, a pair of small hoop earrings, and a spray of Givenchy perfume, and she is ready for her guests and pacing like a nervous feline.

16

An Emotional Reunion

Six o'clock. Buzzing vibrates the walls. Emily flinches and heaves a breath. The swish of her pulse pounds inside her ears, and her cheeks flush. Seems like years instead of days since she last saw them? Of course, who can trust time at this moment?

She peeks through the door. He's still rugged and handsome. Maybe a bit taller. Younger. Still has the scar. Aw, Kyler. Little Kyler. So handsome. The characteristic symptoms of his HGPS are obvious. However, he's much taller than an HGPS child could ever hope to be. And his symptoms appear to be in remission, if that's even possible.

"Travis. Kyler. Oh, my God. Come in, come in."

She kneels and scoops Kyler into her arms—kissing his forehead, cheeks, and neck. She rises and ogles Travis. What a pain in the ass. But God, how she has missed him. He outstretches his long arms and winks.

"Wow, Em, you're beautiful. But what the hell happened to your hair?"

She punches him in the chest. Her eyes well and tears spill over her cheeks. She squeezes into his arms and buries her face into his chest. The scent of leather and spice was real. It lingers. She wraps her arms around his torso and shares a silent embrace.

He whispers, "This always worked on the goats, *babe*."

She pushes away from him, laughing and sobbing—wiping away tears with her fingers.

"Sit. We have so much to talk about, boys."

She plops onto the sofa, and Kyler tucks into her lap. Travis squats into the easy chair opposite of her. His movements seem awkward.

"Travis? I don't think I ever asked you what happened to your leg."

"Lost it in Syria."

He rolls his pant leg upward. "This is a temporary prosthetic from the knee down. They're supposed to fix me up with a better one soon. They tell me it will look, act, and feel like the real thing. I think they're full of shit."

"I never asked you this, but are you the only soldier in your family, Travis?"

"Nah, I have an uncle in the Army...well, had an uncle. He's the reason I joined. He fought in Nam...was a special ops captain. I followed in his footsteps. He became *General* Richard McCallister and spent his remaining years waxing a chair with his ass at the Pentagon. He was more like a father to me than an uncle."

Kyler gazes at her. His unblinking aquamarine eyes cause her heart to flutter. The characteristic beak-shaped nose and bald head of his condition are evidence he continues to be held prisoner by his genetics. She pulls off her scarf and winks at him, provoking a beaming smile behind his thinned lips.

"Geez, Doc...They shaved your entire head? I-I mean...don't get me wrong...it's a beautiful bald head and all... perfect shape..."

"Thanks...I think. It came with my brain surgery. You're just going to have to get used to it, there, Gimpy—until it all grows back."

He guffaws. He seems to delight in antagonizing her . It must entertain him somehow. God, how nice it is to be sitting here with him and Kyler. She jerks. "Dammit, I *hate* that buzzer."

She swings open the door. A teenage boy driving a food cart greets her.

"Your dinner, Dr. Grace. Courtesy of Dr. Steinburg."

"That's a damn nice-looking spread there, Doc. Kyler, let's eat, buddy."

Steak, potatoes with all the fixings, country-style green beans, buttered sourdough buns, and homemade tapioca pudding. *How did they know?*

"How long can you stay, Travis?"

"They're going to send someone to escort us back at ten p.m."

"Ten p.m.? No. I want you both to stay the night."

"Well, I'd love to, Em. But I don't know how that's going to go over with *the man*."

"You're both staying. I'll tell whoever comes to get you, you're staying the night, and they can tell Steinburg to allow it to happen."

"All right. I'm in...Tell that pencil-neck to shove it up his ass, right? Oh. Sorry, buddy."

Kyler bursts into laughter. Neither she nor Travis has ever heard him laugh so hard. His giggles sound like the bleats of a sheep. She snags a bottle of wine and a beer from her refrigerator.

"Look at this, Travis. *Egon Muller Scharzhofberger Riesling Spatlese 2018.* This had to cost them a small fortune. I'm going to drink this one slow. Here's a vintage Coors just for you, Pard."

***

"Doc, what the hell is going on here? Are we sitting here having this conversation, or is this is just another simulation?"

"I don't know...I *honestly* don't. I believe it's real, but who knows? Travis, when they pulled us out of Morpheus, where did they take you?"

"I woke up in a hospital bed. They told me they removed the shrapnel from my brain. I'm so damn confused. They wheeled me to a recovery room, and I saw Kyler in there. A day later, they took us both to a military barracks, and that's where we've been camping out. No explanation. No nothing."

She sighs. "I plan on solving this mystery. They want to put me in charge of the Morpheus program, and I'm going to use that position to get some answers."

"What? Morpheus? Why? You be careful, Em. Don't trust that scumbag, Steinburg."

"Trust me; I don't. I'm going to use this opportunity to find out as much as I can."

The buzzer! She avoids spilling her third glass of wine.

"God, I've got to do something about that darn thing. It scares the crap out of me *every* time. Is it ten o'clock already?"

She yanks the door open to a startled young male staff member. "Can I help you?"

"Uh...Yes, ma'am. I'm here to pick up Mr. McCallister and Kyler...to escort them back to their quarters."

"Well, they're staying with me tonight."

"I'm afraid that's not possible, ma'am."

"I'm afraid it *is* possible. Do you work in the Morpheus area?"

"Yes, ma'am. I do."

"Say hello to your new boss. You can tell Dr. Steinburg that the boys are having a little sleepover with me tonight. You can come back tomorrow morning to pick them up."

"I-I will give him your message. Good night, Dr. Grace."

"Nice work, Doc. Hell, *I* was intimidated.

"Kyler. Get ole Big Mac another beer from that fridge, would ya, son?"

Travis removes his cowboy boots then detaches his artificial leg. He stretches his legs across the sofa. She gathers a blanket and pillow and tosses them over his face in a heap.

"I take it you want the sofa. Let me put Kyler to bed in my room, and I'll sleep out here on my comfy chair."

Kyler's hand fits inside of hers. She tucks him into a fluff of cotton bedding and kisses his forehead. He's asleep almost instantly. Poor guy was tired. She changes into a pair of satin pajamas and snags a pillow and a soft blanket from the bed. She squishes into her chair.

"Ya look a bit too comfortable there, Doc. This is a real nice place they put you in. Beats sleeping in the barracks. Smells like a men's locker room in there."

"Barracks, huh? We're going to fix that tomorrow."

"I have no doubt you will, Doc."

She shouts, "Dim the lights." The room goes dark save for a small kitchen light radiating a calm blue glow throughout the apartment.

"Impressive, Em. I just wanna say something here...Tonight was a great night. I enjoyed it. I also enjoy being around you... you're kinda special to me and..."

She slips out of her chair—listening to Travis ramble on and on. He has no idea she's standing over him. What would his body feel like next to hers? Emily's chest quivers as she inhales a nervous breath. She lifts the edge of his blanket and snuggles into the sofa next to him. Breathing shifts to soft panting. Her heart races. *Is this crazy?* It's bold. Her feelings for him are nothing like the feelings she had for her ex, Brandon. No. This is something unique. Is it love? Maybe. Infatuation? Probably. Sexual desire? Definitely.

"Em? What are you doing?"

She presses her index finger across his lips. "Shut up. It was lonely on that chair."

Her lips caress his. Pushing deeper. Harder. Tasting the alcohol in his breath. Filling her nostrils with his scent. He turns onto his side. His hands cradle her face. He kisses her cheek, then her neck. The warmth of his lips remains on her skin. A surge of passionate kisses ignites. They're like two bumbling teenagers groping for the first time. Clumsy. Fumbling in the dark. Where is this headed?

Her hand glides over heavily muscled pectorals—tugging at its coarse hair. He allows her to explore his body then pulls her hips towards his. She slips her thigh between both of his legs. Rubbing against him. Sensing a throbbing, pulsating response. She's never been the aggressor. It's intoxicating. Empowering.

His fingers glide across her skin inside her pajama top. A whimper rises in her throat. Quivering chills travel along her ribs and moisten her inner thighs with their warmth. If she doesn't stop now, it'll be too late.

"Travis. Let's move slow. I want to make this last—like my expensive wine."

She crawls into his hug. His kiss warms her forehead with a lingering softness.

He whispers, "Doc. Ya have anything in your medical bag for blue balls?"

She sighs and giggles. "There's no such thing."

"Oh, trust me. There is."

Their bodies entwine and fade into blissful sleep. Secure in each other's arms. Is this all part of another elaborate dream?

17

THE NEW BOSS

Institute staff arrived early this morning to escort Travis and Kyler back to the barracks. It must have been before 7:00 a.m. She hadn't checked the clock. Hadn't even opened her eyes. A hot shower and a steaming cup of coffee have her wide-eyed and alert—ready for her expected confrontation with Dr. Steinburg this morning. Not to mention her new role as head of the Morpheus Project at the Institute. Why would Steinburg be so eager to place her in charge of his pet project?

"That darn buzzer again. Geez."

"Good morning, Dr. Grace. I hope you slept well. Would you like a kale ball?"

"I slept better than I have in years...and no thanks, Sierra... Not really a *kale ball* kind of girl. You go ahead. Enjoy those... little tidbits."

"Dr. Steinburg wants me to escort you straight to the Morpheus lab. He wanted me to pass on to you he'd meet you inside the lab this morning."

"Thank you. I love your shoes, by the way. That's a fascinating pattern."

Sierra's eyes sparkle. Her full coral-colored lips widen at the edges, forming a partial grin. She stops walking and extends her right foot—wriggling and modeling her shoe.

"It's an ancient Navajo pattern. One I remember as a little girl. My boyfriend had these shoes custom-made to match this turquoise dress. It's his fave."

"Well, kudos to your beau. Perfect match. He did an outstanding job."

Sierra cocks her head and flips her long raven hair to the side. "Thank you. You think so?"

"Uh-huh. I do. You got it going on, girl."

"Here we are. Security has created a face-recognition scan for you in their system. Look into this window and smile. Dr. Steinburg should arrive soon. Have a nice day, Dr. Grace."

"Thanks, I will. And please, call me Emily."

Emily's smile causes the crimson door to buzz. She pulls the handle and enters the lab. The lights are dim. No windows. One way in and one way out. Three neuropods are standing erect against the far wall. At least they look like neuropods—definitely modified and improved. Four holographic computers sit at a station in the center of the lab atop a semi-round clear desk. The air is sterile and seems to contain a concentrated amount of oxygen. It's exhilarating. A familiar voice abruptly disturbs the silence of the room.

"Have a seat at your new desk, Dr. Grace. I hope you find your new office adequate and up to your standards."

She flinches. "Oh. Dr. Steinburg. You startled me. I didn't see you hovering in the corner over there. You stepped out of the shadows like Count Dracula. A window or two would have been nice...but it'll do...I guess."

Steinburg smirks. She didn't notice it before, but he appears shorter and skinnier than she remembers from her experience with him inside the Morpheus program. His facial features are not as symmetrical either. Programmed cosmetic enhancements, maybe? Or were the enhancements of his appearance something Steinburg's team mapped into her memory for her experience?

"Dr. Grace, let's get started. Allow me to brief you on the Morpheus Project mission and its purpose. Then I will point you in the direction of everything you need to know. All the info you need resides on your new HG computer. The files are there. The data...case studies...even your case study.

"Once you have gone over all the information, we can sit in my office and chat. You can give me your expert opinion and all your observations. From there, we will formulate a new strategy to execute Morpheus. We need to have the project ready for the United States Space Force by the end of this month."

"The end of this month? Twenty-seven days. That's a tad ambitious, isn't it?"

"It's our deadline. I'm confident we can work together and meet the requirements. Please have a seat, and we'll begin.

"The Morpheus Project creates a safe and enriching experience for astronauts and other space travelers. I'm talking *deep* space travel, Emily. Light years away. Placing space travelers into our state-of-the-art catatonic state will allow them to avoid aging.

"We place memories of the environment within the neurons or place cells in the hot zone of the brain. These are only minimal suggestions to these memory zones. We prefer participants to work together to create the rest of their environment and life scenarios on their own and with their team...in unison with their cryo-partners. Thus, forming an environment where symbiotic-type relationships can be established.

"We also place memories for participants to educate themselves on all the technologies and skills they will need for the mission. We instill training programs to allow them to learn the jobs they will do when they arrive at their destination. By the time they awaken, they will be trained and educated and will have formed strong relational bonds with their cryo-partners.

"The effects of living this virtual or dream-like existence also provide the benefits of keeping the brain and the body fit and intact. We preserve their minds and emotional well-being along with their basic needs and desires. The system applies a series of electrical charges to the subject's body at regular intervals to help maintain muscle integrity over long periods."

"Okay, that's the *theory*. What's the *reality*, Dr. Steinburg? This all sounds too perfect, and you're pitching it like a used car salesman. Give me the downside...the failures and dangers you've encountered. What are the challenges you face? Why do you need my help so desperately?"

"Well, Dr. Grace, this is where I leave you. All the answers to those questions exist on the network. Read through all the files, and then we'll talk later in more detail."

"One more thing, Dr. Steinburg. I want Travis and Kyler to move to the apartment next door to mine. That's not a request. I want it done today."

Steinburg frowns, then nods and exits the lab. His pitch sounds good on paper. But she has been a scientist for too many years to be persuaded into thinking this process is without flaws or risk. People used to say, "Trust the science." The people who said this were obviously not scientists. Science is not based on facts. Science comprises theory, hypotheses, observation, and conjecture. Theories evolve with discoveries that redefine concepts. Instead of trusting the science—trust the process.

***

Hundreds of files and documents lie before her. Her eyes throb, and she's developed a crick in the side of her neck. She stands and stretches. She read case study after case study but found no real meat to sink her teeth into. They create trios of participants. The amount of theta brainwave activity in the prefrontal cortex determines a match. Interesting. High amounts of theta brain wave activity result in better dream recollection. But what happened to these other participants? The reports don't say. It is sterile data.

She opens her case study with Travis and Kyler as her cryopartners. Maybe comparing a case study she is familiar with will provide clues to what's missing in the others. She wraps her hands around her chin and snaps her neck. A crackle runs along the vertebrae at the base of her neck like dominoes—relieving tiny muscle spasms. *God, that feels better.*

Hours pass. Dryness in her eyes forces her to blink. She glances over her scribbled notes—notes comparing and contrasting her case to the others.

1 - Our combined theta brainwave activity was three times the level of all other cases.

2 – *We spent two weeks inside the Morpheus program before they terminated it. The other cases didn't last twenty-four hours. One case made it to three days before terminating.*

3 – *Travis, Kyler, and I have near-identical coding systems for time in the context of memories and experiences in our brainwaves. Our temporal organization and grid cell connection as it relates to time are uncanny.*

4 – *Placed memories for our case included the city of Phoenix and all the buildings associated with the city; Vehicles, including the wiener; Functionality of electronic devices and network systems; The orphanage; The ranch, horses, and hideout. All created by us, along with many of the people we encountered. God, I hope the wienie mobile was Travis's idea and not mine. The data contained in the Institute's database was interjected by the program. Therefore it cannot be trusted.*

The questions for Steinburg are mounting. Why did he decide to terminate our case and pull us out of Morpheus? Why are we the only case lasting longer than a day or so? What happened to the participants in the other cases? Where did they come from? Did they volunteer? Were they paid? It would be helpful to interview those individuals in person.

"Wait. Oh my God. All the participants are former cryonic patients of the Promise of Lazarus Program. They didn't die. They're using them to experiment on? Like lab rats—treating them as if they are disposable commodities. What have I done? My program provided them with their test subjects."

18

A Moral Dilemma

How do we define reality? How can we distinguish between what we perceive as reality and what we perceive as a dream? Is reality itself a grand and elaborate illusion? If the mind cannot discern the difference between a world of abstraction and a world of consciousness, then how can we know for sure when and where we exist? Or even how we exist?

"Come in, Dr. Grace. Please, have a seat. What are your impressions of the program?"

She slides a chair away from a long mahogany conference table. Her notes slap the tabletop while her butt plops into the cushy chair. She sighs. Nibbling on the end of her pen, she glares at him.

"I have a lot of questions regarding this program. Give me honest and detailed answers. Otherwise, count me out. I'm done."

"I understand. I'll answer any question you have. I truly need your help, Doctor."

"Why in the hell are all the participants in the Morpheus Project my former patients? Don't lie to me."

Steinburg rubs his temples. He sits back in his seat and crosses his arms.

"Okay. Okay. We used former patients of the Promise of Lazarus Program who survived the process. Some didn't survive, Emily. I'm very sorry. The ones who survived we deemed as suitable candidates to take part in our program. We were unsuccessful in finding living breathing candidates in the outside world to volunteer."

"So, Travis, Kyler, and myself were not the only patients who entered Morpheus?"

"No. We utilized the entire group in exchange for reviving them and healing those we could heal."

"So basically, you used us like monkeys in a lab—without our permission. And you lied to me."

"Dr. Grace, the participants, except for you, McCallister, and Kyler Carson, had complications...technical glitches that cost them their lives. I don't want to see any more lives lost because of our research. That's why I chose you to lead this project."

"Glitches? Computers have glitches. People get sick, people die. I won't be part of a project that risks innocent lives, especially one that doesn't ask permission of the participants."

Steinburg leans forward and places his palms on the table. His brow raises.

"Emily, this is an issue of life or death. Our world is dying. We don't have a great deal of time to waste. *All* of our lives are at risk. Permission is a luxury we do not have. I need your help. Thousands of lives are depending on us...depending on you. And don't you think it is hypocritical to accuse us of using patients like lab animals? Isn't that what you were doing with The Promise of Lazarus Program? I don't want to debate ethics or morals, Doctor. There's no time for that discussion."

"Are you kidding me? You're just now telling me this? Or is this more of your bullshit? Show me. Show me that the world is dying. Prove it to me. I want to see the outside world. No more secrets. If you want my help, then I need to know everything you know."

"I cannot allow you to venture outside the facility. But I can allow you to see the outside world from the safety of our observatory. If I do this, will you commit to directing the project?"

"I'll give you my answer once I have the chance to view the outside world."

Steinburg purses his lips and stands. He sighs. "Follow me."

***

"Oh, God. How many floors is this elevator?"

"The observatory is on the twenty-fifth floor. If you don't like elevators, it will please you to know that this one comes with a unique feature."

The doors close. Her breathing grows shallow. Steinburg presses the button for the twenty-fifth floor. He smacks a large blue button.

"Oh my God. We're on a beach. I can smell salt and fish in the air. I can feel a cool breeze on my face. How is this possible?"

Doors open. An electronic voice speaks. "Observatory. Level twenty-five."

"That was...*incredible.*"

"It's one-of-a-kind and the first virtual holographic elevator in the world."

The entire ceiling illuminates along the hallway—a soft violet glow—almost fluorescent. The floor is black. Shiny. A pair of metallic double doors stand firm like sentry guards at the end of the hallway. Her stomach tightens with anticipation.

The observatory is an enormous round room encased inside a vast glass dome—360 degrees of viewing. Every 45-degree point has a set of stationary binoculars—eight in total. A circular sofa runs along the wall of the dome. They placed a large telescope in the center of the room, mounted upon a circular platform. Next to the telescope is a glass desk. The desk itself is a holographic computer. It appears to be running a program and mapping the stars.

Devastation surrounds her. Leveled buildings. Billowing smoke hovers over smoldering embers for miles. An apocalyptic nightmare. The skies reflect an orange haze. An occasional flash of electricity rips through black clouds. The sun appears like a dwarfish rusty ball.

"This is our world, Dr. Grace. Radioactive and uninhabitable. The masses survive underground—what's left of them, anyway. Starving. Scavenging. Anarchy reigns supreme. This is the reality we face. Everyone living outside our facility is doomed to a fate of sickness and death. Take your time to gather it all in, Doctor."

"If this is all true, who are the thousands we are saving?"

"We have enough spacecraft to accommodate three thousand souls living and working inside our facility. Many are military, and some are civilians. Everyone trapped outside the facility is too radioactive to be saved. They are the *condemned*...which is why they do not make good volunteers."

"So, this is a mission to save humanity...to find a new home in the stars? Am I right?"

"There are several exoplanets in the Proxima Centauri system we are targeting. Three planets, to be exact, exist in the habitable zone of their star. Each vessel will transport one thousand lives and land on one of three planets. Three chances to save humanity from extinction. There are no more resources on this planet to allow for a meaningful life. We must abandon Earth. Time is up. Humankind has overstayed its welcome."

Steinburg exposes his palms to her. He raises his eyebrows, pleading.

"Emily. I have had little success in finding a solution to all the problems with Morpheus. There is no explanation why you, McCallister, and young Kyler were 100% successful in your Morpheus experience. We are desperate for answers. Your reputation and your innovative breakthroughs in the Promise of Lazarus program caught the attention of myself and the Board of Authority. You have an uncanny gift for problem-solving. We need answers fast and solid solutions so we can execute our plans before it's too late. Will you help us accomplish this? Please."

The devastation surrounding her is sobering. "Okay. I'll help. But I need full access to the network and every piece of data that relates to the Morpheus Project. I want full transparency, Dr. Steinburg. I also want full control of the project and the authority to make all the decisions. Understood?"

"I can assure you I will make it so. I'll also ensure that you have every means at your disposal."

"One more thing, Dr. Steinburg. Travis and Kyler are to be considered my family. They live with me and are untouchable. Anything happens to either of them without my knowledge or permission, and the deal is off. I'm not afraid to die. So, don't test me."

19

A FAMILY UNIT

She taps on the door of her new neighbor's apartment. Travis greets her with a crooked grin. Kyler rushes into her arms and hugs her waist.

"Welcome to the neighborhood, gentlemen. I brought you some chocolate chip cookies."

"Ya never cease to amaze me, Doc. Your powers of persuasion could convince a mule he was an Arabian thoroughbred. Look at this place. Rustic, manly. I swear it reminds me a bit of my ranch house. Beats the hell out of the barracks. Kyler has his very own room. Come on in. I'll give ya the grand tour."

"It is uncanny how much this place resembles your ranch house...makes me wonder, and gives me the creeps. Something doesn't feel right, Travis...something is weird, and I need to figure out exactly what it is."

"Doc, I feel like I've mentioned this before, but we need to be careful. Steinburg is a slimeball, but he's a damn smart slimeball. Trust your gut. Pay attention to every move he makes and every word he speaks."

"Believe me; I don't trust him. What's for dinner, Big Mac?"

"I...uh. Well, shit. Let me take a gander in the fridge and see what kind of grub they left for us. I'm sure we can whip something up. You just sit tight, little lady, and let ole Big Mac do the cooking."

She winks at Kyler. "This should be interesting."

***

She pats her lips with a napkin and folds her hands in her lap.

"Well, that was...uh...most interesting. Mac and cheese with hot dog slices. Thank you for dinner, Big Mac. The name *really* suits you now. I think maybe we should leave the cooking to Kyler and me from now on."

"What? That was gourmet mac and cheese. And them dogs were 100% pure beef. How 'bout you, Kyler? What d'ya think? Pretty good, right, buddy?"

Kyler smirks and glances at Emily.

"What are ya looking at her for? Y'all don't appreciate a wholesome manly meal when ya taste one. I'm crushed. Hey, I saw some fudgesicles in the fridge, Kyler. Go grab one."

"Well, gents. It's been a genuine pleasure, but I have a lot of work to do. I'm going next door and calling it a night."

She kisses Kyler on the top of his head. He slurps his fudgesicle, oblivious to her departure. Travis pulls her body tight against his. His lips brush against hers. She caresses his cheeks and presses her mouth hard against his. She whispers, "Get some sleep, cowboy. Don't get any ideas. Good night."

Travis narrows his eyes and grins. He presses his tongue against the inside of his cheek and nods.

"Okay. Goodnight. I get it. It takes time to learn how to handle a stallion. Take your time, princess. I'm in no hurry."

He seems too cocky. She slips through the door then pokes her head back inside the room, pointing at his crotch.

"Put your rope away, Tex. You won't be lassoing any dogies tonight."

She puckers her lips and blows him a kiss before allowing the door to shut.

She sets a hot cup of coffee on the kitchen table next to her computer. The time has come to dissect the Morpheus Project.

***

Emily initiates a holographic notepad that responds to her voice. *Well, that's intriguing.* She rifles through hundreds of notes and documentation, reading aloud areas of importance and significance—piecing a complex puzzle together word by word. Her thought process is quick and focused. Whatever they implanted in her brain has increased her cognitive reasoning and problem-solving capacity one-hundred-fold.

"The trio of neuropods connect to a single server. Groups of three participants match according to brain wave activity and memory-mapping capacity. Once a trio meets the minimum requirement of 70% or greater compatibility, they are secured inside the connected neuropods and placed in a state of cryonic animation. Neuro-headsets are used to stimulate brain activity and initiate memory mapping of neurons. Frequency and magnetic fields are utilized to stimulate, meld and synchronize the minds of the cryo-team."

Emily ponders. *But what's missing here? Oh my God. They died of heart attacks and strokes days into the process. Their vitals show significant stress within hours of initiation.*

"The symptoms of every cryo-team member are similar to Sudden Unexpected Nocturnal Death Syndrome. SUNDS."

But most SUNDS victims were young Asian males—refugees from the Vietnam War long ago.

"Oh God...they must have died from horrible nightmares. Goddamn, Steinburg. This is exactly what I warned you about. You freaking killed them inside a hellish night terror they couldn't escape from. Like...like Freddy Krueger."

Think, Emily. Think. SUNDS was later cured by introducing a correct balance of hormones. Without enough acetylcholine, REM sleep isn't possible. Too much melatonin leads to lucid dreaming and nightmares. The concoction they gave us is all wrong. Idiots.

"Increase acetylcholine by 25%. Reduce melatonin by 40 to 50%. Add oxytocin to enhance feelings of trust and maintain social connections—The old cuddle hormone we get from sex. This change in the formula should make the experience a pleasant one instead of a nightmare straight out of the pits of hell."

Steinburg sacrificed all these patients for nothing. My patients.

Her eyes itch and burn. A deep yawn overtakes her. The clock on her wall reads 8:17 a.m. She closes her notes and yanks the data slide from her computer. Her heels tap heavy against the floor headed for Steinburg's office.

"Dr. Grace...you can't go in there right now. Dr. Steinburg is in a very important meeting, and you cannot disturb him."

"I don't give a damn. Nothing is more important right now than what I have to tell him, and I'm not in the mood to be told no."

She pushes past Steinburg's administrative assistant and barges through the conference room door.

"Dr. Grace? I'm in a meeting here. Can you please wait outside?"

"No. We need to talk. Right here, and right now."

"Um...Colonel Pomeroy, this is Dr. Grace...our new Director of the Morpheus Project."

Colonel Pomeroy rises and extends his hand. "Pleasure to meet you, Dr. Grace."

"Yeah, well, the pleasure's all yours, Colonel. I need to speak with Steinburg. Alone."

"Emily, Colonel Pomeroy is the Commander of Research and Development and the overseer of the Morpheus Project. If your urgent need to speak to me regards Morpheus, the Colonel would be interested in what you have to say."

"Fine. Suit yourselves, gentlemen."

She slides a chair from the end of the glass conference table where Steinburg and Pomeroy sit facing each other.

"I figured out your problem. You had the doses of neurological hormones wrong. Many innocent patients...*my* patients...died because of your negligence and ineptitude."

"Now, please calm down, Emily, and explain what you mean."

"I'm not going to calm down, but I'll explain what I mean. Simply put, the percentages of hormones in your sleep concoction were all wrong. The excess melatonin by itself was enough to cause intense lucid visions—goddamn night terrors. Imagine your worst nightmare where you can't wake up? The obvious result is a stress-induced stroke or heart attack. That's why they all died. All except us. Travis, Kyler, and myself. Our bodies must have had enough of a balance of hormones to allow us to survive *our* nightmare. But you kept experimenting, killing more patients...or should I say, *victims*. It kind of qualifies you as a serial killer, Steinburg. A real mass murderer."

"Dr. Grace, I'm sorry. I apologize for our failed attempts and the unexpected casualties. But if you've found the answer as you say, we need to implement your solution as soon as possible. And I promise you will oversee the entire operation to ensure no more lives have to be sacrificed. Your remaining patients will be completely in your care."

Colonel Pomeroy leans forward and lays a meaty right palm on the glass tabletop.

"Dr. Grace, I concur with Dr. Steinburg's sentiments and regrets at the loss of our patients. *Your* patients. It's a travesty. But sacrifices are made to ensure the development of a workable solution to our dire situation. We are running out of time. We will give you anything you need. Everything is at your disposal to get us where we need to be. We need your help and cooperation to move forward."

"I'm going to hold you both accountable. I'll send my revised formula over to the pharmacy lab and have enough doses developed for testing. Then I'll choose the next trio of participants. We will set up the next experiment for only one control group. If they succeed, then we will move to another three test groups. If those are successful, then you have a certified process, and you can begin the next phase, which brings me to my next question. What *is* the next phase?"

"Boarding the vessels, Dr. Grace. Boarding the vessels and preparing all the passengers for the long voyage ahead. Three-hundred and thirty-three cryo-team trios. One thousand passengers will board each vessel."

She sighs. "Then we better get to work."

20

THE MORPHEUS DECEPTION

Mercedes Santini was a wife and mother of three beautiful boys. At age forty-two, she discovered a lump inside her left shoulder. Two weeks later, she was diagnosed with stage four lung cancer. She was given three to six months to live.

Waylon Hayes was a farmer. At age fifty-seven, he was diagnosed with Huntington's disease. An inherited affliction causing the breakdown of nerve cells in the brain. No cure. He left a wife, a son, and four grandchildren behind.

Lola Swanson was a business owner. She ran the largest bakery in Sioux Falls, South Dakota. On April 3, 2020, Lola fell into a coma following a serious auto accident, leaving her paralyzed.

All three were Emily's patients. She knows every detail of each of their cases. She supervised their cryonic inductions. Yesterday, they were released from Morpheus, after seven days of immersion. The process didn't encounter a single issue with any of the three patients. All their vitals are perfect. All three were cured of all their conditions. Today, they will reenter society and have their lives restored.

Nine more of her patients are preparing to experience Morpheus under her care. Another seven-day trial will be underway by the end of the day. If successful, this will end the experimental phase of the evaluation and will initiate the implementation phase.

She totes her NERU Pro-HG along the hallway towards a conference room. Her insides flutter. Her mouth is dry. She hasn't spoken to these patients for the better part of a century. What will she say to them? How will they react to her? Will they thank her? Hate her? Love her or even remember who she is? The unknown teases her mind with the worst possible scenarios. Why is that? Why are we always negative in thinking through the outcomes of our life situations? We expect the worst instead of hoping for the best. She heaves a breath and opens the opaque glass door to her inaugural patient reunion.

Lola Swanson sits upright. She's bald. She appears bewildered. Confused. No signs of paralysis or even a handicap. Her brow furrows over darkened eyes and a tight frown.

Waylon winks and smiles. *I always loved his East-Texas drawl.* He sits, hands folded on the conference table. Patient, polite, and content. A gentle giant with a full head of wavy silver hair.

Mercedes appears broken-hearted. A familiar reflection of pain glints inside her olive eyes—a reflection Emily has seen in Travis's eyes from time to time. Mercedes glances at her, then lowers her eyes, focusing on the table.

They are all dressed in standard-issue white jumpsuits with an Institute of Cryonic Technology logo attached to the sleeve. *How am I ever going to explain all this to them?*

"Good morning, everyone. I don't know if you all remember me. My name is Dr. Emily Grace. I was in charge of the Promise of Lazarus program for The Institute of Cryonic Technologies over eighty-seven years ago. You were all my patients. As promised, your conditions have been cured, and you have been revived. You can live out your life, healthy and free, in a different time and place. I am sure you are all shocked to be alive and sitting here. I know I was. Are there any questions I can answer for you? Anything I can help you to understand?"

Her eyes dart between three blank faces. What could they be thinking? Waylon raises his hand.

"Uh, yes. Mr. Hayes. Please..."

"Dr. Grace, ma'am. Is there any chance you can introduce me to members of my family? I guess that would be my great-great-grandchildren? Do I have any family alive?"

"I-I think we can research whether you have living family members...and maybe reach out to them. I will do everything in my power to find an answer to your question, sir."

"Thank you, Doctor. And thank you for all you've done for me. Very much obliged, ma'am. Gonna take some getting used to, I'm afraid. But I'll get along just fine, I'm sure."

"You're welcome, Mr. Hayes. I will do everything I can to help you with your transition back into society. Does anyone else have a question? Yes, Mrs. Santini?"

"Can I change my mind? Can I choose to die instead? I don't want to be here. And why are you here? Shouldn't you be dead?"

"Well...I don't know the answer to that question, Mrs. Santini. I can schedule an appointment with our resident psychologist... um...and maybe he can help you work through this. Similar to you, I suffered a fatal condition and entered the Promise of Lazarus program years ago, and...well...here I am." Emily's nervous laugh raises prickly heat along the back of her neck.

"I don't *want* to work through it. I have nothing to live for. I'd rather die. I wish you all would have just allowed me to die."

"I'm so sorry, Mrs. Santini. I will see what I can do to help your situation.

"Ms. Swanson? Do you have a question?"

"Uh...I don't...really. I'm looking forward to seeing the brand-new world and starting my new life, I guess. I'll wait and see. If I have questions later, how can I reach you?"

Emily sighs. "I'm pleased to hear that, Ms. Swanson. You can reach me anytime. Just ask one of the staff to contact me to set an appointment to sit and talk.

Waylon raises his hand again.

"Yes, Mr. Hayes."

"Dr. Grace, was the experience I had with these two fine young ladies an actual event? How did y'all manage that?"

"There is a briefing after this one that will cover everything you need and want to know regarding the Morpheus Project. They'll answer all of your questions and explain the program in detail.

"Well, if there are no more questions for me, I will leave you in the capable hands of your sponsors. Welcome to 2108. Your journey is complete. And your new life begins. Congratulations."

Mrs. Santini smacks the table and stands. "I want my journey to end here and now. I want to die. Please."

Emily stumbles backward and fumbles for the door handle. She slips through the doorway. Her heels tap rapidly along the empty hallway. She wipes warm tears from her cheeks with a trembling hand.

She cannot remember a more awkward meeting in her life. Mercedes, Waylon, and Lola are off to the next phase of their transition back into modern society. A meeting on the Morpheus Project where researchers will pick their brains and document their experience. More lab work for the lab rats. Then they will join an unknown world. An unfamiliar world. A world she is responsible for introducing them to.

The next three cryo-teams are beginning their journey into Morpheus. If these cases go as well as the last, the project will ramp up to accommodate the thousands destined for the stars.

She checks her ePhone: 7:28 p.m. Her ankles swell. A deep yawn overtakes her, causing her jaw to stretch and her eyes to tear. She runs her hand across her scalp, tugging at her thick hair. *Almost an inch, now.* She stumbles through the door into her apartment. She kicks off her heels, launching them one at a time across the living room floor.

"Siri. Call Travis."

No answer. She walks next door and knocks. Still no answer. The door is unlocked.

"Travis? Kyler? Anybody home?"

She peers into Travis's bedroom, then Kyler's. Where are they?

"Dr. Grace?"

She jerks and turns towards the sound of the voice.

"Oh, my God. You scared me. Who are you?"

"I apologize. I'm here to escort you to meet with Dr. Steinburg. My name is Sergeant Phillips. Please come with me, ma'am."

"Do you know where Mr. McCallister or Kyler Carson is?"

"Yes. They are with Dr. Steinburg as we speak. Please accompany me, ma'am."

"Why should I? Where are we going?"

"Ma'am, as I said, I am escorting you to meet with Dr. Steinburg."

"Yeah. I remember that part, sarge. But I want to know where."

"If you will follow me, you will know soon enough. It's confidential, ma'am."

She shrugs. "All right. Let me get my shoes."

***

Two elevators, five steel-reinforced doors, and one staircase later, she finds herself in a ten-by-ten room. A single stainless-steel table sits between two metal chairs in what looks more like an interrogation room than a conference room.

"Please have a seat, Dr. Grace. I will let Dr. Steinburg know you have arrived."

Why do I get the feeling this isn't going to be good news?

"Hello, Emily. I apologize for all the secrecy and short notice. After our meeting last week, Colonel Pomeroy asked me to meet with you in a secure location. Away from any risk of a compromise of our privacy."

She scoffs. "What's going on, Steinburg? What are you up to? Cut through the crap."

Steinburg leans back and steeples his fingers and glares.

"You've done an outstanding job, Emily. And in such a short period. A simple answer to a complex problem. I can't believe we missed it. But *you* sure didn't."

"When you're done stroking my ass, can you get to the point of this meeting?"

He inhales, then sighs. "You're right. We should get to the point. We appreciate your quick solution to the technical difficulties we were struggling with. But we've determined that we can take it from here. We can't wait another week for the latest test group. We need to get our people on those vessels now."

"Why do I get the feeling you're going to pull a hypodermic needle out of your pocket and jab it into my arm?"

He crinkles his brow and shakes his head. "What?"

"Never mind. So where does that leave me? And where the hell is Travis and Kyler? Did you move them somewhere?"

"You have three choices, Dr. Grace. One: You can remain in our facility along with Mr. McCallister and young Kyler as our guests and stay out of our way until we launch in one week. Then you can have a free run of the place and live out your days in peace and security.

"There is enough power, food, water, and supplies to support five thousand people for two hundred years or more. You can choose to revive the remaining participants in the Promise of Lazarus program and introduce them to this world if you like. Or you can terminate them and spare them a life of confinement and confusion.

"Two: We can place you, McCallister, and Kyler back into Morpheus where you can live out your days...forever.

"The remaining choice you have is to leave our facility and take your chances in the outside world. It would be a death sentence, but a slow death sentence."

"Oh, my God. You're a dick no matter what world I meet you in, Steinburg. You're unbelievable. If this is a joke, it's not funny."

He chuckles. "No joke. So, what's it going to be, Dr. Grace?"

"Gee, let me think. Hm. I'm not going outside, so that option is out. I'm not going back into Morpheus, so scratch that idea. I guess we'll just have to stay here as your guests. Now, where are Travis and Kyler?"

"They're in a secure area. I assure you they are comfortable. Once we depart, I will release them to you. Until then, they will stay put, and you will remain in your apartment. I may call on you if we feel we need your assistance."

"Goddamn you. I want them released now, or I'm not assisting you on anything."

"You've already given us what we need. You're no longer in a position to negotiate anything, now are you, Doctor? Sergeant

Phillips will escort you back to your apartment. We'll be in touch if we need your services again...although, I do not expect that we will."

21

T-Minus 24 Hours

The facility buzzes with the frenzy of a disturbed anthill. Rumors say the vessels are ready for boarding. The passengers and astronauts are preparing for cryonic suspension. A skeleton crew of scientists and technicians will navigate the vessels and enter neuropods a week into the flight—once they've verified all systems are stable.

Emily was told they are holding Travis and Kyler in a secure bunker below ground. Bunker #3. Steinburg assures her that within thirty minutes after launch the doors to the bunker will open and release its occupants. It's confusing why Dr. Steinburg has separated them. It makes even less sense why he's leaving them behind.

Two military guards sit outside her door. There's nothing for her to do at this point but wait and worry. An annoying feminine voice echoes through the hallways every hour on the hour.

T-minus twenty-four hours! Please follow the assigned colored line to your vessel and prepare for launch. Red crew report to deck seven. Green crew report to deck fifteen. Yellow crew report to deck twenty-four. Doors will lock in T-minus twenty-three hours, fifty-eight minutes, and seventeen seconds. Passengers who miss their scheduled report time will not be allowed access and will remain behind. Passport identification is required for all civilians.

It's maddening. Patience was never a virtue she possessed. Why didn't Steinburg consider taking her, Travis, and Kyler with them? They are a perfect 98.7% match. Are they a threat? Do they know too much? Maybe there weren't enough neuropods. It makes little sense.

***

T-minus two minutes. Prepare for launch.

A jolt of adrenaline surges through her heart, forcing her eyes open and her body to sit upright. *What the hell? How long was I asleep?*

Lights dim and the building quakes. Dishes and glasses shudder—several glass bowls fly off her china hutch and shatter across the tiled floor. She stumbles to the front door and flings it open. The guards are nowhere in sight, and the hallway radiates with an eerie crimson glow. Floors tremble and pitch beneath her feet like a cruise liner in the middle of a typhoon.

She sprints along the hallways balancing herself by pushing off the walls. Her untied laces tap at the floor, keeping rhythm with her pace. Scurrying down the stairwell in leaps and bounds, she reaches the bunker floor. She bursts through the stairwell door and jogs to bunker #3. The doors to all ten bunkers remain closed. She paces like an animal about to give birth. "Open up, damn it."

The rumbling of walls and floors subsides. A deafening silence follows. Metal scrapes against metal as all ten bunker doors open in unison. She rushes inside bunker #3. It's empty. Her breathing grows rapid and shallow.

"Travis! Kyler!" Echoes respond to her cries.

She checks the other nine bunkers. All are empty.

"No! Travis? Kyler?"

She collapses, squatting on a concrete bench inside bunker #3.

"What is happening here? Steinburg, you liar. What did you do with them? Oh, my God...my God. I'm all alone here. Where did they take them? No, no, no, no...this can't be happening." Emily returns to the stairwell and navigates her way back to her apartment.

***

Broken glass glints across her kitchen floor. Her mouth is agape and dry—her heart devoid of emotion. She plops into her lounge chair and cuddles a fat pillow wedged between her thighs, rocking her body forward and backward.

What could have happened to Travis and Kyler? Are they lost in the facility somewhere? Surely, they could find their way home? Are they trapped? Maybe Steinburg took them aboard. But why would he? And why would he abandon her here like this—leaving her all alone? Did she underestimate the depth of his cruelty?

The crackling hum of a nearby lamp resonates inside her ears. She's aware of her breathing and the pulsating echoes of her heartbeat. Her fingertips tingle. Her innards gurgle. She tosses the pillow aside.

She slips into a pair of khakis, utility boots, and a T-shirt Travis gave her and slicks her hair with gel. It's going to be a long day. Her new mission: Find Travis and Kyler no matter how long it takes.

Hours pass wandering deserted hallways, searching each section of the facility—calling out to Travis and Kyler. *The observatory. Maybe they wandered outside somehow. Maybe Steinburg kicked them out of the facility.* She rides the twenty-five floors in a simulated paradise to reach the observatory. The dome is quiet. The desolation outside hasn't changed since her last visit. And why would it? She peers through each set of binoculars, scanning the horizon for any clue of life or movement.

Smoldering mounds of rubble cover the landscape. She stares through the dome across miles of destruction. She notices a structure towards the city of Tempe. The old Hayden Flour Mill has stood preserved for centuries. A weathered white building with a tower and seven adjacent silos. A landmark that stood out to her from her years as a student at Arizona State University. She directs her binoculars to view the old building. As she gazes, bricks fall and the foundation crumbles into a massive heap of dust and debris.

What's the point of this? The sooner she accepts her fate, the quicker she can get on with her life of isolation. An enormous prison with everything she needs to live a long full life. Alone. She plops onto the leather sofa that encircles the dome interior and leans her head against the wall. Her eyes close. *Five minutes. I just need five minutes to rest my eyes.*

***

Her snort startles her. She must have been asleep longer than the five minutes she promised herself. Her left leg tingles with shooting sparks of electricity. She shakes the fog from her mind and stretches. It's odd. The sun appears to be in the same place it was when she closed her eyes earlier. Maybe she *was* asleep for only five minutes. She scans the countryside. If Travis and Kyler ended up outside, they wouldn't survive this gruesome scene. Nobody would.

A glint of white light catches her eye. She peers through the binoculars. *What the hell?* She zooms in. The Hayden Flour Mill is standing—like when she first observed it.

"What is going on here? This is nuts. I know I watched that building crumble to the ground. I'm sure of it."

She hovers her hand over the login sensor of the holographic computer next to the main telescope.

"*Dr. Emily Grace. Permission granted.*"

She scans folders of data and examines the list of computer programs. One program, in particular, stands out from the rest. *NERU Metaverse.* She taps the icon to activate the program. A variety of orbs appear across the top of the glass desk—each displaying a unique three-dimensional scene of nature. One orb is larger than the others—a world of destruction and chaos. She taps one of the other orbs. The dome inside the observatory darkens then transforms the landscape into a beautiful Amazon forest, stretching out for miles.

She leans back in her chair with her mouth agape—stunned into silence.

She mutters. "You have *got* to be joking. What the *hell?* Steinburg. You...son of a bitch."

She taps another orb. The landscape morphs into an arctic wilderness of ice.

"This is un-fucking-believable. Oh, my God, everything you said and did was one big fat pack of lies. *Everything* was a lie."

One orb stands apart from the group. It doesn't display a landscape. It's solid black with a scarlet X in the center. She reaches to tap it, then withdraws her hand, hesitating. She stares at the orb. *Come on Emily. Stop being such a wuss.*

She grits her teeth and squints, then smacks the black orb.

A sultry female voice speaks. "Program deactivated."

The dome fades into a deep inky blue darkness. Shimmers of turquoise glint through the glass.

"What is this? Another program?"

She rises and eases her way to the concave glass of the dome. The surface is frigid against her fingertips. A silvery glow flashes past the glass. She shrieks and lunges backward.

"What the heck was that?"

Another silvery glow streaks by. Then another, and another.

"Oh my God. Those are *fish.* Those are *goddamn* fish. Where in the hell am I?"

Emily collapses onto the cushioned seating that encircles the room. Her jaw slackens. She sucks shallow breaths through her mouth, trying to calm her racing heart. Warm, wet tears stream along her cheeks and spatter across her boots. She wipes her face with her hands and shakes her head. Her breathing turns ragged. *Stay calm, Emily. This is not the time to panic.*

She whispers, "Oh, my God. Oh, my God. Where the hell did Steinburg leave me?"

She heaves a breath and raises her eyes toward the top of the dome. Her world exists beneath a deep indigo ocean. She is confined within a dark, watery prison.

22

LOST IN AN OCEAN OF TEARS

Even from beneath its surface, the ocean radiates serenity. The ocean's cognitive effects on the mind stimulate chemicals in our brains that ease our minds and spirits of tension and anxiety—inhibiting the release of stress hormones. The horror of being trapped beneath the ocean's magnitude is an ironic and tragic absurdity. Its suffocating weight bears down upon her.

She rises and glances at the panel of orbs spread out across the glass computer desk. The black orb has changed to green. It now reflects a white triangle icon in its center. She grimaces and smacks the green orb, anticipating the reaction.

The sultry voice declares, "Program activated."

She taps an orb to select a new scenario. The dome illuminates and displays a landscape of the Arizona desert in full bloom against a fiery sunset backdrop. She pushes the double doors open and marches along the hallway towards the elevator.

"Twenty-five floors...I can do this. No scenic route this time."

Emily enters the elevator and presses the button to the first floor. She holds her breath for a moment, then blows the air from her lungs. She slaps the blue button to initiate the scenic route.

"Okay, maybe I can't do this..."

***

Steinburg's office resides on the first floor near the military section. Her credentials allow her access. His office is half empty. The furniture remains, but the photos, plaques, and awards that once hung on his vanity wall are gone. Faded, yellowed shadows are reminders of his once self-proclaimed accomplishments. The desk is empty save for a few scattered pens, pencils, and candy wrappers. Atop the desk is a small NERU HG mini-computer.

"How convenient is this? I can't wait to listen to the message he left for me. I know, I'm going to regret this."

She initiates the computer. A holographic folder appears across the desktop. She taps it.

"Hello, Dr. Grace. My apologies for this inconvenient method of communication. It wasn't my intent to be forced to brief you in this manner. Yet, here we are. I'm sure you have a laundry list of questions for me. You always were a woman with so many inquiries—too many at times.

"As you listen to this message, we are traveling across the galaxy headed for unknown worlds and fresh beginnings. Reaching out to the stars to ensure the survival of humanity. I'm sure you will understand and appreciate our mission, and I want to express my deepest appreciation for all your hard work and contributions to the Morpheus Project. Without you, it would not have been possible. Your name is part of its legacy and memorialized in its history. Thank you for your exquisite service.

"Dr. Grace...Emily. There are some very important matters I need to discuss with you. Or, more accurately, pass on to you since this isn't an actual discussion. You may wonder what became of your friends, McCallister and young Kyler. I regret to say they had to be removed from the facility. They are both liabilities and would hinder the work you will need to focus on in the coming months and years. We needed someone with your skills and competency to stay behind and maintain the operations of our home base. You were the perfect candidate. Your knowledge and skills and ability to solve the most complex of problems qualify you to captain the ship, so to speak—an honorable task.

"In the top-left drawer is a data slide. It contains all the information you will need to do this critical job. At the unfortunate

possibility that one of the three planets we intend to inhabit turns out to be uninhabitable, we will return the vessel to Earth—to the base you are managing. It is essential you follow all the instructions and protocols and maintain the facility to the utmost of your capabilities. It is necessary for your survival as well.

"*Once you have completed all the tasks I have outlined for you, you must place yourself into a cryonic state and set your recovery date and time to the date specified on the schedule I have prepared for you.*

"*I know you are lonely. I'm very sorry for that inconvenience. You should be happy to know that McCallister and Kyler are alive and well. They are not aboard the facility any longer. Knowing they are safe should put your mind at ease and allow you to focus on the essential tasks at hand.*

"*It has been my pleasure and my honor to have worked with you, Dr. Grace. I trust you will tend to your duties. I have granted you full access to the entire facility. You have enough food and water and resources to live a full and rewarding life—after you wake from your cryonic state, once again. Best of luck to you and Godspeed. This is Dr. Roland Steinburg signing out.*"

She pounds the desktop with her fist. Her eyes well and overflow with bitter tears.

"You arrogant...selfish...bastard! Inconvenience? You're a disgrace to this profession...a disgrace to humanity. Oh, my God...I'm all alone! You've imprisoned me and isolated me."

She removes the data slide from the drawer and stares at it. She inserts the drive into the mini laptop. Several folders organize themselves across the desk. *Power Grid and Hydraulic Systems; Cryonic Schedule; Life Support Systems; Health and Nutrition Systems; Water Management; Sanitation Systems; Computer Information Systems; Medical and Pharmacy.* She spends the next several hours combing through the files and taking notes.

***

"Okay, look at this. I can run this scan to track any warm-blooded creature in the facility. If Travis and Kyler are inside the facility, I should be able to locate them, right?"

She taps the execute button. A three-dimensional holographic blueprint of the entire facility unfolds inches above the desk. A red marker reveals itself on the first floor in Steinburg's office. *That's me.* No other markers are evident.

"Wait. What's that?"

A small red marker moves along the hallway near the housing section. She springs from her seat, tucks the computer beneath her arm, and sprints along the main hallway—darting into adjacent hallways until she reaches the housing section. The hallways stretch into long dreary shadows and empty darkness. She heaves a breath and listens. A low droning from the life-support vents is the only sound.

"Kyler? Travis?" Her voice echoes along the lonely hallway.

"Mew...mew."

"Oh, my God. Where did you come from, little fella? Who left you behind? Aw. You look like you're Siamese...your eyes are blue like Rexy's. Oh...you're a girl. Yes, it's okay, kitty. I got you now. Are you hungry, baby? I'm going to call you, *Roxy*. Let's find you something to eat little Miss Roxy."

She clutches the kitten and strolls into the cafeteria. Roxy's soft purring soothes her frazzled nerves. Roxy's presence nurtures the void of loneliness in her heart for the moment.

"There you go, Roxy. Goodness, you're a hungry kitty. Go on...there's lots more where that came from...like thousands of years more."

She cuddles Roxy and ambles along the eerie and serene hallways towards her apartment. She pushes her door open and falls into her easy chair. Roxy wriggles between her chest and neck and closes her eyes. Purring and clawing herself into a comfortable spot—needing Emily as much as Emily needs her.

It seems Travis and Kyler are nowhere inside the facility. But where could they be? Were they forced to board one of the space vessels? Are they housed in another facility beneath the ocean? Maybe they are on the surface somewhere. The day's events have drained her energy like a visit from a wraith in the night.

"I don't want to think anymore, Roxy. My brain hurts. I just want to crawl into bed and hide from all this emptiness. I'm so happy we found each other. Thank you, God, for sending Roxy to me. If I can ask for another favor, can you please send Travis and Kyler back to me...or me to them? I can't do this alone."

Emily carries Roxy into her bedroom and plops her onto the bed. She strips down to her bra and panties and tucks herself under the warmth of the bedding. She allows Roxy to snuggle into her bosom, and she closes her eyes—emptying her mind. *Tomorrow is another day,* as Miss Scarlett O'Hara would say.

23

A Voice from the Past

Exercise is an activity that improves physical and mental health by teaching the body's many systems how to function together and manage stress. People used to believe that exercise produced a rush of endorphins throughout the body. And it does, but it is the lesser-known neuromodulator norepinephrine that helps the brain deal with stress more efficiently. Half of the brain's supply of norepinephrine is in the *locus coeruleus*. The significance? This area of the brain is involved with emotional and stress responses.

Her body glides along the surface of an Olympic-size pool—the water a comfortable seventy-eight degrees. She taps the edge, then ducks her head and executes a body roll beneath the water. She thrusts her body off the wall using her feet and glides in the opposite direction. *Fifty. Done.*

Her thighs swish against the warm water as she ascends the stairs. She buries her face into a fluffy towel, then dabs her hair. Securing the towel around her nude body, she slips her feet into leather sandals and exits the pool area.

She sighs, then mutters. "Okay. Feed Roxy. Then I need to get busy working on Steinburg's checklist...to keep this place running of course. I think that bastard knows me better than I know myself. He knew I'd follow all the protocols to maintain this facility. Is my OCD *that* obvious?"

It's been nine weeks since the launch. The days intermingle into mundane time and space. A regimen of daily tasks keeps her mind occupied. Maintaining life-support systems; planning meals; exercising and recreation to battle mental fatigue and monotony; searching for clues to the whereabouts of Travis and Kyler. Searches that lead to dead ends, false leads, and dashed dreams.

Hope. The desire and expectation for a positive outcome. A driving force that channels desperation and tethers panic. A remedy for insanity. But hope is a bottle filled with an unspecified quantity that eventually runs dry.

Medical science has advanced in the past century, although certain aspects of modern medicine remain unchanged. Emily sips a glass of Chardonnay and stares at a handful of opioid pills. Calmness embraces her mind and spirit. She has made a decision. Brain cancer isn't so daunting compared to a life of isolation inside a deserted prison beneath the ocean. Too much time alone leads the mind into eventual insanity. She understands this fact. If Travis and Kyler were here, things would be different. But they're not here. They're nowhere.

She fills her mouth with dozens of tiny white pills and a sip of sweet Chardonnay—anticipating the moment she will swallow. Beads of sweat trickle down her temples. The beads combine and roll off of her cheeks as droplets. Adrenaline fuels her heart, creating a rhythmic thumping inside her eardrums. Roxy brushes against her calves, purring and rubbing her whiskers against her skin. Emily's eyes moisten. She hangs her head to weep. Nobody could survive this solitude. Just swallow, and the door to escape this hell will open.

Static crackles and pops over the intercom system.

A faint voice echoes along the hallways. "Doc. Doc...are you there? Emily? Can you hear me?"

She spews the wine and pills across the floor. The wine glass shatters on the concrete. *Was that real?* She leaps to her feet and dashes to the intercom. She crushes the intercom button with the heel of her hand.

"Travis?! Is that you? Please. Tell me it's you..."

Silence. Faint modulation hums inside the speaker.

She smacks the button and screams. "Travis! Kyler! Oh God, please be real."

They must be close by. They have to be. Where does the intercom system extend? She races to her bedroom and snatches her computer—pouncing onto the bed and initiating her login. Two beeps and the intercom schematic diagram forms a three-dimensional holograph. The master computer system resides in the Information Technology section. Intercom units appear in every room throughout the facility. There are hundreds of them. Travis's voice could have originated from any one of them. Or maybe she only imagined it. The mind can create sophisticated illusions that appear authentic and believable in times of extreme stress. Is her isolation causing her to lose her mind already? And did her mind's illusion just spare her life?

"I heard you, Travis. I know I did. You're somewhere close by. I know you are. You have to be."

She re-runs the scan for life forms within the facility. She and Roxy appear as red dots. No indications of other life forms are evident. She squishes a pillow into her lap and stares at the holographic blueprint of the intercom system. Roxy crawls into her lap and snuggles into the pillow—purring and rubbing her whiskers against Emily's arm.

Wait. What's this? An anomaly? She almost overlooked it. One of the intercom units seems to hover outside the facility's walls on the holograph. How can that be? The anomaly is adjacent to the Information Technology maintenance section. She slides her pillow, along with Roxy, off her lap and slips into a company-issued jumpsuit and leather combat boots.

"I'll be back, Roxy. You stay here and be a good kitty."

***

She dashes along the hallways, computer in hand, towards the Information Technology section. Rows of computer banks fill the maintenance area. Black-metal racks support flat computer disks. Tiny lights of reds, greens, and yellows twinkle. Emily sets her computer on a small glass desk. She initiates a holograph combining the blueprint of the intercom system with the life form indicator. She moves around the room, comparing the location of her body indicator on the computer screen to the location of the anomaly.

The computer screen shows her body icon is closest to the anomaly icon near the far wall. It's a blank wall except for a metal panel secured in its center with rivets. There is an intercom unit mounted close to the panel, but it shows up in its proper location on the holograph blueprint. The anomaly seems to be several feet beyond the wall. *I have to remove this panel somehow.*

The intercom crackles and pops. A searing blast of screeching feedback assaults her eardrums. She covers her ears and crouches.

"Oh, my God! What the hell?..."

"Doc. Doc, are you there? Do you copy?"

A surge of adrenaline courses through her veins. She smacks the intercom button with her fist.

"Travis! Yes. I copy. Can you hear me? Travis?"

Her anticipation ramps up her senses. Her heart races. She heaves several breaths of hope. *Answer. Please answer me, Travis.*

The silence is like an eternity. The intercom crackles. "Copy that..." Static muffles the rest of Travis's message.

"What? What was that? Travis? Say again...I didn't catch all that."

Static. Popping. "Doc. Do you know Morse Code?"

"What? No. Who do you think I am? Scully from the X-Files?"

Crackling and static continue to pop. "Stand by...I'm working..." Fizzles and squeals pierce the air. "I'm tuning the modulation and gain..." Droning hum. Silence.

"Travis? Where did you go?" She bangs on the intercom button. "Travis?"

Emily slides a desk chair across the floor and parks it next to the intercom. She plops into the seat, supports her head with her palms, and hums a medley of '80s rock tunes. She taps her toe in rapid rhythm.

Shrieking feedback screeches through the intercom. Travis's voice booms like thunder.

"Doc? How do I sound now?"

She curls into a ball and covers her ears. She fumbles for the intercom button.

"You sound like the voice of *God*. Turn it down. Geez."

"Em, your voice never sounded so sweet, gal. How are you doing, princess? You hanging in there?"

"Oh, my God. That's so much better. Yes. Yes. I'm hanging in there, Travis...especially now that I hear your voice. How are you doing? Is Kyler with you?"

"Yes. My little pard is right here. Say something, buddy."

"Hi, Dr. Grace. I really, really miss you. Can you come and pick us up? I'm hungry, and I'm tired of mac 'n' cheese."

"Oh, hi, baby. I miss you, too. So, so much. You have no idea. Yes. Just be patient while we figure this all out, sweetheart. You can call me Emily if you like, Kyler."

"Can I call you Mom?"

Her throat tightens. She finds it difficult to swallow. *Mom?*

"Of course, you can, sweetheart. I would love for you to call me Mom."

"Em, we need to figure out how we can get back over to your side."

"Where are you, Travis? Do you know your location?"

"I do. We're in a smaller facility next to where you are. Brace yourself for this bit of breaking news, Doc. Are ya sitting down?"

"God, I hate when someone asks if I'm sitting down. Yes, I'm sitting."

"They transported us inside a small sub. We didn't get here through a passageway leading from the main facility. Em...we're beneath the ocean. About a quarter-mile under the surface...and somewhere near Antarctica."

"What? I knew we were under the ocean. I figured that out a few months ago. But...Antarctica? You mean like penguins, walruses...Shamu?"

"Yeah. Exactly. A bit of a jam we're in. A *quandary*."

"*Quandary*? Never heard you use a big word like that before. Have you been studying over there? Memorizing a thesaurus or something? You must be bored."

"Ha-ha. Trying to keep our little guy here educated...and upping my vocabulary at the same time. I have to keep up with you. Are ya impressed yet?"

"I like the old you. The one that always knows how to get us out of a...*quandary*. I need you to be that guy right now, Travis. Can you please be *that* guy? And I need a big group hug with you and Kyler."

"Doc, I know that our section of the facility is connected to yours. But I can't find any plans or schematics that might show me where it's connected. The vessel they transported us in is no longer docked on this side. It must be on your side. I think that's our way out, Em...our way back to the surface."

"Are you, uh...forgetting that the surface is like negative one thousand degrees? I don't recall seeing any parkas lying around, do you? How do we even know what's up there?"

"Good point. Let's focus on getting my little buddy and me back to your side. Then we can figure out how to blow this popsicle stand from there."

"Travis, none of the holographic blueprints in the network show anything about an adjacent facility. It does, however, show an intercom unit that might be on your side of the wall. It's behind a panel in the room I am standing in. The panel is riveted to a metal wall."

"If I knew where you were, I could check around for some kind of panel on this side. I have no idea where I am in relation to you, Doc. You need to remove that panel and find where it leads."

"How do I do that?"

"A couple of options come to mind. Round up some tools. A heavy hammer and a chisel. Or better yet, a blow torch. You know how to man a blow torch, Doc?"

She scoffs. "Travis...uh...who do you think I am? I'm a brain surgeon. A scientist. Not a handyman. *Tool time* isn't my thing. But I'm confident I can handle a blow torch as good as any man."

"Well, ya better learn fast, unless you wanna chat over an intercom from now till forever. Go round up some tools. Come back and let me know what you find. I'm gonna feed Kyler some grub. I'll meet you back here in one hour. Copy?"

"Copy...Commander. Thank you, Travis. Thank you for still being here. You both saved me. More than you'll ever know."

24

A Midnight Rendezvous

The maintenance room isn't an area Emily has visited often. It's a goldmine of tools, equipment, and electronics. She snatches an empty canvas tool bag and fills it with a variety of chisels.

"What's this? *Johnson steel club hammer. Four pounds.* Looks heavy-duty enough to me."

She rolls a small metal cart away from a corner of the wall. She tosses the bag of chisels and the hammer onto the cart. They clank, sending the cart spiraling backward in the direction of the wall.

"Okay, this thingy looks like a torch. And this looks like a storm trooper's helmet. What about this saw? Hm. Looks like this could cut a hole in the wall...or cut my arm off. A drill? I'll take this too...and this flashlight."

The wheels of the cart screech along the hallways. It veers off course each time she turns a corner—bouncing off the walls along the long corridors. She uses her body weight to maneuver it to the center of the hallway—arriving back to the Information Technology maintenance room. She plops into the seat of a chair, heaving breaths and wiping the moisture off of her brow with her sleeve.

"Travis?" She gasps for air. "I'm back. Are you there?"

Silence. She passes the time reading the instructions on each of her newly-acquired tools. Surely, one of these items will do the job of reuniting them.

"Doc? You there? Hey, Doc..."

"Oh! God, can you turn your volume down a notch? Yes. I'm here."

"What d'ya bring me, gal?"

"Well...a big fat hammer...some chisels...a blowtorch...some kind of portable handsaw thingamajigger...and a drill."

"Sweet. Let's start with the big-ass hammer and chisel. Try popping off the rivets."

"I said, big *fat* hammer. Not big ass. Okay. Here goes."

She places the edge of the chisel against a rivet and taps it with the hammer. The chisel scratches the surface, knocking off a few flakes of paint. She stumbles and braces herself. She taps again. The hammer drops to the floor.

"Ouch! Goddammit. Ow, ow, ow. Oooooh."

She sucks her thumb, then blows on it.

"What d'ya do, princess?"

"I smooshed my thumb...damn it. They're stuck on there, tight, Travis. And I think this stupid hammer must have belonged to Thor."

"Okay, forget Thor's hammer. Try the portable saw. See if you can cut the rivets off."

"Alrighty. Here goes."

She braces herself against the wall and places the edge of the vibrating blade across the first rivet. The saw bites into the metal and pops the rivet head, sending it flying and pinging against the far wall.

"Yes. That worked. Five more to go."

"Nice work, Doc. Keep going."

She pops all the rivets from the panel and tosses the saw onto the metal cart with a clank.

"I have them all off, Travis. Now what?"

"Now what? Well, now try removing the panel, gal."

"It won't budge. It's still stuck on the wall."

"Check the edges. Is there anything else you can see that might be holding it to the wall?"

"Um...there are some squiggly things along the edges. Feels like they're made of metal."

"Uh...those would be called welding joints, Em. Ya didn't mention those."

"You didn't ask. How am I supposed to know what those things are? This is my first panel removal. Not my area of expertise. I'm good with a scalpel."

"Just pretend it's brain surgery, Em. See if the saw will cut into the metal panel. Try to make a hole if you can. Be very careful."

"Roger dodger. Cutting on the wall now."

The blade screeches as it bears down on the metal plate. She struggles to maintain her balance. The blade snaps. She lunges forward and drops the saw.

"That didn't sound good. You okay, Doc?"

"Yeah. Scratch the saw. It's um...broken...kind of exploded when it hit the ground."

"Time for your first welding lesson, Dr. Grace. Fire up that torch. Do you have a face shield to wear? You'll need to protect your eyes."

"I do. It feels ridiculous on my head, though. I am *so* glad you guys can't see me."

"You're going to make a hole in the middle of that metal panel. Make it big enough for my big butt to fit through. Take your time. Make it a square and focus on one side at a time. Be sure to stand back when you're close to finishing. I don't want any of your pretty little toes to match your thumb."

***

Emily steps backward expecting the metal panel to drop to the floor. The panel falls inward instead and clanks inside a four-foot-by-four-foot duct. Her flashlight reveals a passage that extends around fifteen to twenty feet and ends at another wall.

"Travis? I'm in. It looks like a tunnel. There's a wall at the other side."

"Okay. You need to climb your buns in there and reach that other wall. Take Thor's hammer with you. When you reach the other wall, start pounding. We'll follow the noise and come to you."

"What? I don't want to climb in there...I-I can't."

"Emily. You have to try. We can't find you if you don't. Stay calm. Keep your eyes focused on the opening behind you and pound the heck out of that wall. You got this."

There is not much room to sling a hammer inside the duct. She crouches, bracing her feet against the narrow walls. Gripping the hammer with both hands, she pounds on the wall using the top of the hammerhead like a battering ram. The opening behind her seems minuscule and far away. She breathes deep and holds her breath, then exhales.

Her shoulders burn. Her grip loosens. She heaves a breath and pauses—allowing the blood to return to her taxed muscles. She lifts the hammer and resumes tapping the wall. "Come on... hurry, guys."

The banging sounds out of sync. She pauses. The banging continues from the other side. "Yes! You found me. Oh, yes, yes, yes, you found me!"

She wriggles out of the tunnel and hits the intercom button.

"Travis? I heard you. Travis? Are you there?"

"I'm here, Doc. I found your intercom. It's red-colored. Maybe it's special or something. It has two intercom buttons. One labeled *Main* and one labeled *Surface*. Sit tight. I'm going to use a welding torch to cut through this side of the wall. We'll be right over. What's for dinner, by the way?"

"Affirmative...uh...roger. Just be careful. I hadn't given dinner a thought yet. I wasn't expecting company."

The opposite end of the tunnel is aglow. A blinding white torch shoots sparks through the metal wall like a 4th of July sparkler. Travis rips the metal plate away and pokes his face into the tunnel.

"Travis. Oh, my God. You have no idea how good it is to see your face. What are you two waiting for? Come on. Get over here."

"We need to let the metal cool for a sec. Then I'll send Kyler through first. Hopefully, my fat ass will make it through that hole."

Travis places an insulated blanket across the bottom of the cutout. He lifts Kyler into the tunnel opening.

"Okay, buddy. You're first. Crawl through to the other side."

Kyler's eyes widen. He scurries through the vent like a mouse.

"Come here, baby. I got you."

"Mom."

Kyler squeezes her neck and buries his face into her shoulder. She kisses his head and twirls him around before setting his feet on the floor.

"Okay, Kyler. Let's watch *Big Mac* try to shimmy his big ole butt through that tunnel. This should be fun to watch, huh?"

Kyler giggles. "Come on, Mac! Don't be scared. Just do what I did."

Travis's voice echoes. "I'm coming, buddy. Save me a seat over there."

Grunts, moans, and thumping echo through the vent. It sounds like a rhino is trampling through the walls. Travis's mug pops through the opening, sweaty and red-faced.

"Holy shit, that was rough. Help me out here, Doc."

Her heart is full. "Come here, both of you. I'm ready for that group hug. Oh, my God, how I've missed the both of you." The warmth of Travis and Kyler in her arms lightens her heart. Emily sobs and giggles at the same time. She refuses to let go.

***

Dinner consists of minced pork, reconstituted mashed potatoes, green beans, cornbread, and cherry pie.

"This grub is a hell of a lot better than the freeze-dried hot dogs and mac 'n' cheese my little buddy and I have been living on. I hate to say it, but I'm glad to be home."

"Kyler, baby, finish eating. I want to introduce you to Roxy."

"Roxy? Who's that?"

"Roxy is a young Siamese kitten I found. She was all alone like me. She's been keeping me company all this time while I was waiting for you and Travis to come home. You can sleep with her tonight. Would you like that?"

Kyler's eyes widen and his jaw slackens. He squirms in his chair and sits upright.

"I would like that, Mom. I-I would *really* like that."

"Brush your teeth and crawl into my bed, and I'll put Roxy in bed with you. I'll sleep out here on my chair tonight."

Kyler's chair screeches across the floor. The pitter-patter of his feet scampers towards the bathroom. Her eyes catch Travis's. He tilts his head and remains silent. The squint of his eyes is slight. His lips widen at the corners, causing his dimples to form. He is so damn rugged and handsome it's intimidating. She looks away, then glances back at him.

"What the hell are you grinning at, *Big Mac*?"

"Nuth'n...just happy to see you, is all. I've missed ya, Doc. I've missed ya so much, Em."

The soft tone of his baritone voice relaxes her. Comforts her. She's missed him too.

"You want to sleep on my couch tonight, cowboy?"

"Thought you'd never ask."

"Yeah, well don't get any ideas, Tex. You best be keeping your hands to yourself."

He chuckles. "No worries. I plan on sleeping like a fat hog tonight. Ya might wanna stay on your side of the room this time."

She scoffs. "Uh-huh. You never stop dreaming."

She tiptoes into her bedroom and tucks Kyler into bed. She sets Roxy on the bed allowing her to burrow in next to him—purring and cuddling into his neck. Emily kisses him on the forehead.

"Good night, Kyler. I love you, sweetheart."

"Night, Mom. I love you too. Good night, Roxy."

Travis stretches out across the sofa with his eyes closed and a goofy grin across his face. She buries that grin with a mound of blankets and pillows.

"Thanks, Doc. Hey, would you mind rubbing my foot?"

"Ugh...disgusting. Good night, Travis."

Travis snores. He's too big for that sofa. His foot hangs over the edge like a large flipper. She lies curled in a ball, nestled into her easy chair. She stares at the shadowy outline of his body. Is he truly here? If this is some kind of hallucination, she's swallowing the entire bottle of opioids tomorrow. It's midnight. She mumbles,

"I wish I could stick a sock in his mouth." She giggles and thinks to herself. *Actually, I wish I could cover his mouth with my lips. Go to sleep, Emily. Don't be a slut.*

She tiptoes across the room and leans in close to his face. Dim light casts a soft purple glow across the chiseled features of his jawline. She tucks his blanket under his chin. The heat of his breath across her face and the scent of leather and spice titillate her senses. She caresses his cheek with the tips of her fingers. His left eye pops open and startles her. She grabs his nose and pinches it closed.

"Shit. What the hell, Doc? What are you trying to do?"

"Um...nothing. You...you snore. Shut up already. Rollover or something."

"Oh, sorry. Maybe just nudge me next time instead of trying to suffocate me in my sleep."

He rolls into the sofa cushions and buries his head under the blanket.

She plops into her chair and snuggles into the cushions and her comfy down-feather pillow. Heaving a deep sigh, she allows her eyes to close.

Travis's muffled voice interrupts the tranquility. "Ya just can't stay on your side of the room, can ya, Doc?"

25

Life Below Zero

Computer Log Entry 01-25-0001. *Master Sergeant Travis McCallister has suggested I maintain a daily log of our life on the facility. I hate it when he's right. I should have been doing this all along to document my time and all the events of my experiences here. It has been over three weeks since my reunion with Travis and Kyler. Our daily lives consist of performing quality control checks on all the life-support systems, food and fresh water supplies, plumbing, computer systems, cryonic labs, and recreation areas and equipment. Boring but necessary. According to Dr. Steinburg's schedule, I am supposed to place myself in a state of cryonic animation tomorrow at noon. Why? To prepare for a potential return of a space vessel that didn't land on a habitable planet. I'm supposed to sit here and wait, on the remote chance a vessel returns to Earth? A round-trip journey to the Proxima Centauri system would take over 140,000 years to complete. How would anybody know if Earth will be around by then? I'm going to live out my life here in this facility with Travis and Kyler. Steinburg's authority is light-years away. That means I am in charge. – Dr. Emily Grace signing off.*

"Are you boys ready to go to the Amazon rainforest today?"

"The Amazon rainforest? All right, I'll play along. How do we get there, Doc?"

"I wanna go, Mom. I finished my report on what happened to the Carib tribes and the other indigenous people who once lived there. I wanna see what the forest looks like. Can we go now?"

"*Indigenous*? I'm liking your vocabulary, Kyler. Yes, we can go right now. And...we are going to take the coolest elevator you two have ever experienced in your life to the twenty-fifth-floor observatory. Well, it's a virtual observatory, as I learned. But it's no less spectacular to experience. Follow me, boys."

It's been months since she visited the observatory. This is the first time she has escorted Travis and Kyler to the attraction. It has all the fun and feel of a day trip to the zoo.

***

"That was the best dadgum elevator ride I have ever experienced in my all my days, Doc. What d'ya think, buddy? Cool as all get-out, right?"

"That was...so weird. This hallway is creepy, Mom. Why is everything glowing purple? Is that the observatory...behind those big metal doors?"

"Yep. Don't worry. There's nothing to be afraid of, sweetheart. It's not as creepy as it looks, I promise."

The scene outside the dome is the same Arizona sunset she selected the last time she visited—everything is just as she left it.

"Wow. Is that real, Mom? Can I look through all those binoculars?"

"Go ahead, sweetie. It's okay. Check out the desert, and then I'm going to take us to the Amazon. Woo-hoo."

"Damn, Em. That's realistic as hell. You're telling me this is some kind of holograph? You gotta be yanking my chain."

"I'm not yanking your chain, Travis. It is indeed a holograph and had me fooled. Steinburg tricked me. I'm embarrassed I fell for it. I felt so stupid. Over here is the computer system that controls the virtual world."

She initiates the computer. Holographic orbs line up ready for action.

"Kyler? You ready to go to the Amazon?"

"Ah, heck ya. Let's go. Can I press the orb?"

Kyler taps the Amazon orb. The dome morphs into darkness, then explodes with vibrant colors and lush forest for miles. It lights up like the inside of a Disney ride.

"Whoa...look! There's the Amazon River. Just like the pictures in my schoolbook, Mom."

"Hm. I didn't notice these discs last time I was up here."

Emily taps a miniature disc with an icon of a nose. A moist, woody scent of vegetation and decaying wood permeates the air inside the dome. The room is also becoming humid somehow.

"Oh, my God. That's so darn crazy...in an amazing way. Can you guys smell that?"

"Smell what? Oh, excuse me...Powdered eggs this morning. Sorry, guys."

She crinkles her nose. "What? No...the air, dummy."

"Oh. Right. Hard not to notice that, Doc. What's this one? With the ear?" He taps it.

Buzzing insects, piercing bird calls, and rushing water resound throughout the dome in stereo.

"Holy sh...uh crap. We need to spend more time up here. This is like a primo vacation spot. What do you think, little buddy?"

"This is great, Mac. I could spend all day up here."

Travis winks at her. "Press the mouth. Go on. I dare ya."

She taps the miniature disc with the mouth icon. A booming voice begins a narration of Amazon rainforest facts and information.

"Hell, Doc, just send Kyler up here from now on for Geology... instead of making him do school. Great idea, don't ya think?"

"*Geography*...not Geology. I do like that idea, Travis. But you want to know an idea I like even more?"

"What?"

"I like the idea of pressing the orb for Antarctica and learning everything we can learn about the land above us. How about we also send *you* to school for a lesson or two?"

"Now that's dang smart, Doc. Maybe we can pinpoint our exact location and find out where we are...maybe scour the local terrain. Might not be a bad idea in case we ever need to bug out of here in a hurry."

She giggles. "Right, Travis. Exactly my point."

***

Computer Log Entry 01-26-0012. *We discovered our location today on the continent of Antarctica. Travis broke into the fortified offices of the military. It took several hours to quiet the alarm that blew out all our eardrums, but if you give Travis enough time, he'll solve just about any puzzle presented to him. Sometimes with a hammer. In Colonel Pomeroy's office, Travis found a series of maps, blueprints, drawings, and other plans locked away in a cabinet.*

One map shows our location near an old museum. It is a former Chilean base located at 63°19'15"S 57°53'55"W, and an elevation of thirteen miles above sea level, and about thirty km southwest of Prime Head, which is the northernmost point of the Antarctic Peninsula, at Cape Legoupil. Of course, we are a little over a quarter of a mile beneath the ocean surface trapped in this massive facility. More precisely, five-hundred and fifty-seven meters below the surface. They historically used the base as a research station called General Bernardo O'Higgins. The U.S. government later purchased it and converted it to accommodate the Morpheus Project, which I now call the Steinburg Debacle.

"Doc, follow me. I found something interesting."

"What did you find, another set of antlers for your den, Gaston?"

He chuckles. "Ya never stop busting my balls on that. Those antlers belonged to a ten-point buck. Do ya have any idea how rare that is?"

He pushes open a reinforced stainless-steel door, revealing a storeroom filled with parkas, boots, gloves, scarves, facemasks, and ski equipment.

"Look at all this, Doc. I'm wondering if this means we're close to finding a way to the surface. Maybe there's a submarine or an elevator shaft, or some other means nearby to reach the top?"

"This is nice work, Travis. You may be on to something."

She doesn't know where the impulse came from, but her body quivers with nervous energy. The solitude and dank, musky air of the compact storeroom are having a puzzling effect on her libido. Travis's scent of spice, leather, and sweat seems intense today. She has no idea why her sense of smell is so acute or why this area is making her so horny.

She shoves Travis further into the room, to his surprise. She takes his hand and brushes her lips along his meaty fingers, then locks eyes with his intense gaze. His coffee-brown eyes glint. A crooked smile forms a dimple on his left cheek. He tugs her body in his direction. His powerful arms enfold her. Her eyes slide closed. Every sense in her body is alert and prickling with sensual heat. Warm, moist breath caresses the flesh of her throat, moving along the nape of her neck to her earlobe. His lips suckle and softly nibble the back of her ear, sending titillating chills along her spine and creating a raging fire begging for his attention.

He caresses her face. Their lips join the passion of the moment. The pounding of her heart forces short breaths, shifting to erotic panting. His lips press deep and hard—covering her mouth with his. Their bodies intertwine, slamming against the wall—wrestling their way to a rack of parkas. He knocks the rack to the floor, creating a pile of fur and canvas. He lifts her into his muscled arms and crouches—gently setting her down.

She grabs the inside of his shirt and rips it open. Buttons pop and fly across the concrete floor. He lifts her T-shirt over her head, sliding it away and tossing it to the side. She's exposed. Braless. Exhilaration raises goosebumps along her chest and arms. His lips brush along her navel, leaving wisps of warm moisture from his touch. Each wisp quickly cools across her skin. *Oh, God. Oh my God, is this really happening?*

They blew past the point of no return moments ago. Too late. Her sweatpants slide down her thighs and land on the floor next to her T-shirt. It's been *so* long. Nobody has ever brought her to these heights of climactic intensity. *God, how is he doing that?*

She's oblivious of the exact moment Travis stripped away his clothes, revealing a chiseled body with the brashness of a stallion. He lifts her off the floor. Brandon could have never performed anything close to this. Brandon would satisfy himself and then fall asleep. Her panting increases with an abandoned frenzy—building to tearful and euphoric moans. She cries out—digging her nails deep into the rippled muscles of his broad shoulders—releasing every ounce of desire and fervor from her mind, body, and spirit. She collapses, submissive inside his arms—like a newborn foal, heaving breaths and self-aware of the shy grin forming on her face. Shocked by whatever possessed her to instigate this moment.

The entire episode is out of character for her. Something her ex-husband made a point to exploit the last time they argued. Today she is spontaneous and she acted on her desires.

Travis is drenched. A sheen of sweat reflects off his skin. His body is reddened and patchy. He collapses next to her.

"What the heck brought that on, Em? I'm not complaining by any means. But..."

Her face flushes with warmth. The corner of her mouth quivers.

"I...I can't say. I don't know. This room...your scent...the moment. I guess I needed that so much. I wanted it to happen, Travis. It was bound to happen. I've never experienced such an incredible...crazy thing like this in my life." She reaches out her hand and strokes his moist cheek.

He lifts his body and rests on one elbow. His pursed lips widen into a broadened grin. He leans toward her and kisses her forehead.

"I've been waiting a long time, Em. I wasn't sure I was capable of this anymore. At least not without the right woman. My guilt has always hindered me. I still feel married to Cheyenne...and I try not to think about her. But you're different. You remind me so much of her. You both share the same fiery spirit...you're both bright...and you both seem to enjoy busting my balls every chance you get. I've missed that...until *you* came along."

His eyes glisten. He glances at the ground. She reaches for him—massaging the rippled muscles of his firm shoulders. She nudges his chin upward with the tip of her index finger. His stare holds hers but seems to be filled with a distant pain. This man loves with all his heart and even decades haven't seemed to cool the love he has for his wife and son. A broken heart weighs heavy on the soul.

"Travis. It's okay. Being here with me doesn't mean you don't love your wife anymore. She'll forever live in your heart...and I-I would never want to take that away from you. You're such a good man. She was a lucky woman to hold your heart the way she has. I'm sure she was an incredible person. I understand how deeply you must miss her and your son."

Tears trickle over her lashes and patter across the parkas beneath them. She sniffles. Her words betray her heart. She wants his love. All of it. She doesn't want to share it with his past.

His eyes widen. He sighs. He folds his hands over hers, squeezing and caressing her fingers between his.

"It's not that, Em. It's just...I never thought I could feel like this again. Never thought I could lie with another woman. Cheyenne will forever live in my heart, and she will always be the love of my life. But I...I wonder...ya know...wonder if a man can have two loves of his life. I don't know how that works...How to allow myself to find love again, Em? But you're making it so dang hard for me. Confusing my heart...and I just..."

She covers his lips with her fingers. "Sh. Let's get dressed. Kyler must be wondering where we ran off to. We can talk more later."

26

TREMBLORS

Once per week is "explore day" in the vast facility. All of its compartments, rooms, equipment, and secrets are yet to reveal themselves. The uniform of the day is khaki overalls, boots, long-sleeve sweatshirts, boonie hats, and backpacks.

"Today, campers, we are going to continue our exploration of the military section. Our mission is to locate and identify our means of escape to the surface...should that scenario present itself. Search for a marine craft, elevator, stairs, or other means of escape. Is everybody's radio and laptop charged and operational?"

"Yes sir, Commander Mac. Charged and ready for service. Mom, can I be on your team today? Commander Mac farts when you're not around. And can we take Roxy?"

"Ha-ha. Of course, you can, Kyler. You and I are going to find the target before Commander Mac. Roxy can ride in your backpack. Bring some food and snacks along for Roxy."

"Sounds like some friendly competition, team...and it appears we have a whistleblower in the group." Travis frowns at Kyler.

"Okay. You're on. The first team to locate the target gets a coconut cream pie tonight made by the other team. Deal?"

"Deal, Commander Big Mac. We're gonna kick your butt, so you better be ready to put your apron on."

Travis guffaws. "You three take the transport cart. I'll walk. We'll meet up in front of the parka room at 1600 hours. Don't be late. Report in with me on your radio every fifteen minutes. Get moving, troops."

"Where's the parka room, Commander Big Mac? Is that a secret hideout?"

"Nope...ask your mom. She knows where it's at. She enjoys modeling the parkas... All at once."

"Travis." She swats his arm.

Emily, Kyler, and Roxy glide along the hallways in a food delivery cart. Its top speed is ten miles per hour, allowing them to enter the military facilities long before Travis.

"We'll park here, Kyler, and walk."

Static crackles and pops. "Report in, team. Sound off."

"Kyler here, sir. Checking in at 1315 hours."

"Emily checking in, *Big Mac*."

"That's Commander Big Mac to you, soldier."

"Yeah, well, over and out, Rambo...or whoever the heck you think you are today."

"Come on, Kyler. Let's explore these rooms and see what we can discover."

"What's this room, Mom?"

"Looks like a gym. I never knew this was here. I'm going to come back and work out. This is prime equipment. Your tax dollar at work...literally. Oh, and look. A dance room."

The floor rumbles.

"Mom! What was that?"

"I don't know, Kyler. It's gone now, baby. Stay close to me."

Walls rattle for several seconds, then the shaking subsides. Kyler's fingers dig into the flesh of her thigh.

"Travis? You copy? Did you feel that?"

"Copy, Doc. Yeah, I felt it. Hey, listen, I think I might have found something. Use your laptop to track me. Both you and Kyler need to come to me."

"Roger. I hope those rumbles aren't a sign of something bad about to happen."

"It's common in this part of the world, Doc. Lots of volcanic activity. I don't think we have anything to concern ourselves with, though. Head my way, and don't dilly-dally around like a couple of tourists."

"There. I see you on my screen, Travis. We will head your way."

Kyler clicks his radio on. "Yeah, we're on our way, Captain Kangaroo."

"Okay. Now that's just disrespectful. Show some love for your commander, troops. And Captain Kangaroo was way before your time, buddy. I think I can guess where that one came from. Over and out."

They walk along the narrow hallways, through briefing rooms and, down a large hallway. The floor vibrates and pitches—like a cruise ship on rough seas.

"Travis? I see you, but you're on the other side of this wall. We can't get to you. I'm worried about these quakes."

"Doc, go back down the large hall you just entered and go through the door on your right. Follow that skinny hallway around, and you'll run right into me. Try to stay calm."

"In here, Kyler. Come on.

"There you are, Travis. What'd you find that's so urgent?"

"Look at this. I think we found our way up to the surface. It's a shuttle. Looks like it shoots up that shaft until it pops out the top. The problem is...how does the thing work? We need to search around this room and see if we can find instructions or an operation manual."

Kyler and Travis scavenge through drawers, closets, baskets, file cabinets, and every nook and cranny they come across. There is a computer desk sitting next to the shuttle. She searches the desk for the access port to initiate the computer. She glances into the computer screen and places her thumb on a sensor on the side of the desk. A prompt beeps, initiating a holographic screen in front of her.

"Guys. I've got something here."

"Whoa. Can you log in, Doc?"

"*User identified. Dr. Emily Grace, lead surgeon and operations manager of the Morpheus Project. Access is denied. Insufficient security clearance.*"

"Darn it. It won't let me in. Steinburg didn't grant me access to this part of the facility. That bastard. Sorry, Kyler."

"Okay. Well, I still think there's a manual somewhere...a backup. Another way to figure out how to use this system, Em."

"Yeah, but what if we need to access the computer system to operate the shuttle? If so, we are totally screwed."

"All right, let's uh...punt. Let's gather our things and make our way back to Homebase. We'll try to figure it out from there. We'll come back tomorrow with fresh minds and continue to work on the problem. Let's head home, troops."

***

"Kyler's asleep. He is pooped, poor guy."

"He's a good soldier."

"Stop. We're not playing soldiers for the rest of the night, okay?"

"You sure ya don't wanna play a little *Capture the Flag* in the parka room?"

She crosses her arms and rolls her eyes—refusing to give him the satisfaction of a grin.

"No. Let's pretend that never happened."

Glasses and dishes rattle—several dishes fall from their shelves and explode in tiny shards across the tile. The floors quake and the walls rumble. A booming crash follows a powerful jolt.

Kyler shrieks. "Mom! Mac! I'm scared!"

She rushes into her bedroom and scoops Kyler from the bed. She darts into the kitchen and scrambles beneath the kitchen table. Travis slides a chair away from the table and joins them.

"What the hell, Travis? What's happening?"

"I'm not sure. That was a strong series of tremblors. Feels like something's brewing out there on the ocean floor. We need to figure out how to use that escape shuttle and do it fast. Whatever is going on, it has calmed down for the moment. Let's all sleep together here in the living room. Kyler, crawl in with me on the sofa, buddy."

"Hey. I want to sleep with you guys too. Make room for me. You're not leaving me all by myself with all that rumbling going on out there. Come here, Roxy. Come here, baby. There you go. Crawl in there with Kyler."

"All right, family, let's try to get some shuteye. Em? Can you remove your knee from my groin, please? Okay, nobody move. That's perfect. Nighty night, campers."

Five minutes later, Travis is snoring. How the heck can he fall asleep like that? She stares at the soft purple shadows cast across a soft gray ceiling. How can she gain access to the military's shuttle system? There has to be an entrance point she can compromise. God only knows what these quakes are telling them or what they might lead to.

27

A FURIOUS TIMEBOMB

5:37 a.m. The floor jolts and the walls shudder, followed by a tremendous boom that rocks the apartment. Emily squeals and leaps to her feet. She loses her balance and falls face-first into her lounge chair. Kyler claws at Travis's chest like a wildcat scurrying up a tree. Roxy hisses and vaults straight into the air. When she rebounds, she hits the sofa and scrambles into Emily's bedroom, darting beneath the bed.

"Hang on, Kyler. It's okay, buddy. It'll subside in a minute. Em? You, okay?"

"Yeah...I think so. I face-planted into the arm of the chair. Feels like someone socked me in the nose."

"We need to get dressed and figure out that shuttle, pronto."

The uniform of the day is the same as yesterday. Literally. Same clothes. No time to waste on fashion this morning. They head out the door in eight minutes flat. Rubber squeals and echoes along the hallways the moment the food cart hits full speed—ten miles per hour.

"Can't this darn thing go any faster, Travis? I can walk faster than this."

"Nope. Top speed, I'm afraid, princess. Sit tight, and I'll get us there. Use this time to figure out that network and get us inside their system."

"Aye, aye, Captain. I'll get right on that. You just keep your eyes on the road. This isn't one of your four-wheeling escapades."

***

"Okay, jump out. Kyler and I will continue to search for documentation. You work some of that hacker magic, Doc. Make use of that education your daddy paid for."

Emily stumbles to the right, then slides to her left. Her palms sting, smacking the floor. Walls crackle. The floor quakes. Travis scoops up Kyler and slides under the computer desk like a runner stealing second base.

"Em! Gimme your hand."

Lights dim and flicker before complete blackness envelops them. Silence. No hum coming from the vents. The air is still. Kyler sucks in a nervous breath and whimpers. A crimson glow emanates along the hallways and inside the shuttle room.

"We are on backup life support, Travis. If we don't get these systems back online, we'll run out of air in twelve hours, and the temperature will drop to below freezing."

"Well, if we ain't breathing, we won't notice the cold."

Travis points in the shuttle's direction.

"Hey! The lights just activated on that control panel, Doc. It looks like it woke up or something."

The floor has stabilized but continues to vibrate and hum. She crawls towards the control panel, followed by Travis and Kyler.

"It's active, Travis. What the heck?"

"Maybe it's a fail-safe programmed into the system, Doc. Say...if we lose life support, maybe it overrides the system or something. Let's see if we can activate it and figure out how to launch this thing."

A cramp in the base of her throat prevents her from swallowing. She bites her lip and glances at him.

"What? Why are you looking at me like that?"

"There are only two seats, Travis. We have to go on separate trips."

"Shit. You and Kyler go. I'll take the next one out."

"You know zilch about this facility, Travis. I know how to check the life-support systems and keep this place operational. You don't. You have to go...you and Kyler. If you were to get trapped down here, you're hosed. Game over. *I'll* take the next shuttle."

"Ah. Goddammit. I can't leave you here. You know I can't do that. Wonder if we get to the surface and can't send the shuttle back down? Let's see if we can bring the facility back online and figure out a better plan, Em. Deal?"

She sighs. "Right. Okay. We have eleven hours and forty-seven minutes of life support remaining. If we can't bring the systems back online in say, eight hours, then we need to fire up the shuttle and go."

"I set my watch. Show me what to do. Teach me everything you know about the facility's systems and how this joint operates, Doc."

"There isn't time for that. My God, you're such a cowboy. It took me weeks to figure all these systems out."

"Ya, but you didn't have a mentor. Just teach me what you can. I'm a fast learner."

***

"Travis. How much time do we have left?"

"We're out of time, Em. Like forty-five minutes ago."

"What? Why didn't you tell me?"

"Because. You're making significant progress. You got this. Just use that ASU nerd education and piece this shit back together."

"That leaves us three hours of life support, Travis. Damn it. You should have said something."

"We're almost there, Em. Take a deep breath and relax. You already have most of the power restored...we just need the most important one restored, now."

"You make this sound so easy."

Sweat drips off her brow and splatters onto the desktop. The life support system is the most complex and difficult to override and reroute. Every combination she tries ends up a failure.

"Travis. I think if I use grid #37 that supplies the power to purify our water and grid #12 that controls our lighting, I might be able to bring back the life support grid. We'll just have to live without water and light is all."

"Well, we have forty-two minutes left, so we should give it a try. Give me five minutes to round up a couple of power cells. We'll need to see when the lights go out."

"Okay, go. Hurry. I'm about to complete the patch."

***

"Slow down, Travis. I can't see what's ahead. We don't need to break a world record on our way back to the shuttle room."

"No need to pitch a hissy fit. This food cart only has a top speed of ten miles per hour. I'm doing five."

"Yeah, well...it seems faster in the dark."

The power cells illuminate the shuttle room as they roll to a stop just inside the doorway. They're still breathing, and the air remains a constant seventy-five degrees. Kyler fell asleep in the back of the cart with Roxy tucked beneath his arm.

"Doc, there are no lights on the shuttle's control panel anymore."

"Oh, my God. We're so stupid. The panel must have activated when the life support system failed. I think bringing it back online must have reset the system's security protection. We'd have to turn life support off again to use the damn thing. How can we be that dumb?"

"Don't beat yourself up, Doc. Hey, we're still kicking."

"Wait. There were over three thousand people who boarded those space vessels, right? There's no way they'd use this shuttle system to transport all those people to the surface two at a time in an emergency. This must be an exclusive ride to the top. There has to be another means of transport to the surface—one that could accommodate three thousand plus people. Don't you think?"

"See there? Now you're thinking again, Doc. Ya ain't so dumb after all."

She rolls her eyes and opens her mouth to speak. No words come out. She scoffs and shakes her head.

"Let's keep looking, Travis. Where is the most logical place to locate a mass transit?"

Travis's eyes widen. His dimples deepen.

"Doc. We need to check out that launch area. I know that seems obvious, but if you're transporting three thousand bodies to the stars, you should have the ability to transport three thousand bodies to the surface from that same location? Make sense?"

She places her hands on her hips and sighs. "It makes perfect sense. You may be on to something, genius. We need to get inside one of those launch areas. There are three of them on different floors. I haven't tried to enter a single one since I've been here."

Vibration travels through her boots, reaching her knees. Rumbling erupts inside the floors and walls, escalating into violent quakes. The floor pitches and quavers. She dances and scrambles, then dives into the back of the food cart. Kyler whines and trembles beneath her body. She hovers over him and Roxy. Travis grips a metal support beam in the center of the shuttle room, holding on like a tree-hugger. The tremblors continue for several minutes then subside. An eerie silence surrounds them.

Travis slams the power cells into the cart and sits in the driver's seat.

"Everybody okay?"

"These earthquakes are getting stronger, Travis. We've got to find a way out of here."

"Hold on, Em. Stay down, buddy, and take care of Roxy."

Travis reverses the cart and zips out the doorway, headed down the hallway towards the central stairwell.

"What levels are those launch pads on, Em?"

"Um...let me think. Red is level seven...I think green is fifteen and yellow is on twenty-four."

"Red it is."

The cart skids to a stop in front of the central stairwell. Travis lifts the power cells in each hand and stands near the door.

"It's three floors up. Can someone get the door for me, please? Thank you."

A thick red line runs along the center of the hallway on level seven. The line leads to a set of stainless-steel double doors.

"Oh God, please let me have access."

She smiles into a small reflective portal set in the panel of the left door. A soft-blue light scans the features of her face.

"Dr. Emily Grace. Access granted."

She exhales and sighs. *Thank you, Lord.*

Inside is a massive hangar. The facility's builders inlaid huge windows within a curved wall. She stares into the deep shadowy bowels of a daunting ocean. A metal staircase leads to a single door set above the windows. This must be where the space travelers exited the facility and boarded a one-way flight to Eden...or maybe Hell.

"Travis! Look."

Three open chambers house marine craft—each the size of a small bus.

"That is the same type of craft they transported me and ole Kyler in. I paid attention to how the pilot operated it. I think I got this."

A scarlet glow blazes in the distance, illuminating the deep ocean floor. An underground mountain explodes, spewing radiant golden lava and sending a killer shockwave in their direction.

"Oh, my God. Travis, grab Kyler! We need to get inside one of these subs now!"

The facility rocks and jolts from side to side. Roxy leaps from Kyler's arms and darts up the metal stairway.

"Roxy! Come back. Mom...Mom, we need to save Roxy."

"Ah, crap. Travis put him inside. I'll be right back."

"Em. No, we gotta go. I'm sorry. Leave the damn cat."

"Put Kyler in the sub. I'll be right back."

She dashes up the stairway and scoops Roxy into her arms. Time stops. The facility is rocked like a twenty-megaton bomb. She's airborne. Flung into the air like a child's doll—tumbling and spiraling over the safety rail.

The impact steals every ounce of air from her chest. The ceiling blurs and spins—fading in, then out—keeping rhythm with the high-pitched squeals resonating inside her ears. She struggles—sucking in air that refuses to fill her lungs. Her head throbs. She can't move or cry out. She can only lie motionless and wait.

Her body is lifted into the air and whisked away. *Travis?*

"I got you, darlin'. Just relax. Breathe in slow. That's it. Ya got the wind knocked out of ya, that's all. Just relax and breathe, girl."

"Mac, is she going to be okay? Where's Roxy, Mac? We have to save Roxy.

"Roxy is gone, buddy. We have to go, son. I'm sorry."

She fades in and out of consciousness. Beyond the glass, a furious underground volcano erupts. Kyler's teary eyes reflect terror and heartbreak. She listens to Travis's voice as he reassures her—his words jumble—turning into gibberish. Kyler's sobs fade. Her world dissolves to silent blackness.

28

THE FROZEN DESERT

Antarctica is Earth's fifth-largest continent. Over 99% of the land is covered in ice. The irony? Antarctica is classified as a desert. No sand for your toes, but plenty of ice for your tea.

Shades of pastel and gray swirl before her eyes. The swirls morph into the concerned face of Travis. He caresses her cheeks. Moisture from his kiss cools as it evaporates from her lips.

"There she is. Welcome back, darlin'. Ya had us worried for a spell, Em."

"Where are we, Travis? Where's Kyler? And Roxy?"

"Well, we're the only residents of an old research station called *General Bernardo O'Higgins*. Kyler's here. He's stayed glued to your side the past few days. I couldn't pull him away, even for supper. Roxy didn't make it, Em. I'm very sorry. We were very fortunate to escape when we did. A little longer and we'd all be permanent residents of the South Atlantic Ocean. We just didn't have the time to find Roxy."

"Oh, God. Poor Roxy. Poor Kyler. How long have I been unconscious?

"It's been three days, darlin'. Ya took a hell of a spill off those steps. Scared the shit out of me. Ya did a Peter Pan right off that metal stairway, but ya didn't land on your feet."

"And the underwater facility? Did it survive?

"No way to know for sure. But if I had to speculate, I'd say... no, probably not."

"God, my head is pounding. Do we have food? Water? Are we safe?"

"We're okay, Em. I'll debrief you when you're feeling better. You get some rest now. Kyler and I are fixing to whip up some supper soon. We'll wake you up when it's ready."

"*Please.* No mac 'n' cheese."

He guffaws. That's the least of your worries, Doc. Here, I found some pain meds. It'll help you rest."

***

The aroma of burnt toast fills her nostrils and interrupts her slumber. She sits upright on a narrow canvas cot. She heaves a breath and scoots her feet to the side of the cot and onto the floor.

"Ow. What's this? Well, Travis did a commendable job bandaging my ankle, I have to admit. Hm. My toes look like purple grapes."

"Hey...hey now...don't get up. Let me help you into the kitchen. You did a nasty number on that ankle. Not broke, but a real bad sprain. At least I'm not gonna have to shoot ya, anyway."

"That's...that's not funny, Travis. What are you doing? I can walk. Put me down."

"No. You can't. Let me help you."

She slaps his shoulder. "Yes, I can. Put me down."

"Suit yourself." He sets her feet on the floor and releases her. Her head fogs and whirls. She hobbles three steps, then collapses to one knee.

"Come on, Em. I told ya that was gonna happen. You are so darn pig-headed, gal."

She raises her head and flips him off. Travis lifts her off the floor and sets her in a chair at the kitchen table. Her temples pulsate. She steadies her vertigo by gripping the tabletop.

"Okay. What did you two chefs create? I'm starving. Something smells burnt."

"We made breakfast for supper, Mom. I made the oatmeal, and Mac burnt the toast."

"Way to throw me under the bus, buddy. I asked you to keep an eye on it. Ya just can't get good help these days."

Travis yanks Kyler's ball cap over his face and sets a plate of eggs, bacon, toast, and a bowl of oatmeal in front of Emily. Someone scraped the burnt toast and wasn't too clever in concealing it with butter and jam.

She stabs her eggs with a fork. "What would you classify these eggs as, Travis? Over easy or scrambled? Mm. The bacon is...interesting. Thank you both so much for making me food. I was famished. It looks and tastes...*delicious.*"

The kitchen is a quaint fifteen-foot-by-ten-foot room filled with vintage appliances. The small weathered table sits in its center. Bits of white paint chips flake and curl from its edges. The walls are sterile white. The area is cozy and warm and filled with something she hasn't seen in a very long time. Sunshine. Even if it's only filtered sunshine.

"This is surprisingly good. Did you guys have time to check the facility out? You didn't explore the place without me, did you?"

"Uh...well...we did. Kyler and I did some exploring while you were resting. I pulled him away from your side for a couple of hours. Most of the buildings haven't been occupied in a very long time. There is, however, one building that has some modern equipment and electronics. I'm guessing Steinburg and his cronies made use of it. And hey, I found the other end of your red intercom attached to the wall in that room."

"Where do we stand as far as food and fresh water?"

"I'd guesstimate we have a solid six to eight months of food for the three of us...if we manage it well. Water? Well, Antarctica contains most of the world's freshwater supply, so we're good in the *agua fria* department. That's Spanish for *cold water.*"

"Yeah. I...took Spanish in college."

"We found a small storage room with some parkas, bunny boots, iron pants, and even some skis and fishing gear. I think once you're feeling better, we'll take a brief trip around the area and see what else we can find. We found a swordfish boat in the bay and a smaller fishing boat down by a storage shed. Maybe the sword boat will help us sail across the salty seas to get back home? I think South America is north of us. Did you know that only 3% of the Earth's water is fresh water?"

"Wow, Travis. Spending all that time in the observatory has turned you into Captain Trivia. No, I didn't know that, Mr. Wizard. But thanks for sharing that tidbit of info."

He chuckles. "Em, I can show you the parka room later when Kyler's asleep if you like?"

"Very funny, Travis. Hilarious. But while we're on the topic of exploring, I'd love to go on a tour after supper. You boys up for it?"

"That's a negative, princess. Besides your gimpy ankle, you suffered a serious concussion. You need some time to heal, gal and, Kyler and I are going to make sure you do just that. That flop you did on the floor just now confirms you're not ready for duty."

She sighs. "You're right...I guess. Thank you, both for taking such good care of me. I'm going to sit over here in front of this window and close my eyes. It's been too long since I felt sunshine on my face. I just want to soak it up for a little while."

***

Eleven days of enjoying the beachfront property of beautiful Antarctica has swept by. The purple has faded from her toes, and the swelling has decreased, thanks to Travis's freezing snowpacks. He has amazing first-aid skills from his military days. Her headaches have subsided. The pain meds were a godsend. But the medicine cabinet is bare other than a few bandages, splints, and antiseptic gel.

She cannot contain her excitement. Today is "explore day." The uniform of the day is a heavy parka, bunny boots, iron pants, gloves, beanie, facemask, and goggles. She glances in the mirror. *I look like a fat, green polar bear. But a cute, fat, green polar bear.*

The Antarctic air penetrates her thick gear. She doesn't care. Being outside and breathing fresh arctic air is an acceptable trade-off to freezing her butt off. The skies loom dark and ominous. The sea appears to have more ice than water. Milky blocks of icebergs fill the bay, floating along, headed in no particular direction. The world around her appears in black and white. The only splash of color is the rusty-red buildings of the General

Bernardo O'Higgins research base. Even the penguins are black and white. The ground is composed of rugged volcanic rocks mixed with patches of pure-white ice and snow. The footing can be treacherous, especially for someone with a bum ankle.

"Kyler and I are gonna show ya the fishing boat we discovered last week while you were sleeping. We took her out for a short spin. It gave me a chance to teach the boy how to fish. He landed a big one. Didn't ya, Kyler? We packed a nice haul of cod in the icehouse."

Kyler points. "There it is, Mom. You ready to go sailing?"

"Good, Lord. You mean that thing actually runs? It looks like an old rusty tub."

"Ha-ha. Yep, she runs, all right. What she looks like on the outside isn't what she is on the inside, Doc. Kinda like me. Don't judge a sword boat by its hull. Someone did an outstanding job of converting it into a modern and seaworthy vessel. You're gonna be our capitán today. That's Spanish for 'captain.'"

"Me? Why me? I don't want to be captain or capitán. How about I just come along for the ride, okay? One of you guys be the captain."

"Em, you need to learn how to operate this boat. It's our ticket off of Antarctica. And if anything happens to me, you will need to know how to sail this vessel. It's easier to navigate than those submarines from the underwater facility. You can do this. I promise."

"Come on, Mommy. You can do anything Big Mac can do, can't ya?"

She nibbles on the inside of her cheek and glances at Kyler, then shifts her eyes toward Travis and squints.

"You bet I can, Kyler."

"Climb aboard, mates. Kyler, take your seat over there and rig that fishing pole just like I showed ya. Captain Grace, step on over here to the wheelhouse."

She climbs into the wheelhouse and lays her hands across a solid oaken wheel—polished from years of sailor's hands and nautical navigation.

"Okay, I'm ready for my first lesson."

"Alrighty. That there thing you are holding in your palms is the wheel, Captain. It steers the boat."

"No kidding. I gathered that much. What's this button do?"

He chuckles and grins. "Pay attention now. Don't touch that yet."

"A small nuclear cell powers this boat. See this yellow box? It's all contained inside here. No dangerous waste or anything like that. I understand it's a very safe method of fusion used to fuel this vessel. I don't understand the science behind it, and I can't explain how it works...but I know it works. She's about a fifty-foot boat. Top speed is around thirty knots. The manual says the synthetic oil used for the engine will last for years. We could sail around the world hundreds of times without having to worry about fuel or oil."

"Thirty knots, huh? What's a knot?"

"A knot is how fast a boat travels on the water. Thirty knots is around thirty-five miles per hour, I reckon. Check this out. Press this button to start the engine. Use this lever to move the boat forward or reverse, then use this lever to set the speed. This computer screen shows ya all kinds of cool information, like what time the tides change...how deep the water is...temperature...and important shit like that. You can even program the boat to sail to any destination using the autopilot function. It's pretty darn simple. It doesn't require a brain surgeon to operate."

She chuckles. "I see what you did there. If it doesn't require a brain surgeon to operate, then you be the captain."

"Looky here. This is a map of the Americas. We could plot a trip up the coast of South America, travel along the coast of Mexico and enter the Gulf of California...and then land in Puerto Penasco. Good ole, Rocky Point. We can slam back a few brewskies and check out the tourists."

"That's hilarious. I'm sure the party days of Rocky Point are long gone. I don't think we'll be seeing Jimmy Buffett or Kenny Chesney singing in any of the bars. How far is Rocky Point from Phoenix?"

"Around a hundred and fifty miles as the crow flies. We'd have to find some sort of transportation to get ourselves through the Sonoran Desert and up to Phoenix.

"All right now, Captain. Hit the button and fire up those engines. Push that lever forward and take us up to ten knots. Head for the bay."

The engine makes a slight hum. It's nothing like driving a car. Flutters tickle her insides as the boat reaches ten knots and enters the bay unannounced. Freezing air exhilarates her senses and chaps her nose. Ice sloshes off the sides of the boat, leaving a wake of slushy dark waters rippling behind them.

"Okay...all right...we're sailing, Travis. I can get used to this. What's this thing do?"

She pulls a lever that blasts a horn. Kyler screams; Travis clamps his hands over his ears and crouches.

"Holy shit, Doc. I wasn't ready for that. You're scaring the fish away."

She yelps, then giggles. "Oops. That was really loud. Sorry."

"Let's keep our little pinkies off that lever. Deal? Let's park here, Doc...er, Captain. We'll let Kyler fish for a spell, assuming there's still fish in the area, then we'll head back. In the meantime, let me give you the full tour.

"Climb on down. This is the bottom deck. We have a couple of small cots, a nice heating system for the cold, and a fancy cooling system when it's hot. Over here is our water supply. We have enough fresh water for about a month if we ration it well. The beautiful thing about this contraption is this: Turn on this pump and voila—The system can convert salt water to fresh water. And we have tons of freezer space to store a couple of month's worth of food.

"I believe we can do this, Em. But whatever we end up finding at home in good ole Arizona...well, your guess is as good as mine. Getting to a warm climate might be worth the risk, I reckon." Travis leans in close to her ear and whispers, "Because my nut sack is frozen to my leg right now." Emily slaps his shoulder. "Can you stop? Kyler might hear you. God, you're so crude."

"Mac! I got one...I got one."

"Attaboy, Kyler. Sink that hook into his lip and pull him in. A couple more and it's codfish for supper."

"Do you *really* think we can do this, Travis? We can actually go home?"

"If we do this right, I'm confident we can find our way home. Speaking of home, why don't you turn us around, capitán, and take us back into port."

The fishing boat's autopilot executes a perfect docking.

"Mom! Penguins! Can we go play with them?"

"Oh wow. Those penguins are so close. No, honey. We should only observe and keep our distance."

"Why? They look friendly. Are you scared of them?"

"No, I'm not scared of them. We shouldn't interact with them. They're wild animals, Kyler. We need to respect that and respect them. This is their home, not ours."

"Listen to your mom, Kyler. She's right."

An ominous rumble shakes the ground beneath them.

"Travis? Did you feel that?"

"Yep. I think that Roman candle under the ocean is throwing another hissy fit."

"Kyler. Stay away from that edge. That's a long way down, sweetheart."

"I'm okay, Mom. I just wanna look at the ocean from up here."

"Kyler. Step away from there. Please. You're making me nervous. Kyler...Kyler. Oh, my *God*. Travis! Grab him!"

The ground trembles. Rocks and ice crunch, then slide like a conveyer belt carrying Kyler over the ledge. Kyler's eyes widen. He stretches his arms towards Travis, then disappears. Travis leaps over the hill and rides debris of rock and ice to the bottom with the agility of a mountain goat.

Her heart flutters. She scoots down the hillside, using her boots and her butt as a skid. Kyler is sprawled across a milky-white block of ice. A puddle of pink oozes from his skull and runs along the ice block, dripping onto the rocky ground beneath.

"Don't move him, Travis. Let me look at him first.

"Oh, baby... Oh, Kyler. Mommy's here, sweetheart. Lie still. We're going to get you back inside. Don't move, honey."

"He's semi-conscious, Em. His back and neck look okay. But he cracked his head open pretty bad. We need to get him inside quickly. I'm going to carry him."

"Keep his head supported, Travis. Don't let his neck turn."

"You run ahead, Em. Prepare whatever you need to prepare inside to save our boy here, okay? Deep breaths now. Kyler needs us to keep our wits. I'll be right behind ya."

29

SEARCH AND RESCUE

Kyler's brain is swelling. He fractured his skull. Contusions and bruises cover his body. She needs to operate now! She's performed dozens of craniectomies in her career. The implant and nanotechnology Steinburg inserted into her brain accelerates her analysis and formulates a viable strategy for performing the procedure. She feeds Kyler a dose of liquified pain meds through a tube into his stomach. He's unconscious, and the pain meds should keep him sedated long enough to complete the procedure.

"Travis, I need tools...Knives as sharp as you can find. See if you can locate any type of saw blade...and a drill. Everything has to be sterilized."

"I am all over it, Doc."

"See if you can find alcohol and some clean gauze pads or clean linen. Quickly, Travis. Kyler can't wait much longer."

She wheels Kyler on a stainless-steel kitchen cart into a small bedroom area. She covers his partially nude body with a clean sheet and rolls another kitchen cart next to him to prepare a make-shift surgery table.

"I found a bottle of rubbing alcohol, a drill, and a fine-tooth hacksaw blade. What size of drill bit do you need, Em?"

She points. "I want that one. The skinny one. Dip it in the alcohol and don't touch it with your fingers. Sterilize the saw blade while you're at it...and those knives...everything on this table."

"You got it, Doc."

"I'm going to need you to assist me. Are you okay with that?"

"I'm a former soldier, Em. I've seen worse."

"Good. The swelling is right here. See that contusion? Hand me that knife. I'm going to create a flap of skin to expose the bone. I have to open his skull to relieve the pressure."

"You're doing good, Doc."

"Hand me the drill. I'm making a few small holes to help remove a piece of skull bone. Now hand me that saw blade. Travis, I'm going to need a sterilized glass container to store the skull fragment. We have to keep it frozen."

"Shouldn't be too hard to keep anything frozen around here. How about this jar?"

"Perfect. Fill the jar with alcohol and rinse it. Let it air dry. Okay, now I'm draining the blood and fluids. I have to bring the swelling under control. Can you hand me that towel?"

"You're a hell of a surgeon, Em. Kyler's damn lucky you know what you're doing."

"All done. I'm going to stitch him up for now. He'll have to stay this way for a few days until the swelling in his brain subsides. Then I'll reattach the skull fragment and, if all goes well, he should be fine."

"You make this whole procedure sound as easy as cleaning a skinned knee."

"Let's let him rest for now. We have enough pain meds to keep him sedated for several days."

Travis lays his hand across Kyler's shoulder. His eyes are misty. "Sleep tight, buddy. You're in excellent hands, son."

"Travis, I need to talk to you. Kyler is at high risk for infection. We have no antibiotics in this building. We had enough antibiotics in the medical wing beneath the ocean to last a lifetime. I hate to say this, but we need those drugs."

"I'll go, Em. I'll take the sub and go back down and bring 'em up--assuming the facility is still intact."

"It's not that easy. The drugs are locked away in a medical lab. I'm the only one with access to get inside. You're not authorized. I have to be the one to go."

"Yeah, but you don't know how to operate the sub."

"Then teach me. I have to be the one, Travis. We have no other choice."

Travis sighs and scratches the back of his neck. "All right, then. Let's teach you how to drive. No telling what you're gonna find down there though. That volcano might have already chewed that facility up and spit it out like a chaw of tobacco."

"If that's the case, then I'll turn around and come back. But if it's still intact and I can get inside, I have to try. Kyler's life depends on it."

"Time is a wasting. I'll put Kyler in his bed, then give you a crash course in maritime submarining."

***

Beams of light from the front of the vehicle penetrate the inky darkness as the submarine dives deeper into the abyss. The submarine's autopilot function tracks a homing beacon transmitted from the facility. There's very little she needs to do. Travis made this sound more complicated than it is. The downside? It's like being buried in a coffin underwater. Rhythmic beeps from the control panel increase in volume the deeper she travels. Soft green light reflects off her face and into the glass window in front of her. A terrified expression gazes back at her.

"Oh, God. Breathe. Just breathe. I don't know if I can do this. Come on...come on. I have to...it's for Kyler. Suck it up."

The hull creaks and grinds the deeper she dives. An enormous shadow passes in front of the small craft.

"What the hell was *that*? Some kind of sea monster? Do they have those down here? Please don't swallow me...please, please. Oh, God. Hey...Is that an Orca? They're friendly, right? Like Shamu..."

The homing beacon guides the sub deeper and deeper until she reaches the ocean floor. Blurry obstruction lights of the facility emerge from murky obscurity.

"Lights? Maybe the exterior lights are on a separate grid from the main lights. Please be a smooth landing. Why isn't the door to the hangar opening? Come on!"

"Hangar eight jammed. Rerouting to the substation entrance."

She jerks. "I didn't know this thing spoke. Where the hell is the substation entrance?"

The craft navigates around the facility and positions itself in front of a smaller wing next to the primary structure. A hangar door opens. The craft enters the first door and hovers in front of a second door. The first door slams behind her. Water drains like a flushed toilet. The second door opens.

"Arrived on the substation, hangar four."

She sighs. "Now what? Now...I...go find the medical lab."

She grabs a small utility bag containing a flashlight and several hand tools. The hallways are a maze that twist and turn and stop in front of random doors and dead ends. There are no security scanners at the substation. It's open access everywhere.

She whispers. "This is the hangar where Travis and Kyler were confined. What was this facility even used for? Storage? God only knows. It's so creepy down here."

She stares down a long dark passageway. The substation is noisier than the primary facility. Sounds of clanking and twisting metal are continuous—like the walls are going to buckle any second. Musty air fills her nostrils. Steam from her breath is visible in the dim emergency lighting. She shivers.

"Well, this was a great idea. I have to find the tunnel we made to access the main facility. I should have asked Travis to tell me how to reach it. Damn it, Emily. Why didn't you think of that? I suppose I could call him on the red intercom...but...oh yeah. Guess where that is? Right next to the tunnel."

She explores room after room. Hallways dead-end. She stumbles across maintenance rooms and barracks with dozens of cots lined along the walls. Wait. An office. *Lieutenant Melvin Sharp.*

"Wow. He must have been important. An office the size of a broom closet. Is that a computer?"

"Facial recognition failed. Please log in with your password."

"Ah...damn it."

"Incorrect password. Try again."

187

"Huh? Okay...okay. Let me think. Lt. Sharp. Melvin Sharp. Maybe a simple password. S-H-A-R-P."

"Incorrect password. Try again."

She rifles through his desk. Styluses, data slides, thumbtacks, gum wrappers. A badge. The number AR02-01-2003.

"A, R, zero, two, zero, one, two, zero, zero, three."

"Incorrect password. You have one more attempt before system lockout."

She nibbles on her lower lip. Scanning the room. A weathered photo of a German shepherd clutching a ball in its mouth hangs on the wall. The glass is broken. She slides the photo from the frame. On the back of the photo is written *Oliver May 2nd Kiwanis Park.*

Can it be that easy? "Oliver, 5, 2."

A holographic keyboard appears across the old wooden desk. Holographic folders organize themselves in front of her. *Conduit/Wiring System; Personnel Records; Disciplinary Actions; Substation Schematics.*

"No way." She touches the Substation Schematics folder. A three-dimensional design of the substation appears.

"There. There you are. Third floor. Control Center."

She limps and jogs along the hallway until she reaches the stairwell leading to the third floor. She lifts the red intercom. "Travis? Travis, can you hear me? Do you copy?"

Static crackles and pops. "I copy, darlin'. How you doing down there, girl?"

"Well, I made it to the tunnel. I'll check in again on my way out. Stand by and wait for me, okay? How's Kyler doing?"

"You got it, Doc. I'd wait an eternity for ya. You just take care down there and get your butt back up here where we need ya. Kyler is doing fine. Just worry about yourself for now and focus on the mission."

"Copy. I'm entering the tunnel now, Travis. Wish me luck."

Occasional static and crackling pops interrupt the silence. She lifts herself into the tunnel and slides through to the other side.

"Now, this is *much* better. At least I know where I am."

***

"Welcome back, Dr. Grace. Access granted."

She snatches a large leather satchel and stuffs it full of antibiotics, painkillers, and other medical supplies and drugs. She adds a bag of scalpels and surgical tools to the satchel. The floor beneath her feet vibrates.

"Oh...hell no! Not you again. No, no, no. Come on!"

She crams a handful of gauze pads and surgical tape into the satchel pocket and zips it. With the satchel strapped across her left shoulder and the utility bag in her right hand, she rushes out the door and down the stairwell. An enormous impact of energy rocks the facility. Muffled echoes resonate inside her ears. An explosion sends shockwaves through the hallways and floors, collapsing walls and ceiling tiles along the passage leading back to the tunnel.

She dances over debris, glass, twisted metal, and plastic. She scurries along the hallways, bracing herself against sections of a solid wall.

I have to make it back to the tunnel...for Kyler.

She enters the Information Technology room. The tunnel has collapsed. No way back. Massive blocks of machinery and razor-sharp metal jam the entrance. The floor rumbles and booms. She catapults into the air. Her body suspends in mid-air—pauses— then slams into the ground. The strap of the satchel tears away and slides across the floor into a pile of rubble.

Wavelike tremblors continue to ripple through the building, followed by exploding quakes. The emergency lights extinguish. The room flashes with a dim crimson light. She fumbles through the utility bag and flips on a flashlight.

She snatches the satchel and stumbles along the hallway, back into the stairwell. There is no way is she getting in that elevator. The idea of being entombed in an elevator is not happening today. She scrambles up the stairway to level seven. She enters the launch bay. Every marine craft in the bay is sitting on its side or crumpled like an old soda can.

"Why? God, please help me. If you truly exist, and you can hear me...help me. Prove to me you are real, not for my sake, but for Kyler's sake. Show me the way out! Please."

She climbs the stairwell, headed for level fifteen. At level twelve, the stairwell has collapsed. She heaves a breath and squats onto a steel-grated metal step. That's it. Nowhere to go. If there are marine craft in the fifteenth and twenty-fourth-floor bays, she'll never reach them. She can't communicate with the surface, and her path to the substation is sealed off. The only thing left to do is to die. She must hope that Travis can somehow figure out how to replace Kyler's skull fragment and nurse him back to health. Without antibiotics, Kyler's chances for infection are extreme, and his chances for survival are minuscule.

She rests her elbows on her knees, allowing her hands to support her face. Why didn't she stay in 2021 and face her brain cancer? Cancer seems insignificant now. Imagine. Cancer, an insignificant problem. Twelve hours. That's all she has remaining of life support.

"So. What do you want to do, Emily? How do we *kill* twelve hours? Pun intended."

The last time this happened, they brought the life support system back online. This time there is way too much damage. Last time?...wait.

"Last time the life support failed, the power to the shuttle in the military section turned on. Please, God. Let me have one clear path. Just this one time. I'll never ask you for anything again for the rest of my life. I promise."

She braces herself on the handrail and shuffles down the stairwell. The heavy damage, debris, and dim lighting create a confusing environment. Wrong way again.

"I thought it was this way. No. This way leads to the labs. No, wait. That goes to the cafeteria."

Her flashlight flickers. She smacks it.

"You would think they would have better flashlights in the future."

The floor beneath her feet explodes. She drops to her knees. The flashlight flings from her hand and clatters across the floor.

Creaking and crackling turns into a crashing boom above her. She flinches. A six-inch pipe swings from the ceiling towards her head. She ducks. White lightning rips through her eye sockets into the base of her skull. The floors blur and rotate. The constant rhythm of an alarm echoes through the hallways and pulsates through her ears. Her eyes dim.

***

Red lights oscillate across her retinas. The pitch of the pulsating alarm increases. She lifts her head and peers down a dark, crimson hallway. Her temples throb. She rolls over and runs her fingers across a knot on the front of her forehead. *Ah, damn. I thought I ducked.*

The floor pitches and shifts. She pushes her body off the floor and rises to one knee. Her head whirls in foggy confusion. She pinches the bridge of her nose and heaves a breath.

"Get up, Em. Get going."

Debris blocks the hallways. *They all look the same. Which way?* She rises to her feet and braces herself against the wall. She shakes the haze from her mind and wanders along the hallway. Crimson light fluctuates and reflects off the walls. Dark alternates with light. She navigates the trash and debris along the corridors, roaming hallway after hallway. Walking in circles. More dead ends. She leans her back against a wall and slides to the floor. She buries her face in her hands. Sobs convulse her body. It's hopeless. Where's the hallway to the shuttle room? Why can't she find it?

A faint whimper echoes. *There it is again.*

She rises to her feet and listens. A faint mew. "Roxy? Roxy! Come here, baby."

Roxy scrambles over debris and darts between her legs. She purrs and wraps her tail around Emily's calf. She's dehydrated and weak. Emily scoops her off the floor—hugging and kissing her.

"Oh my God, Roxy. You always know when to find me. You always come and rescue me, sweet girl. Which way did you come from? I think, maybe, that way. That's as good a hallway as any. Let's see where it leads."

The ocean floor has calmed for the moment. A low, resonating rumble continues to vibrate through the floors. She hurries, clutching Roxy in her arms.

"The parka room! Okay, okay. We're almost there."

***

The shuttle room is just as they left it. Tiny, twinkling LED lights never looked so beautiful—better than Christmas lights on Christmas Eve. She opens the holographic computer connected to the shuttle. *Please be active.*

"Well, boys. Here are those instructions you two were searching for: inside the computer and right where I said they would be."

She straps Roxy into the left seat of the shuttle and places the satchel and pouch next to her. She straps herself into the other seat and initiates the launch sequence. *Deep breaths. Don't think about it. This is for Kyler.*

"Get ready, Roxy. You're going to hate this." She hums '80s tunes and squeezes her eyes shut.

You know that thrill ride at the amusement park?...The one that catapults you straight into the air like a Roman candle on the 4th of July? The one that leaves you puking on the sidewalk? Yeah. Well, that ride is for wimps.

30

A NUCLEAR FAMILY

Maybe life in Antarctica isn't such a terrible prospect. What if Antarctica is the only habitable continent left on Earth? Who can say if only remnants remain in the civilized world? Could living in this frozen desert keep them safe from an apocalypse? Or maybe the apocalypse was Steinburg's ultimate hoax to manipulate her compliance into advancing his ambitions to the stars. What if the world is exactly as they left it? Wonder if there was never an apocalypse? Dare they risk leaving the secure solitude of their new environment in search of unknown lands like fifteenth-century explorers?

"Mom, my head hurts."

"Oh, you're awake, baby. I'll give you something for the pain. You're doing so well. Let me look... Ooh. That's healing well. You're going to have a cool scar just like Big Mac."

"Not like Big Mac...like a *pirate*."

"Ooh. A pirate. I've never met a real pirate before. Especially one as handsome as you."

Kyler giggles and slips his hand inside hers—wriggling his fingers around her thumb.

"Mom? I'm happy we're together. My parents knew you would take good care of me."

"Huh? Your parents knew I would take good care of you? How do you know that, Kyler?"

"They told me I should find you when I go to sleep, and you would be my mom until I wake up again. They were *right*."

"Oh my God, Kyler. I *am* your mom, sweetheart. And you've already woken up."

"I'll see my parents again. I spoke to them when I died."

"When you died? Kyler, what are you talking about, sweetie? You didn't die. You're fine. You're here...with me...and Travis."

He pats her hand. "It's okay. You'll see. My dad told me that heaven has many mansions. I've seen my mansion. My parents are there...and I have a little sister. Her name's Bella. They promised me you would take me home when the time is right. They're all waiting for me."

"Oh, Kyler, honey. Sometimes medicine can do crazy things to us. You've had a terrible accident and bumped your head. But you're going to be okay now. Just rest, my love. Those are all wild and crazy dreams."

"Okay...but can I tell you one more thing?"

"Of course, you can, sweetie. What do you want to tell me?"

"*Bo* is your horse. Not Jasper."

"Bo...is my horse...not Jasper? Okay...uh...*Bo* is my horse. I'll remember that. Thank you, Kyler. And I have a big surprise for you, now that you're awake."

"Really? What is it? Tell me."

Emily lifts Roxy off the floor and lays her next to Kyler. Roxy purrs and wriggles her nose into Kyler's neck.

"Roxy? Oh, Mom. How did you find her? I thought we lost her forever. Hi, Roxy girl. Aw, I missed you so much. I'm so glad you came home. Thank you, Mom. I can't believe it. This is the best surprise I've ever had in my life."

Kyler grins and closes his eyes—hugging and kissing Roxy. Roxy snuggles into his chest, purring and rubbing her face against his. Emily kisses Kyler's forehead. *Poor thing must have been experiencing terrible hallucinations throughout his entire ordeal. Pain meds can disrupt communication in the brain and spinal cord and interfere with serotonin levels. In cases of traumatic brain injuries, the frontal lobe can interfere with the parietal lobe causing hallucinations. He should be back to feeling normal in a few days, poor little guy.*

She closes the bedroom door to Kyler's room. Travis sits at the kitchen table, looking rugged and handsome. Jeans, a torn white T-shirt, an unbuttoned green-flannel shirt, sleeves rolled to his elbows, and scruff across a chiseled jawline. It's disgusting. He shuffles a deck of cards and flashes his dimples.

"Did ya get your patient to sleep, Doc? How's our boy doing?"

"He's doing well, Travis. He's healing much faster than I expected. The swelling is under control...and he has a cool scar. Seems all my men these days have cool scars. He is over the moon with excitement holding Roxy. You should have seen his little face light up. And what the hell are you grinning at? Where'd you find those cards?"

"I have my ways, gal. How's about a friendly hand of rummy? One hand...Winner gets their feet rubbed, or in my case, foot rubbed. You in?"

She smirks and slides a chair away from the table. She slinks into the seat and folds her arms, enhancing her full cleavage. He sits stone-faced—his eyes twinkling with orneriness—crinkled at the corners and narrowed—tongue pressed against his cheek. *I just want to slap him sometimes.*

"You must enjoy losing to me, cowboy. Stop shuffling and deal.

"Travis, what should we do? Do we stay here and live out our lives at the South Pole, or do we try to find our way back home?... If there's even a home to make it back to."

"I've been pondering that same question myself. It's cold as hell here, but we have food and water and an ocean full of fish. The housing is well built and has a nuclear generator that'll last for centuries after you and I are long gone."

He lays an ace of spades on the discard pile. She smacks the table and snags it. She lays a run of ace through ten in spades on the table and sticks out her tongue at him. He scoffs and shakes his head.

"Well, Doc, we can't go anywhere until our little pard is feeling well enough to travel. The tip of South America is about six hundred miles north."

"I don't know. Maybe we should play it safe and stay here, Travis."

She slaps the table. "Rummy, *dummy*." She adds the nine of spades to her run.

"I *wanted* you to have that one."

"Uh-huh. Sure, you did."

"Em, I found an old ham radio and a lot of spare parts inside a bunker. Radio maintenance was one of my specialties back in the day."

"Oh, my God. Really? Does it work? Can we call somebody?"

"Don't know yet...I'm still tinkering around with it. I'll let ya know if I make 'first contact'...Anyone, in particular, you wanna call? Maybe we can order a pizza? Think they deliver to Antarctica?"

Travis slaps the table and slides the king of hearts into his hand. He lays a run of king through seven on the table and smirks.

"Bastard. I knew you wanted that."

"Then why did ya lay it down, genius?"

"I...you distracted me...with your radio maintenance news."

"Oh...okay. It's your turn. Go, princess."

"I had the weirdest conversation with Kyler before he went to sleep. I think the meds and his brain injury caused him to experience some bizarre hallucinations."

"Why do you say that?"

"He imagined he died and talked to his parents. He told me he has a baby sister. Oh, and he said that *Bo* is my horse, not Jasper."

Travis chuckles. "Well, we all know Jasper was *my* horse... so that's not earth-shattering news. I named Bo after my kid brother. I told you that story. Maybe Kyler was just having one of those...what do ya call 'em?...flashback memories. The boy's probably just a bit mixed up."

"Yeah. Maybe. Can you *go*, please?"

"Why ya so anxious, sweet cakes? Trying to go out or something?"

Travis pulls a card from the deck. He swats the table with his cards. "Hah. I'm out. Add 'em up, loser. Whatcha got?"

"Eighty-five. What do you have?"

"A hundred and ten...which, if my math is correct, is greater than eighty-five. I reckon that makes me the winner."

She mocks him. "Oh...reckon that makes me the winner... whoop-de-do."

He slides his boot off and slams his foot atop the table. His sock is twisted and sweaty, and he waves his floppy toes at her.

"What are you doing? That's so gross. Get your foot off the table, Travis. Ew. We eat meals on this table."

"I won. You owe me a foot rub. Pay up."

"I'm not touching that thing. Are you kidding me? Rub your own gnarly foot."

"Hey now. You gotta pay up. We had a bet. Are you gonna renege? That's cheatin' where I come from. People get shot for less."

"Call it what you like, Sheriff, I ain't touching that thing...or those knobby toes. But...I'll let you sleep with me tonight if you promise to be a good boy."

"I ain't promising shit. I'm disappointed in ya, Doc. But I'll sleep with ya. And I think you're the one with the wandering hands...so stay on your side of the bed unless you intend on paying off your debt and rub my foot."

***

Travis sits on a wooden chair facing a small table where the ham radio rests. He reaches both hands inside an access panel. He places leads of a voltmeter across the tiny solder joints of a circuit board. His arms jerk in sync with the crackle of sparks and the smell of ozone.

"Ow! Goddammit. Come on, man! You worthless piece of shit."

"How's the troubleshooting coming along, Mr. Radio Maintenance? Here, I made you an omelet. Mushrooms, green peppers, anchovies, and jack cheese. Just the way you like it."

"Just zapped the piss out of my finger with two hundred and sixty volts. How are your CPR skills, Doc?...Just in case I electrocute myself?

She lays her palms across his pecs and straddles him. She presses her mouth over his and suckles his lips—nibbling on his lower lip. He groans. His body slackens. She seals his mouth with her lips then blows hard, expanding his cheeks.

"Ah. What the hell was that?"

She giggles and rises from his lap. "My mouth-to-mouth skills. I think you're safe."

He guffaws and shakes his head. "I could think of a better use for that talent."

"Uh-huh. I'll bet you could. Focus on your work, pervert. Let me know if you need my help reading those schematics." He scoffs, then chuckles.

Kyler continues to sleep. He needs the rest. She tucks his blanket beneath his chin and kisses his hand. He looks peaceful in his sleep. She whispers, "I don't know what I'd ever do without you, Kyler. I love you, sweetheart."

March is the end of summer in Antarctica. The thermometer reads seventeen degrees Fahrenheit this morning. Today is a perfect day to stay indoors and curl up with a delightful book. She found a variety of old books in one of the dorm rooms. Fiction; Non-fiction; Biographies. She stretches her legs across a small sofa. Metal springs pop beneath her butt. Rough textures from the fabric stab through her jeans, creating an annoying itch. She flips through the pages of a romance novel. The kind with the sexy stud-muffin sweating all over the cover, his shirt and long hair blowing wild in the breeze, exposing his rock-hard pecs. Meanwhile, the slutty damsel in distress hangs off his biceps, begging him with her eyes to bend her over. Travis interrupts her the moment the book gets juicy with raunchy details and savage sex scenes.

"Doc. Come here. We're broadcasting to the world, campers. Let's see if anyone's out there."

"Wow. Nice work, soldier."

"This is Travis McCal..."

She grabs the mic and clasps his mouth.

"Travis, I don't think it's a good idea to tell the world who we are or where we are, do you?"

He slides her hand from his mouth and removes the mic from her hand.

"How do expect to escape the coldest goddamn continent in the world, Doc?"

"I-I don't know. I'm just thinking...what if the world has gone crazy?...and what if this is the only safe place left to hide? Do we want people to know we're here? Maybe it's better if we stay isolated, Travis. Maybe we should listen and see if someone answers, but not tell them who we are...or where we are."

"Em, this is an extreme environment. It's dangerous. Weather like this can kill in a matter of minutes. I think we need to move to a warmer climate—maybe take the loss on the house."

She slides a chair next to him and grasps his hands. How can she make him understand? She's had her fill with unknown worlds. Why not settle down?

"Travis...sweetheart...why don't we live out our lives here. You and I and Kyler. Maybe we can have a baby together? Start a family. I'm tired, Travis. I want to settle down and be happy. We can be happy here. Can't we?"

His face grows solemn. His jaw slackens and his lips purse. Her words awaken the pain hidden behind his weathered eyes.

"Emily, I don't know if I could do that, to be honest. I had a son...and a wife. I mean, I'm falling for you, but I don't know that I'm capable of moving on and forgetting about my son or Cheyenne, quite yet. I'm sorry...I'm not ready to cross that boundary. Can you give me more time?"

"They're gone, Travis. They've been gone for nearly a century. You have *me* now. You have Kyler. We both need you. I need you. Why can't you see that? We don't know what's out there. We're safe here. We have everything we need right here."

"My heart still aches." He pats his chest. "She still lives inside here. I see her face. I hear her voice. It's not that easy, Em. Yeah, they both died decades ago, but to me, it was only four years ago...the day they resuscitated me."

"Well, the truth comes out. I believed in my heart that we had something special, Travis. I assumed you felt it too. So, even the last man on earth can't love me enough, and I guess I'll never know what it is to bear a child."

He places his hands on her shoulders. He sighs and lifts her chin with his knuckle—forcing her eyes to his. She pushes him away.

"No. Don't. Don't feel sorry for me. I don't want your pity. I'll be fine...just...just leave me alone. Go ahead and play with your radio. See who answers. I should go home alone."

"Em, please. Feelings aren't right or wrong. They're simply feelings. I can't help how I feel. You know I'm crazy about you. I'm falling for you deeply...but these old memories bind my heart... and I don't know how to unbind them yet. Just give it time...that's all I'm asking for. Just a little more time. Please. Be patient."

"It's okay, Travis. Really. It's okay. Your old memories are just that—old memories. I'm here with you in the flesh. My body is warm, my breasts are firm, and my lips are moist. Why can't you let go of the past? Live in the present. Look at me. I'm standing right here in front of you. My arms are open; my heart is aching. What is it, Travis? Is there something the matter with me? What keeps you from loving me? Am I doing something wrong?"

"No...Em. Ya aren't doing nothing wrong. Truth is, you're doing everything right. There's not a damn thing wrong with you, girl. Fact is...I *do* love you—more than I allow myself to admit. But I'm broken, Em. Like a horse with a broken spirit. The hurt never goes away. Memories of Cheyenne and Sage still haunt me. I miss them so damn much. I want to move on with you, but I-I can't...I just can't right now. I need time. Just give me a little more time."

Her heart crumbles like parched clay. She may never realize her dreams of a family. She's left with only Kyler to fill the voids of her despair. The depth of Travis's broken heart is far deeper than she imagined. A bottomless ocean trench too deep for her to reach. He wants time. But the problem with time is that there is never enough to give. Time always runs out.

31

Love's Bitter Sacrifice

The weather is a savage negative five degrees Fahrenheit. Emily zips her parka and ambles through the kitchen towards the back door. Travis rises from the kitchen table and grips her sleeve.

"Em. Where are you going? It's almost zero degrees out there. Ya can't just go for an afternoon stroll."

"Yes, I can. I need to go for a walk because I'm suffocating inside here. I need time to think, Travis. I won't go far, I promise."

"It's an ungodly cold outside, Em. Are you crazy?"

"*Yes*. I'm crazy. Okay? I'm crazy to have fallen in love with you and crazy to believe I could be a mother to Kyler. I'm crazy to want a baby...or to believe I could live my life in Antarctica with someone I've fallen in love with. Just listen to how crazy all that sounds. Yes, I'm crazy, Travis. Let me go. Please."

"No. I can't let you go out there. There's a storm headed this way. It's too dangerous. Please don't go, Em. I begging ya. The risk is too high."

"I'll be back. I'm going to walk down to the storage shed and bring back some hamburger for dinner...and maybe walk past the cliffs."

He narrows his eyes—his lips part, and he doesn't blink. She pats his cheek with her gloved hand.

"You don't have to worry about me. I'll be fine. I love you, Travis. With all my heart, I do."

"Em. I love you too. Believe me, I do. Here. Please take a radio with you."

The chill bites exposed flesh. She tucks her nose inside a scarf and waddles across the snow and ice. She follows a trail leading down the hill to an old shed of perishable supplies. There's plenty of hamburger meat in the freezer back in the kitchen. But she needed an excuse to escape. She strolls past the shed and stands at the edge of the cliffs. The ocean is solid ice for miles with giant glaciers locked together. The sky is a haze. Thick clouds form a low ceiling and create a silver and white backdrop to creation. Colorless. Lifeless. Reflections of her own heart.

Why is she even out here in this weather? To punish him? Probably. It's easy to become absorbed with self-pity in this environment. Desolate and gray. Why not leap from this cliff into the icy waters and end this charade? There is nothing for her here. Travis and Kyler will be fine. They've survived without her before and they can do it again.

"Why am I so pathetic? Standing here...feeling sorry for myself. If you're going to jump...then jump. End it."

She squats and plops onto the cliff's ledge. Her boots dangle over the treacherous drop-off like a child teasing fate. Gusts whip and push against her. Snow spits and swirls. Winds howl as flurries blow into frenzied eddies. Visibility drops within seconds.

"Oh no. This isn't good."

Emily stands to face powerful winds that assault her body and drive her to her knees. Her left foot slips off the rocky ledge, and her body slides over the edge of the cliff. Her feet catch a cranny, preventing a fatal fall. She yanks the radio from her pocket. It crackles with static.

"Travis. Travis, are you there?"

"I'm here, angel. Where are you? It's looking nasty out there. Em, you need to get back here *pronto*, girl. The weather has turned bad out there. It's concerning."

"I'm afraid that won't be possible because I'm stuck on the edge of the cliff...a little bit past the shed. Travis, I can't climb up. What do I do?

"Stay there, sweetheart. I'm on my way."

Winds hiss and howl. Gusts roar with the rage of a hurricane. Snow and ice whip into a blinding white frenzy. Her radio clicks and pops.

"Em. I'm tying the rope to the kitchen door. I'm heading down the hill. Stay where you are and hold on tight to something."

"Travis. Be careful. I can't see anything. It's terrible out here."

She shivers and her teeth chatter. She grasps a small boulder and hangs on—It's all she can do.

Static crackles. "Travis? Where are you?"

"Sit tight, darlin', I'm almost there. I'm coming to get ya, my love. Don't you worry none. I'm so sorry about last night. I acted like a fool. You were right in everything you said."

"I'm the one who's sorry, Travis. Let's talk about it later."

Through the blinding snow and ice, a tall shadow materializes in the distance. It's Travis. Her heart flutters. A rope glides through his gloved hands and across his left shoulder. He inches his way towards her, battling fierce winds and blinding snow.

Her shoulder cramps from waving her arm. "Travis! I'm here. Right here."

"I see ya, sweetheart." The end of the rope lands within her reach. "Here. Tie this around your waist. Let me know when it's secure. I'm going to hoist you out of there. You're gonna be all right, I promise. Are you ready?"

"Okay. It's tied. I'm ready."

She grips the rope with both hands, bracing herself against the cliff wall. Her foot slips. She's back where she started. Rock and ice pelt her, followed by Travis's body sliding next to her. He grips the rope, hugs her, then positions himself behind her.

"Em, I gonna push you over the top, okay? Pull yourself up with the rope, while I push you from behind. Got it?"

"Yes. Got it. Almost there...

"Okay, Travis. I'm up. Now what? Travis? What do I do now?"

She slithers on her belly to the cliff's edge and peers over. Travis has slid down the cliff more than twenty feet. He grasps at the loose rocks and ice that appear to be sliding downward.

"Travis! What do I do?"

"Toss me the rope, Em! I don't know if I can hang on much longer."

She unties the rope from her waist and tosses it towards him. He lets go of the rocks and stretches his arms—reaching for the rope's elusive end. Rocks and ice collapse and crumble beneath him. Travis disappears into a roaring explosion of white blindness. The rope slackens.

"Travis! Oh, God. No! Travis! Talk to me, sweetheart. Please. Please, God...tell me you're still there. Travis? Travis!"

A frigid blast of air sends her spiraling over the ledge. Emily snatches the rope and digs her heels into the rock and ice, ending her slide. She fumbles with the rope. Bracing herself against the rock, she reattaches the rope around her waist and lowers herself several feet down the cliff. "Travis! Travis, answer me!" Her cries are swallowed up by the fierce winds.

She grips the rope and pulls herself over the ledge, inching her way up the hill, battling deafening winds. There is no sense of direction. No forward. No backward. No up or down. Only white blindness. She tugs at the rope, guiding herself to safety and exhausting all her strength. She loses sensation in her fingers and toes. Bellowing howls of icy winds devour her screams and cries of despair. The outline of the building emerges from within the white chaos. She's almost there. Adrenaline fuels her heart and pushes her burning muscles onward. She collapses onto the porch and crawls inside the kitchen, kicking the door closed behind her, shutting out the storm.

She heaves breath after breath. Every fiber of muscle inside her arms and legs cramp. She drags herself next to the kitchen wall and crumples.

"Mom! Where were you? What happened? Where's Mac?

She rips off her parka, iron pants, and boots, then tosses them into a corner of the room. Ice and water melt and pool along the kitchen floor.

"Come here, baby. Come here."

He rushes into her arms. She squeezes him and kisses his face and the top of his head. She buries her face in his young body and sobs.

"I was caught in the blizzard outside, Kyler. Travis came to rescue me...and I don't know what happened to him. I don't know, baby...I just don't know...There's a blizzard outside. I can't see anything. It's too dangerous to go back out there. We have to pray Travis can hang on until the storm dies down."

She whimpers and moans. Tears roll off her cheeks, adding warm spatters to the pools of melted snow. This can't be happening. It's a nightmare. What was she thinking, going outside with the onset of an impending storm? *Oh God, forgive me. Travis, forgive me. This is all my fault. I'm to blame for everything. I'm too afraid to go back out there.*

She tucks Kyler into bed along with Roxy. She crawls in next to him and cradles him. Sobbing. The image of Travis disappearing over the cliff replays over and over in her mind. Whirlwinds whistle through the rafters and loose window sills. The building shudders at its foundation. She waits. Listening. Hoping the fierce winds die down so she can return to the cliff.

***

Emily awakens to soft amber light bathing her face. She slips out of bed, careful not to disturb Kyler's slumber. She dresses and rushes outside. The sky is somber. Remnants of the storm remain, but the weather is calm. She scampers down the hill past the shed to the edge of the cliff where she last saw Travis. She gazes over the ledge. Squinting. Searching for any trace of him.

"Travis?!" Remorseful echoes whisper along the steep ridges and icy crags.

Travis is gone. The drop is a direct path to the ocean. His body must lie somewhere beneath the obsidian water and ice. She tosses a canoe paddle and a gaff pole inside the bed of a small fishing boat. She loads the boat onto a trailer and guides them along the road leading down to the ocean. Using the hook of the gaff, she pushes away from the shore. She paddles along the shoreline until she reaches the area where Travis either drowned or froze to death.

She dips the gaff into the black waters, feeling around for any signs of a body. The tranquil waters swirl with icy debris. Hours pass. She lays the gaff across the seat of the boat and rises—staring across miles of indigo and ice-capped ocean. Her tears freeze before they can drip off her cheeks. She wipes frozen slush from her nose with her scarf. Her heart fractures and empties.

How could she be so selfish? So prideful? He gave his life to save hers. Her foolishness killed him. How will she ever explain this to Kyler? Travis McCallister was a man unlike other men. A man with a deep and loving soul. A mentor. He helped her see the world as it exists—teaching her how the pieces of life and nature fit together. Travis loved his wife and son with all his heart and all his spirit. How could she be jealous of a love like that? Love she yearns to know herself. A love so rare takes time to nurture and grow. That's what he was trying to tell her. Give him time, he said. *Why didn't I give him time?* Now there *is* no time. Just an eternal void. *I had everything I ever dreamed of in my hands. Why couldn't I see?*

Her cries echo across a white ocean of broken glass. "Travis. Please forgive me. I would trade my life for yours if that were possible. I'm so sorry, and I'm such a wretched fool!"

She wipes moisture from her eyes. Using the tip of the paddle, she turns the boat around with a single push off the cliff walls. Where will she find an absolution for the dreadful tragedy she caused?

Her body goes numb. She's horrified by the shriek in her voice and drops to her knees. Floating ten feet away from her is the frozen, lifeless body of Travis McCallister. Ice crystals highlight his brow and hair. His bluish lips are parted. An ashen face stares into an ominous sky. His arms and legs lie stiff and sprawled across the mild ocean ripples—cradled by vast still waters.

She shudders. Her wails and screams carry away into the winds and oblivion. "Travis. My Travis. Oh God, what have I done? What have I done? My love...my heart..."

Emily hooks the hood of his parka with the gaff after countless moments of staring at him. She pulls his body towards the boat, creating a soft wake of ice and water. Using the rope from the gaff's handle, she secures his wrist to the boat, then paddles along the shoreline towards the dock. She stumbles onto the rocks and ice and drags Travis's frozen body ashore. She rests his head upon her lap and caresses his frozen cheeks. Sobs and wails rattle her body. Her warm tears drip and trickle along his cheeks—bathing his face with her anguish.

32

Dark Skies

Ham radio provides a voice to speak to the world's ear. It also provides an ear to listen to the world's voice. She broadcasts to the world to learn if there is anyone remaining who can hear her. Will their journey be free of human contact? What are the risks, and what should they prepare for? Will they encounter pirates on the high seas? Bad weather? Maybe living alone in a frozen desert remains their most rational option.

They laid Travis to rest early this morning. They converted a small storage shack into a shrine, where his body will lie at peace in Antarctica for eternity. Kyler is unusually quiet. He strapped Travis's buck knife to his waist and tucked the GI Joe Travis gave him for his birthday into the makeshift coffin. He didn't openly weep, but his reddened eyes glistened like fragile glass orbs.

"Come on, Kyler. Help Mommy load the wagon."

"What for? Where are we going?"

"We're going home, baby. We need to fill the freezer and the pantry with all this food for our trip."

"Are we going to take Big Mac home with us?"

"No. No, sweetheart. His home is here now. He would want it that way."

"Don't cry, Mom. Big Mac is home in his mansion in heaven now. He's with his family...and I-I think they're all going to watch over us and keep us safe on our trip. You still got me." Kyler rests his hand on the buck knife. "I'll take care of us now."

"Oh, sweetie. You are such a brave boy. I couldn't do this without you. Put those big muscles to work and help me load the boat."

The freezer holds close to one hundred pounds of meat and fish. A compartment below deck holds another two hundred pounds of frozen goods, packed tight with ice and snow. Dry goods fill the pantries, and the freshwater reservoir is full. She programs their route into the navigation system—the tip of South America. Cape Horn. A notorious area for treacherous waters from high winds and strong currents. They'll follow the western coast to Central America, Mexico, and into the Gulf of California. They'll make port at Rocky Point, Mexico. God only knows what awaits them, crossing the arid deserts of Mexico and Arizona. But the idea of being in the middle of a warm desert seems like Nirvana at the moment.

"Kyler, let's go, baby. Let's say one last goodbye to Travis. Then it's time."

***

The ocean presents a myriad of hazards this time of year. Massive icebergs create an obstacle course of treacherous ice floating along deep, dark waters. The closer they get to the icebergs, the more intimidating they become in size and stature—almost mocking their attempt to leave. The autopilot guides the vessel through the bay and into the open sea. If all goes as planned, they should be near the coast of South America in approximately eighteen hours.

The indigo waters of the South Atlantic are glass-like. White crests of foam surround the boat, leaving a wake of waves fading into the Stygian waters behind them—a remnant of the life they must abandon. The air is brisk and salty. Beams of sunlight penetrate thick clouds and cast their light across the ocean's surface, appearing as a beacon of deliverance for their long journey. The drone of the engines adds to the peaceful melancholy. Frosty winds toss her hair about and bite at her reddened cheeks.

"Kyler, look. Whales. Oh my God. They're humongous...and so majestic. At least we know there's life in the ocean, right?"

"Wow, Mom. That's the biggest bellyflop I've ever seen. He is so cool. He must be the daddy. I wish Mac could see this."

"Me too, baby. Let's go inside. It's chilly out here. Are you hungry?"

"Uh-huh. Can I have some mac 'n' cheese? Roxy wants mac 'n' cheese too."

"You're both going to turn into a box of mac 'n' cheese, Kyler. Are you sure you don't want some real food? How about a hot dog? Or a ham sandwich?"

"Nope. Mac 'n' cheese. My head hurts, Mom."

"Here you go, baby doll. How about after we eat, we both take a nice long nap, huh? I'm going to be in the wheelhouse working on a couple of things, okay? Come and get me when you're finished eating."

She logs into the command station network and initiates a Captain's log.

March 8: 0612 – It is the onset of fall in Antarctica as we begin our voyage home to Phoenix, Arizona. We buried our beloved Master Sergeant Travis McCallister at the General Bernardo O'Higgins station in Antarctica in a makeshift tomb near the ocean. We have stocked enough food and water to sustain us for at least three months. All systems are operational, and I have charted a course along the western coast of South America, Central America, and into the Gulf of California. God help us. We do not know what to expect. The day seems quiet. An uncomfortable sort of quiet. Kyler spends his time fishing. I believe it connects him to Travis and helps him to cope with his grief. I can hear him talking to Travis when he's fishing. It's breaking my heart.

March 9: 1152 – We reached the tip of South America late this morning. The autopilot navigation maintains our course, miles off the coast, and keeps us at a safe distance from the treacherous waters. Seeing land and trees to our east is comforting. I am very concerned with Kyler's frequent headaches. He had a mild seizure last evening. We have no antiepileptic medications onboard, so if his seizures increase in occurrence, I will have to treat them without drugs. I keep him quiet and force him to lie on his cot and rest, which is, of course, a very tough thing to ask of a boy his age. Roxy keeps him company. His headaches grow stronger, and my worst fear is he may have new internal bleeding inside his skull. We both had to take meds for seasickness. The waters around Cape Horn are very choppy today.

1307 – The autopilot program sounded an alert early this afternoon. It scared the crap out of both of us. Two tropical storms are developing northwest of our location. I will continue to monitor this development. We may need to head to shore to wait it out if conditions worsen. The autopilot program is advising us to reroute our course, which will take us further out to sea. That makes me nervous. I don't want us to be out of sight of land. Why would it recommend that? I don't get it. Kyler's condition has stabilized somewhat. He's back to attempting to catch fish as we continue our journey at twenty-five knots. He's wearing one of Travis's tattered and faded ball caps. A University of Arizona ball cap, of course. Just to try to get under my skin, I suppose. There is nothing more offensive to a graduate of Arizona State than anything with a University of Arizona logo on it. The sun is high and blazing. It felt great being able to sunbathe in its warmth. The added vitamin D will be a nice boost for both Kyler and me.

March 10: 0932 – The skies ahead look threatening. I've never seen clouds so angry or evil in my life. I'm not liking this development at all. The roiling clouds almost seem alive and menacing. The autopilot keeps screaming at me to change our course. I don't know if I should trust it or not. I'm so afraid to head out into open waters. Especially with this monstrous creature bearing down on us in the distance. Wouldn't it be safer to stay near the coast? I'm not sure how we'd make it around the storms if we listen to the stupid autopilot. The charts show the two storms colliding by early morning. One of the storms is now a Category 2 hurricane or typhoon. I never understood the difference. I'm naming it "Hurricane Steinburg."

We've been riding the coast of South America for over a day now. We've seen no signs of human life. Maybe the areas we are observing are uncivilized forests. We spotted a family of monkeys in the trees earlier. They were so darn cute. I know little about this part of the world. Travis spent so much time in the observatory learning geography he'd know everything there is to know about this place. I miss him so much. He was the glue that kept us all together. The rock that kept us safe.

1425 – Kyler isn't feeling well. His headaches continue to torment him. I have him below deck, resting with a warm towel over his eyes. So far today, no seizures, thank God. But his continued headaches are of great concern to me. I spotted a few dolphins swimming alongside our boat earlier today. Maybe it's a sign of good luck. We can only hope. Massive clouds continue to form in the distance. Lightning streaks through them, illuminating everything around them. The waters are getting more and more choppy. Several waves crashed over the bow of the boat. I try to remain calm so as not to alarm Kyler. But he's too perceptive and sees right through my attempts.

March 11: 0817 – The skies appear even worse this morning. I slept little. Kyler tossed and turned all night. He had a nightmare but couldn't remember what it was about. The skies are growing darker. Blacker. This must be the colliding storms the alert warned us about. Winds have already picked up. I have secured Kyler below. I'm keeping him busy with schoolwork, and I asked him to study the South American continent. He's a very smart boy and an excellent student. The autopilot has slowed our speed to ten knots. The lights have turned on all over the boat. We also appear to be sailing into the storm at a 45-degree angle. I hope Mr. Autopilot knows what the hell he's doing. I'm petrified. I tried to take over the controls and steer us towards land, but the autopilot restricted my request and has taken full control of the vessel. The winds are too strong to stay on deck. I'm going below with Kyler and we are going to pray that we can ride out this storm. God willing. Dr. Emily Grace signing out for now.

33

AN IMPERFECT STORM

Winds screech and pound the vessel. A surge of powerful waves crashes into the bow, thrusting the boat upward into the clouds, then allowing it to drop like a rollercoaster ride from hell. Seawater drenches the inside of the cabin, and it has become a nauseous prison. Emily's eyes squeeze closed, and she heaves a breath. Kyler buries himself inside her arms. They take turns vomiting into a garbage bag. Water from the deck drains down the steps and fills the cabin floor several inches deep. The engines scream in protest, trying to compensate for the onslaught—grappling with the mighty ocean to keep the vessel upright.

"Mom...Mom, are we going to sink?"

"No, baby. We're not going to sink. Just hang on to me. I got you, sweetie...Mommy has you...I promise I won't let go."

Hours pass. Emily's stomach twists and turns into a solid knot. Dry heaves cramp the muscles in her throat. She shivers. Kyler shivers. Neither has the strength to continue grasping the support beam. Bruises cover her elbows and knees. Their clothing is saturated and clinging to their bodies. As suddenly as the storm began, it subsides. The foot-deep water on the cabin floor no longer swishes or splashes. Cushions and debris float around their knees.

"Kyler. Maybe it's over. Stay here, sweetheart. I'll be right back, okay? Don't move. All right? Promise me."

"I promise. Be careful, Mom. Please hurry. I don't want to be in here by myself."

"You're not by yourself, sweetie. Take care of Roxy. Try to dry her off."

Chalky-gray clouds scatter across the heavens, overlaid by patches of cobalt sky and amber sunlight. The winds have calmed—an eerie sort of calm. Silent but threatening. The engines sputter and squeal. Black smoke rises from the stern. Mammoth walls of boiling, blackened clouds surround them. Lightning irradiates throughout these monstrous barriers that have them trapped inside a cylindrical nightmare. Thunder rumbles and explodes with a sinister clamor. A soft wind peppers her face with icy droplets. *Oh my God. No.*

She stumbles down the stairs, swishing through the water and debris. She snatches two life preservers from the cabin wall.

"Kyler. Put this on, baby. We have to do this one more time. I promise it'll be over soon."

"No, Mom. I can't do this again. I'm scared. Please. Make it stop."

Kyler's eyes roll white and his teeth gnash. He falls backward onto the mattress, kicking and flailing his arms and legs. Pink-tinged foam bubbles over his lips and cheeks. Roxy darts onto the countertop and crawls into the sink.

"Kyler! I got you, baby."

She cradles him, wedging a small towel inside his mouth. The vessel pitches to the left then rolls to the right. Winds whistle and hiss. The insides of the boat creak and snap with every jolt. She wraps her legs around the support beam next to the bed and bearhugs Kyler.

"God, please help us. Hang on, baby. Mommy has you."

Deafening roars besiege them. The boat surges upward, twirling out of control, and drops onto its side. The cabin floods with waves of saltwater. They are leaning at a 45-degree angle. Her legs slip away from the beam, causing her and Kyler to slam into the cabin wall. Kyler continues to convulse. The engines have stopped. They are at the mercy of the ocean and being tossed and battered like a splintered shard of driftwood. Burnt rubber seers her nostrils. Blackened smoke scorches her eyes. *We've got to get out of here.*

She wraps an arm around Kyler's upper torso and swims toward the cabin door. She yanks at the doorknob. Water and debris have sealed it shut. An explosion rocks the boat and shudders through the walls of the cabin. The lights extinguish, and the boat rolls and whines like the death cries of a wounded beast. Kyler's body jerks from her arms and tumbles into the watery darkness. She's pelted with objects. Her head slams against a corner of a heavy wooden beam, causing her ears to chime while flashes of light shoot through the back of her eye sockets. Emily's grip on the beam relaxes. Her mind fades into a luminous, soft white light and the muffled bellows of howling winds.

***

Rhythmic thumping echoes inside the hull. Seawater sloshes along the walls of the cabin. Amber light peers through a large hole in the ceiling. She squints and shields her eyes with her hand. The sun is ablaze across a golden backdrop. She lifts her head and scans the debris. She's floating and sprawled across swishing waters inside the cabin. Reaching for the doorknob, she manages to pull her body upright and places her feet on the cabin floor. The water level reaches her waistline. The door dangles on a single hinge. She rescues Roxy from the metal sink and cradles her in one arm.

"Kyler! Kyler? Where are you, baby? Kyler."

She searches through the floating debris of the cabin. If he were here, he'd float like her, right? She wades along the floor, using her free arm to swim, searching for him, prodding the waters to give him up. Praying he's alive and lying behind the next pile of floating rubbish. But he isn't. She wriggles through the door and climbs the steps. Her heart seizes. Half the boat is underwater, and the half she is standing on is sinking. Kyler is nowhere in sight. Emily catches hold of a seat cushion floating next to her and rests Roxy on top of it.

"Kyler! Can you hear me? Please, baby, answer me. Where are you? No. Why God? Why him and not me? Please don't take him away from me...please. I'm begging you."

The boat is foundering. A bright orange object catches her eye. "Kyler!"

Emily swims and splashes, pushing the floating cushion towards the orange life jacket. Kyler peeks through one eye and wheezes, "M-Mom?"

She cradles his ashen face and kisses him—sobbing and clutching him to her bosom.

"Oh, baby! Thank God you're okay. Kyler, I'm going to put you on this cushion with Roxy. I want you to lay back and relax, okay? Hold on to Roxy."

Emily glances in every direction, struggling to get her bearings.

A small island. Maybe a mile or less away. She launches them away from the boat with a thrust of her legs. Only six feet of the wheelhouse remains above the water's surface. She paddles and kicks, propelling them towards a small tropical island. She dips her arms into the cool turquoise water to relieve cramps in her shoulders and the sting from her reddened skin.

After two hours afloat, her feet stumble upon a flat rocky beach surrounded by massive boulders and sparkling aquamarine ocean. She drags the cushion with Kyler and Roxy into the shade of a hundred-foot cliff and collapses atop spongy sands. She pulls Kyler and Roxy next to her. Soft waves splash against the rocky shores while gulls squawk and dip in and out of the ocean. An arid breeze absorbs all the moisture from her skin and hair. The air is cool in contrast to the warm sunlight. It carries an odor of salt, fish, and sand. Roxy crawls off the cushion and plops next to Emily, exhausted and frightened.

Why couldn't she land on an island paradise? Or maybe Gilligan's Island, instead of this giant rock in the middle of the ocean? There doesn't appear to be a clear path up these cliffs to reach the rich greenery at the top. And God only knows what awaits them up there.

No matter what lies atop the island, nothing will erase the horror of almost losing Kyler. Nothing weighs heavier on her mind. She's responsible for Travis's death, and now she's brought Kyler to a deserted island somewhere in the middle of the Pacific

Ocean. Maybe things would be different if she had heeded the advice of the autopilot and steered the craft out to open sea. What does it matter now? Travis is gone. And there will be no escaping this rock surrounded by miles of a pristine and turquoise ocean. Fate condemns them to a lifetime of seclusion on an island prison.

She slides her arms out of her lifejacket and tosses it onto the ground. The cushion is springy against her back. Puffs of clouds glide like ballooned mainsails across a baby-blue sky. They'll have to climb the jagged rocks to reach the top of the island. But not right now.

"Let's just lie here for a little while, Kyler, and rest."

"Mom? Where are we? Is this Arizona?"

"No, sweetheart. This is an island. We'll explore it after we rest. Okay?"

"I don't think we should explore this place. I just want to go home. Why couldn't we stay in Antarctica?"

"Ow. Ouch. What the hell are those? Biting flies? Get off of me. Get away from me."

"They're biting me too, Mom...and Roxy."

She swats dozens of sandflies swarming her legs and arms. She leaps off of the sand and rushes to the edge of the smallest cliff. "Come on, Kyler. We have to climb. Hold on to my shirt and follow me."

Placing her hands across razor-sharp boulders, she climbs. A small path reveals itself between the volcanic rock leading to the top of the island. Halfway up the path, her sneakers flop, and her toes pop out. Blood oozes from her left knee and trickles along her shin. Six of her fingernails are broken and ragged. The tips of her fingers sting with cuts. Roxy follows them, lingering close to Kyler's heels.

Stepping over one last crevice, they reach a plateau of grasses. The edge of a forest lies around fifteen yards away. A dense mixture of various trees of different thicknesses awaits their curiosity. She observes miles of nothingness across a vast ocean in every direction. Nothing but turquoise water as far as the eye can see. Her throat burns. The tender flesh of her lips split from her grimace. No signs of fresh water anywhere. No signs of life other than trees, grass, and an occasional gull. She sits in the shade of a plush tree at the edge of the woods, cradling Kyler in her lap. She leans against the thick base of the trunk and lowers her head and weeps. Her tears run dry. Roxy crawls into Kyler's lap and lays her head across his thigh. Kyler runs his fingers through Roxy's ruffled fur. Emily leans her head on the tree trunk and allows her eyes to close. "Let's rest here, Kyler. Just for a little while. At least the flies can't get us up here."

34

A ROCK IN THE OCEAN

Scurrying. The crunch of leaves. Her heart palpitates. She must have fallen asleep. She peers through one eye. A rat. Another one. They're everywhere.

"Oh, God. We landed on the island of rats and flies...paradise if I were Shrek."

She launches a stone at the rodents. A feeble toss. They scatter. Several rats scamper up a nearby tree. Roxy follows the rodents and disappears into the branches and leaves. *At least Roxy won't starve.*

Her throat swells and her tongue sticks to the roof of her mouth. Finding fresh water is crucial. Without it, their organs will shut down. The effects of dehydration on the brain create cognitive issues, fatigue, mood swings, and headaches. Her inability to reason and make logical decisions is already noticeable. "Kyler. Wake up. We have to keep moving."

She pushes against the tree, helping her to rise to her feet. They have no other choice but to push their way through the dense foliage. The treetops create an umbrella of filtered sunlight. Fallen leaves and branches crunch and snap beneath her tattered sneakers. They amble along, winding through brush and greenery—stumbling into a small clearing. Her heart races. She heaves a breath.

"Look, Kyler. A small pond. Ugh. Gross. It stinks. What's all that slime and crap floating on top? Yuck. There is no way we are going to drink that nasty brew of garbage...Oh, hell no. Creatures are swimming around in it."

She slumps onto a flat boulder and wipes her brow. The onset of confusion and disorientation is of deep concern. They may have to drink from that disgusting soup of bacteria and insects or become part of it.

She removes her T-shirt. A sports bra, shorts, and ribboned shoes that look like a dog ate them are her uniform of the day. She dips her T-shirt into the water and wipes Kyler's forehead. Kyler is barely responsive. He whispers, "Mom. I'm thirsty. Can I have some water, please?"

"We don't have any water, baby. I'm so sorry. Wait. Are those coconut trees? Keep your slime and your bugs, ya filthy pond...We're going over there...What did you say? Did you say something? No. You didn't, did you?"

"What? Who are you talking to, Mom?"

"I...um...I'm arguing with a filthy pond, Kyler. I'm sorry, baby."

Emily staggers towards a small oasis of coconut trees, dragging Kyler by his armpits. She lays him across a mound of soft earth while snatching a coconut off the ground. She positions the coconut on top of a smooth rocky area, then grabs a jagged fist-sized stone and strikes the hull. Over and over. Fifteen minutes later, she punches a hole. Rotting stench belches from inside the cavity. She gags and tosses the coconut into the woods.

"Gross. Please tell me I don't have to climb one of these trees to find a fresh coconut. Okay. Wait. I got an idea..."

She launches fallen coconuts underhand—like shooting a basketball—but instead of swishing them through a net, they fly into the tree fronds and hanging coconuts.

"Oh my God. I'm such a terrible shot. Please fall...just one of you...I don't care who."

Exhausted, she flops onto the ground next to Kyler and gazes at the forbidden fruit dangling above them. Green coconuts are cast against a powder-blue sky and white puffs of luminous clouds—tantalizing her tastebuds and fueling her raging thirst.

She whispers. "I just want to lie here and die. I want to see

Travis's mansion in the sky, and I don't want to be here anymore. God, please take us...take us away from here now. Daddy? Daddy, can you hear me? If you can hear me, help us. Please."

The trees blur, and her temples throb. A coconut crackles and loosens, falling next to her head with a thud.

"What the hell?...You missed, God! Oh, but thank you, coconut."

She sits upright and places the fresh coconut on her lap—securing it between her thighs and bracing it with her left hand. She pounds at the husk with a sharp rock for over an hour. Her knuckles are skinned and her fingers ache by the time she can sheer away the rugged husk.

"Great. A shell within a shell. Just like one of those Russian nesting dolls."

She rests and massages the cramps from her right hand and fingers, then begins pounding the inner shell of the coconut. Kyler is unresponsive. His lips parch and crack. White flakes of skin peel from his reddened cheeks and forehead.

She continues to pound on the sturdy shell of the coconut. Soon, the coconut splits and leaks fresh clear coconut milk along its exterior. She lifts Kyler's head and drizzles coconut milk across his lips and into his mouth. He awakens and grabs the coconut and sucks at the juice. "Slow down, baby."

She shakes the empty coconut over her mouth and allows the dryness of her swollen tongue to absorb the remaining drops. Emily takes one more strike at the shell, splitting it into unequal halves. She scrapes bits of coconut meat with her teeth—chewing it into a pithy mesh. Its nourishment is pure ambrosia—nectar of the gods. Kyler gnaws at the other half.

She tosses the empty shell—amused at the splash it creates in the disgusting pond. Emily notices a shaded area laden with fronds and leaves. She drags Kyler and lays him atop the fronds and leaves and then curls into a ball next to him on the cushy mound. Images of her and Kyler in the boat haunt her. His screams and cries echo through her thoughts and torment her mind as she falls into a deep slumber. Their two bodies lie still and unresponsive, caressed and serenaded by a warm tropical breeze.

***

Waves crashing against cliffs and jagged rocks mix with the cries of gulls. A wet, sickening shredding sound catches her ear. She peers through the slit of one eye. Roxy lies next to her, mutilating the body of a small rat. The rat screeches and squirms. She pins it with her paws, torturing the rodent before devouring it alive. Emily lifts a fist-sized rock and crushes the rodent's skull. Roxy screeches and hisses at her.

"Oh, Roxy. Has it come to this? Just don't eat *me* when I die, okay?"

The island is a mile long and a half-mile wide. Cliffs rise hundreds of feet above the ocean. The scenery is the same wherever she wanders: forest, cliffs, grasses, rats, sandflies, mosquitoes, and endless ocean. She squints. Her grimace aggravates the chafing across her cheeks. A dry, burning itch. *Shouldn't a deserted island in the middle of the ocean be humid?* Apparently, she picked the only island on Earth that isn't.

Waves roll and crash against the rocky shoreline, blending with the hush of a salty ocean breeze. Gulls squawk, mixing with the chirps and tweets of a variety of birds that have made their home on the tiny island. The aroma of brine and fish travel across the ocean surface in warm gusts reaching her nostrils. She never realized how noisy "quiet and peaceful" could be.

***

For days, Emily and Kyler feed and nourish themselves on coconut milk and the rich sweet pulp. But coconuts are high in potassium and act as a laxative. The hope for fresh water and a new food source fuels her repeated exploration of the island. Fried rat is beginning to sound appealing—if she could only create a fire and snag one of Roxy's victims.

"Mom, I don't want to explore today. I just want to sleep. My head hurts, and my tummy burns."

"Rest, baby. It's okay. Mommy is going to see if she can find some fresh water and food. I'll be back soon, okay?"

"Okay. I'll be here waiting for you. Mom?"

"Yes, sweetheart."

"Mac told me everything is going to be okay. He said he doesn't want you to worry and that he loves you... and he said it wasn't your fault."

Emily kneels next to Kyler. "You spoke to Travis? Oh, baby. I wish that were true." Her palm absorbs the heat from his moist forehead. His eyes glaze, and his breathing is shallow. She runs her hand over his eyes, forcing them closed. "Rest, sweetheart."

The center of the island has a narrow land bridge leading to a bulbous section on the other side. Endless turquoise waters sparkle and surround the island. It appears there might be another island several miles to the west—all the good that does. This is her initial exploration of the small, bulbous side of the island. Same foliage. Same rocky cliffs. But something is different. Towards the edge of the farthest cliff are several squared rocks supporting a six-foot smooth slab. The stones are purposely arranged. A well-worn path leads to the stones. A twinge of foreboding and tingling apprehension fills her insides as she approaches.

There are strange petroglyphs on the sides of the stone slab: weird shapes, moon phases, stars, and the sun. The slab has a small groove carved into its center. It decreases in width towards the bottom edge.

"Oh my God. Is that rust...or...blood? It runs from the slab over the cliff. How old is this thing? Please be ancient."

She creeps to the cliff's edge and peers over. Her body flushes with itchy, prickly heat. The drop is a straight shot downward. About two hundred feet or more. She pants. The water is deep aquamarine-blue. Sharp rocks peek out from the cliff base like a fortified wall. Anything falling from here would plunge deep into the ocean.

"Please tell me those aren't bones down there. Oh, come on. Maybe this thing is an ancient altar or something... where natives sacrificed their virgin daughters to the island gods. Ugh, this gives me the creeps. Please be a thousand years old."

A sickening sensation inside her gut forces her to backpedal from the ledge. She steps on something and stumbles, flopping on the ground.

"Ow. Goddammit. What's this? A knife? What the heck?"

A four-inch bone handle supports a razor-sharp blade made of some sort of black, opaque glass. It's daintier than it looks. She flips it from hand to hand—dabbing the blade with her index finger—testing the weight of it.

"I'm taking this. It's mine now. I'll bet this will split a coconut... but...what if it's cursed? Come on, Emily. Really? Since when are you superstitious?"

Emily sighs and rises. Her knees wobble and buckle. She rests her hands on her knees and closes her eyes for a moment. She heaves a breath and looks towards the path. The land bridge seems narrower from this side. Emily tiptoes along the rocks like a dancer performing a solo over hot coals, wielding the knife and slashing at the air. There are a lot of coconuts waiting to be sacrificed by her hand.

On her way back to camp, Emily discovers a small path leading to a small sandy beach on the opposite side of the island. Her feet skid along the loose rock and sand as she makes her way down the mountain. The water is as pristine as crystal and remains shallow for several yards into the ocean before turning deep aquamarine. She yanks off her ragged shoes, allowing her feet and calves to find relief in the cool waters. The disturbance of the soft white sands beneath the water causes small crustaceans to flee—shooting away from her toes like tiny torpedoes.

Emily turns and faces the island, scanning the small beach for anything useful. She shields her eyes with her hand. A glint of reflected sunlight catches her attention. Plastic bottles and debris are scattered across the tiny beach.

"Ugh. Plastic will be here long after humans are extinct from Earth. Oh my God. These are full bottles of something. This one is a Coke?"

Several feet away is a small broken ice chest. Emily salvages the bottom half and drops three sealed bottles of liquid inside. She grabs an empty plastic liter bottle and slices it in half with her blade. The sand stirs in the water around her feet as she wades along the shoreline. Emily scoops up as many small crustaceans as she can and empties them into the ice chest. She fills a clear plastic bottle with seawater and adds it to her bounty. She lifts the ice chest and struggles her way up the path, headed back to camp.

***

"Kyler...Kyler...wake up, baby. Sit up. Look what I found."

Kyler's eyes are swollen red slits. Sweat soaks his clothing, and his skin is patchy and pink.

"What? What'd you find, Mom?"

"Here. Drink this. It doesn't taste good, but it's water, sweetheart. It'll make you feel better."

Kyler sips the brownish water. He chokes and spits. "Slow down...just a little at a time, baby."

"It tastes rotten. Like toilet water."

"I know, but it's all we have. We have to drink it. Here, try this one. It's a Coke. It's flat, but it's still sweet."

"That one's a lot better." Kyler swigs and chugs, emptying the old soda bottle.

Emily gathers dry fronds, branches, and small driftwood. Daddy taught her many things as a young girl besides horseback riding. She uses the clear plastic bottle filled with seawater as a magnifying glass—focusing a pinpoint of sunlight through the bottle like a prism onto the dried foliage. Once the dry fronds and leaves start to smoke, she blows the tiny embers until they burst into flames. She adds larger sticks and branches until she has created a respectable fire. She places the tiny crustaceans, mollusks, and fish on two thin sticks and roasts them over the fire. The burning scent of seafood creates a gurgling in her stomach.

"Here, Kyler. This one is yours. Try to eat, sweetheart. Keep sipping on your water bottle."

"That's so cool, Mom. How did you make that fire?"

"Well, my daddy didn't raise no city girl. He taught me a couple of cool tricks when I was a kid. Oh, this tastes so good, doesn't it? Our very own seafood buffet."

"Thank you, Mom. Thank you for always taking care of me. I can't eat anymore. Can I lie down now? My head is hurting again."

"Of course, you can, sweetie. Close your eyes. Mommy will look for more food later."

Emily fills several coconut shells with the putrid water from the pond and boils them over the fire. After they cool, she lays her T-shirt across the ice chest to act as a filter and pours the sterilized water from the coconuts through the tee-shirt and into the ice chest.

***

Days blend into repeated monotony. A week has passed. Maybe two. A diet of coconut milk, coconut meat, insects, and small crustaceans has stolen precious pounds from her already-slender frame. Kyler grows weaker by the day. He can't keep food down, and his headaches and seizures have intensified. The boy is suffering. He doesn't complain and talks more and more about his family in Heaven and the beautiful mansion that awaits him when he gets there. Kyler's pain is her pain. His suffering is her suffering. She's helpless to relieve him of his torture. She's tormented day and night, observing Kyler's agony. It has broken her spirit.

What if she and Kyler are the only human survivors left on Earth? And if true, wouldn't their prayers be the only prayers that could reach the ear of God? Wouldn't they be first in line to have their prayers answered?

Roxy is surviving on a rich diet of rats, insects, and birds. The rancid pond doesn't seem to affect her. She's healthy and almost full grown. Something peculiar is happening to her. She's becoming more and more aloof. Wild even. She spends less time accompanying Kyler and more time hunting. Sometimes she disappears for days. Her absences seem to increase in length.

Daylight fades, bringing an end to another countless day. The night sky sparkles with trillions of tiny specks of light. The moon bathes the two of them with soft blue hues. Kyler is resting after a rough day of vomiting, convulsing, and crying. He has no tears left, and he is voice is hoarse and faint.

Emily's mind fades away, drifting into deep rest. Visions burst within her mind—vibrant colors splash across a dark canvas. Soft strokes of a mandolin harmonize and mix with angelic voices. Emerging from the colorful canvas is a shadowy figure.

"You've done a great job caring for Kyler, gal. Never have I had the pleasure of knowing a more loving and protective mother than you. I want you to know how much I love ya, Em. With all my heart and soul, I do. You've completed my life in ways you can never understand, and I don't want you to blame yourself for how my life ended. It's time to say goodbye now, darlin.'"

"Travis? Travis, don't go. Please don't go. I need you...I love you. I'm so sorry for all the pain I've caused you and Kyler...I've missed you so terribly. Please stay with us."

Travis scoops Kyler into his arms. He winks and softly smiles. She watches as her two loves fade into a thousand shimmering hues.

"Travis! No...don't go. Kyler! Where are you taking him? Don't leave me here."

***

The early morning sun kisses her cheeks with warmth. She rises and kneels next to Kyler.

"Wake up, sweetheart. Here, drink this. How are you feeling this morning? Kyler?"

Waves of emotion flood her heart and mind. Her heart shatters into a thousand shards of glass. Emily lifts Kyler's lifeless body and cradles him. She sings to him and rocks him in her arms for the better part of an hour.

She kisses his forehead and lays him on the ground—wrapping him in her T-shirt and removing his shoes. Emily carries him to the other side of the island and sits on the altar and stares at waves crashing into the rocks and shoreline below. His body is a frail set of bones in her arms. She squeezes him and rocks him back and forth, raising her swollen eyes to the heavens.

"God, please tell Kyler I love him and one day, I hope he can show me the mansion you promised him. I'm giving him back to you now. He belonged to you first. Thank you for ending his suffering so peacefully."

She stands and walks to the edge of the cliffs and allows his body to fall from her arms into the deep blue waters hundreds of feet below.

***

Emily visits the altar every day now. Maybe to pass the time or maybe to prevent herself from losing what's left of her sanity. Or maybe she seeks hope. The hope that whoever created the strange relic will return and sacrifice her life to their gods and end her misery. Each day she has taken a sharp rock and etched her thoughts into the smooth surface of the stone slab. Today is no different.

Life is finite. Love is eternal.

True love sacrifices life to give life.

Images of God are not worthy of God. Our will is not God's will.

I've loved with all my heart only twice in my lifetime. Their names were Travis McCallister and Kyler Carson. I am to blame...

Freedom to choose doesn't always lead to a choice for freedom.

My name is Dr. Emily Isabella Grace. I am 33 years old. I once stood on these cliffs and gazed across these waters. I might be the last remaining member of the human race. Does anyone even care?

Emily removes all her clothing and lies naked with her body stretched across the stone altar. Puffs of serene white clouds float across a deep-blue sky. The sun bathes her skin with its arid warmth. Ocean waves crash along the rocky shoreline hundreds of feet below—whispering her name. Seducing winds call to her spirit. Gulls serenade and celebrate her. Warm breezes caress her skin like the adoring hand of a lover. Her heartbeat is calm. Her breaths mimic the rhythm of her heart's echoes. Tranquility fills her spirit. She sits upright and stares into a blazing sunset, watching its leisurely descent, heralding the death of another day. Its life-giving light is snuffed out as it dips below the horizon. With its final breath, it explodes into warm glorious hues.

"Into your hands, God...I've given you my prayers. I have yet to hear your voice respond to my tears. I have no tears left to cry. No heart left to break. Please reach out your hands and receive my spirit...Forgive me."

She stands, facing the remnants of the sunset. Her toes curl over the cliff's edge, gripping the gritty sand and rock. She raises her arms to the heavens, closes her eyes, and inhales. She lets go and allows her body to fall forward. Wind rushes past her, flowing through her hair and filling her nostrils with exhilaration. The world is hushed until her body plunges. Plunges deep and silent. Blue turns to indigo. Flickering beams of turquoise fade away. Her lungs extend with burning saltwater.

Daddy? Are you really here with me? Can I go with you now?

"Darlin', I never left ya. I've always been right here, my little Biscuit-Cakes. I've been watching over ya and feeling so dang proud of the strong young woman you've become. Pleased to see ya climb back in a saddle again. I want to ask you something, Cakes. Can ya show me your dance? The one I missed at your recital? Dance for me one more time, my precious baby girl. Daddy loves you with all his heart and soul. Nuthin' in Hell or on Earth can ever separate my love from you."

Daddy? Daddy, don't go. Come back...Daddy, come back. Please...don't leave me here alone. I need you. I've missed you so much.

Blinding light cradles her spirit like a blanket and bathes her with waves of loving warmth.

35

THE ILLUSION OF DEATH

The space she occupies is suffocating. Her lungs blister from gasping saltwater. She's trapped. Her body shudders and spasms. Agonizing cramps ripple through her legs and arms. Emily's eyes cannot penetrate the fog that encompasses her. Her legs kick and her arms flail and her heart races. *Where am I? Help me! Help me, please! God, please save me!*

A dazzling white light bursts into shimmering colors. The swoosh of a vacuum dissipates the fog. Warmth rushes over her body like a summer breeze. She can breathe again. Her heart rate slows. The spasms fade to quivers. Her body relaxes. *Thank you, God. I'm ready to go with you now.* A familiar voice penetrates the peaceful brilliance.

"Emily. Just relax, Mija. Your body rejected the antifreeze thirty minutes into the process. You're going to be fine. We will restart the procedure and slow the feed this time. Just breathe in and out. Slow and easy. That's it. Very good. It's just a minor setback."

She chokes, then coughs, forcing shrills and garbled words through her voice box. "No. Oh my God. Eduardo. Get me out of here. Please. I've changed my mind. I don't want to do this anymore."

Eduardo shuts down the system. He glances at the technician. "Help me lift her out of here."

Emily collapses into Eduardo's arms. Her body quivers and shakes. She whimpers. Eduardo wraps a thermal blanket around her near-naked body and guides her onto a small hospital bed.

"I've changed my mind, Eduardo. I want to go through therapy...I want to fight my cancer, and I want my life back."

"Gracias a Dios! I'm so happy to hear you say that, Chica. We can beat this. Together we *will* beat this. Anything you need, just say the word. I'm always here for you."

***

Two months pass. Emily absorbs the aesthetics of the Arizona sunrise from the window of her Chevy pickup. Blazing reds, oranges, and purples splash against a backdrop of pastel blue sky with a single stroke of the Creator's nurturing hand. Emily now grasps its beauty and significance for the first time in her life.

Emily entered cancer treatment. She instructed the surgical team on removing an ATRT tumor similar to hers. Her advanced knowledge of neurosurgery and her profound understanding of the once-hidden processes and functions of the human brain baffled the surgeons. When they performed the first MRI scan of her brain and spinal cord, they discovered the tumor and her cancer to be gone. There was no evidence it ever existed. They did, however, notice a tiny implant in the hippocampus of her brain.

She no longer questions the paradox or the mystery of her intimate understanding of neurology. Dr. Emily Grace is credited with a new technique in removing these types of ATRT masses, *The Procedure of Grace.*

Her appointment months ago with Mr. and Mrs. Carson runs through her mind. A sense of bittersweet sadness fills her spirit. A twinge tickles her insides as she awaits today's follow-up meeting with the Carson family. How will it feel seeing little Kyler's sweet aquamarine eyes blinking at her?

"Mr. and Mrs. Carson. So glad to see you both. Please come in and have a seat."

Two-year-old Kyler's eyes penetrate her heart with their innocent beauty. His smile is as shy as she remembers. She glances at Mrs. Carson and extends her arms.

"May I?"

"Of course, Dr. Grace."

She squeezes Kyler. She glances towards the ceiling to stem the flow of welling emotion.

"Can I hold him for a few more moments?"

Mrs. Carson raises an eyebrow and hesitates. "Uh...sure. He seems to be very fond of you. He doesn't normally go with strangers. I've never seen him do that before."

"Please have a seat, Mr. and Mrs. Carson. Let's talk about little Kyler. Have you both decided on how you would like to proceed?

"Yes. We have. And thank you, again, Dr. Grace for seeing us. My husband Jeremy and I want to take you up on your offer. We'd like to enter Kyler into the Promise of Lazarus program. We'd like to tour the facility and have you show us what to expect."

"Mrs. Carson? Mr. Carson? I appreciate and respect your decision to enter Kyler into our program."

She glances at Kyler and hands him over to his mother.

"I have an alternative option to propose to you both. Kyler has a good twelve to thirteen years of life left to live. These are precious years. Years he can get to know and love his parents. Years you both can pour your hearts into. There is no guarantee HGPS will have a cure in the next decade or even the next century. But research is promising, and maybe...just maybe, they will find a cure to extend his life and his time with you. This might allow him to get to know his baby sister."

The Carsons glance at one other. Mrs. Carson raises an eyebrow. Her lips part, but she hesitates to speak. Her smile is crooked and slight.

"Well...um, Dr. Grace, Kyler doesn't have a baby sister. I-I mean we plan on having another baby, but Kyler is our only child."

"Oh, I meant figuratively speaking...ya know...if he *had* a baby sister at some point...it would be great for him to have a relationship with her."

Mrs. Carson takes Mr. Carson's hand into hers. "What do you think, Jeremy?"

"You know what I think. I never liked this idea. I don't want our son waking up decades from now...all alone...with no family. The thought scares the hell out of me."

"You're right, Mr. Carson. There is a possibility Kyler could be awakened and cured long after you both have passed. The idea is difficult to rationalize."

Mrs. Carson sighs. "Thank you, Dr. Grace, for your honesty. I think we'll take our son home and take more time to consider your suggestion. It seems like we still have a lot to discuss before we make our final decision."

"Yes. I think that is a wonderful plan. And please don't hesitate to contact me...for any reason at all. I've grown attached to my little buddy, Kyler. I hope this doesn't come across as odd, but do you think I could visit him from time to time? You know, to check on his HGPS and see how he's doing? Maybe update you both on breakthroughs in research...if you don't mind. Completely on my own time, of course, and outside of these walls."

"Um...sure. We appreciate your interest in his welfare. I think that would be fine. Can I ask what changed your mind about, Kyler?"

"The advice of an old friend. It's complicated."

***

She leaves state route 87 and turns East onto highway 260. She opens her windows, allowing the wind to toss her long chestnut hair around, blasting the radio set to a station that plays classic hits from the 1980s. The fresh scent of pine fills the cab. Brandon had a change of heart and wanted to try to make their marriage work. He begged to come home and promised to start a family with her. The relationship with his young girlfriend didn't work out so well. It was far too easy for Emily to say, "hell no." If she'd ever had feelings for him, they had departed her heart long ago. She warned him not to drive so recklessly in that damn red Ferrari. He didn't listen.

She turns off of highway 260 and enters Rim Road, headed North. The pine forests are thick and abundant. A small group of whitetail deer lopes across the road in front of her. She pulls into a familiar overlook and parks. She steps out of her pickup and gazes over miles of land stretched out across Phoenix and the Valley of the Sun. Tears stream down her cheeks.

"I see the entire picture now, Travis. You taught me to understand all the pieces. You helped me to say goodbye to Daddy. I will be forever in your debt, my old friend. My love."

She continues along Rim Road towards Woods Canyon Lake. Forty-five minutes later, she pulls into the driveway of a familiar ranch house. It comes into view like a painting from a faraway dream. Emily steps out of her Chevy and straightens her jeans. She braids her hair and places a brand-new straw cowboy hat atop her head. Heaving a breath, she walks towards the front door.

"Oh, hi, Emily. It's so great to see you. Dang. You are looking smoking hot, cowgirl. Are you ready for your ride today? My little man, Sage, has Blondie all saddled up for you and ready to go. I think he wants to join you on your ride."

"Thank you, Cheyenne. And where is my handsome young guide?"

"He's waiting for you inside the stables. He's very excited about your visit. Have a pleasant ride. I'll have lunch ready for the two of you when you return."

She strolls into the stables and places her hands on her hips. "Hey, Sage, I'm ready to go, cowboy. Like my new hat? It's a Resistol. An authentic George Strait."

Sage's dimples outline his crooked smile. Travis's smile. "Yes, ma'am. That's a darn fancy hat. Can I come along? We can race across the field again today."

"Of course, you can. You deserve a rematch. Don't expect any mercy, though. When I'm done whipping your little behind, I'll be ready for some of your mama's amazing fry bread and beans."

Sage's eyes fixate toward the stable entrance. "Hey, Uncle Bo! You wanna ride with us?"

Uncle Bo? She turns and faces a young cowboy striding towards her.

"*This*...is your uncle Bo?

"Yes'm. He's two years younger than my daddy."

Bo removes his hat and extends his hand. His resemblance to Travis is uncanny, except his eyes are hazel and his hair a sandy blonde. He's thinner and taller. *But oh my God.*

"Pleasure to meet you, Dr. Grace. Sage and Cheyenne have told me nuthin' but nice things about ya, ma'am."

A rush of warmth flushes over her chest and neck. She takes his hand in a very firm but gentle handshake.

"I...um...am very glad to meet you, Bo. So, do you and Travis go to the same hairstylist?"

"Uh, what?"

"Never mind. Would you like to join us on our ride, Bo?"

His face flushes. He lowers his eyes. Dimples form on his cheeks, just like his older brother. The genes for dimples are strong in this family. *He's a shy guy, I suspect.*

"Well? You gonna cowboy up or just stand there like a big ole pussy?"

He grins and chuckles. "Give me a few minutes to saddle up, gal. I can't be having ya calling me a pussy, now can I?"

***

February 13, 2022. Today is the day of Travis's transport to the Institute. They will process him into the Promise of Lazarus program. Emily's appointment with Major Benson is set for 1400 hours sharp. She has five minutes to reach the conference room. Clipboard in hand, her heels tap the tiled floor in quickstep rhythm. Major Benson rises as she enters the room. His kelly-green uniform is crisp. Colorful ribbons cover the area above his left pocket. Salt and pepper hair is trimmed in his usual crew cut. His piercing dark eyes squint in her direction. He's over six feet tall, and his presence is intimidating.

"Ah, Dr. Grace. It's a pleasure to meet you in person and put a face to a name. I have all the paperwork ready for Master Sergeant

McCallister, and here is the check from Uncle Sam covering all the costs."

She sits across from the major and crosses her legs. Major Benson slides a stack of manilla folders across the table towards her. Emily shuffles through each document, scanning and reading the diagnosis and condition of Travis's injuries. She closes the folders and glares at him, tapping the folders with the nail of her index finger. The tapping causes Major Benson's left eye to twitch.

"Major Benson. Master Sergeant McCallister's wounds and his condition are treatable. I can save him. As you know, I am a skilled neurosurgeon, and they have credited me with several new and innovative surgical procedures. I would like the chance to operate on the Master Sergeant before we consider enrolling him in the Promise of Lazarus program. May I have your permission to do so, sir?"

Benson sits back in his chair. His eyes widen, and he strokes his chin.

"Dr. Grace, Master Sergeant McCallister's prognosis is fatal. Our finest doctors and neurologists informed me that his condition is not recoverable."

"It is now. I can perform the procedure to remove the shrapnel and save his life. Would you deny him that chance? He has a wife and son waiting for him at home. How would you feel if you were in his position? Would you want to be taken away from your family by no choice of your own? Wouldn't you risk your own life to be with your family? Or how about just the opportunity to make your own decision?"

"Well, I...I suppose I'd want to take that chance if it were me... Dr. Grace."

"Good. Then we agree. Just sign here, and we will take him into surgery immediately."

Major Benson crosses his arms and smirks.

"Entering Master Sergeant McCallister into the Promise of Lazarus program has more implications than merely saving his life for the future, Dr. Grace. He is the property of the United States Army. We need his skills and expertise, even if it means sending him into the future to use them. I appreciate your desire to save his life, but the decision has been made by an authority greater than mine. Good luck to you, Doctor."

"What the hell do you mean? You have no right. He's a disabled veteran and entitled to be honorably discharged from service. He served his country well, Major. I can cure him and reunite him with his family. He has a wife and son waiting for him at home. Do you understand that?"

"Another good reason to put him into suspended animation. He's a soldier. He'll understand and follow orders."

"The hell he will. That's a crock, and you know it. He isn't coherent. How can he follow an order?"

"It doesn't matter, Doctor. He's being processed into the program as we speak. It's too late. You'll have to move on to your next patient. Why are you so invested in Master Sergeant McCallister, anyway?"

She snatches her documents and storms out of the conference room and rushes to the lab.

***

"Where is he?"

"Dr. Grace? Where's who?"

"McCallister. Travis McCallister. Where's he being processed? Which lab room?"

"Um...the schedule says Lab Number18."

She bursts into Lab 18, startling the three technicians preparing Travis for cryonic sleep.

"Stop what you're doing. I need to check on this patient before we can proceed."

"But Dr. Grace, he's prepped and ready to go under. We have instructions from Dr. Diaz to complete the process."

"Who's in charge of this project? Me or Dr. Diaz?"

"Well, you are, but Dr. Diaz is in charge of the department."

"Okay. You three let me worry about Dr. Diaz. You work for me. If you value your jobs here at the Institute, then step aside and let me do my job. Now!"

"Yes, ma'am."

Ugh, Travis, I have to get you out of here and into surgery.

She deactivates the neuropod and slides him onto a gurney. She covers him with a sheet and rolls him out the door. *Ugh. Major Benson. Shit.*

"Dr. Diaz, please have your employee step away from the Master Sergeant. McCallister is 'government issue.' He is our property. I need to ensure we enter him into the cryonic program, and I intend to do so. I'll have Dr. Grace detained if it comes to that."

"Emily. You need to step aside. We cannot interfere with government business. Please."

"You don't understand, Eduardo. I can save this man's life. He doesn't need to enter the Promise of Lazarus program. I need to operate on him immediately, and I already explained everything to the major. He doesn't care."

"I'm sorry, Emily. Please step aside, or I'll have to call security and have you restrained. Please don't force my hand. We have no choice here."

"Oh God. You people. You're all the same. Fine."

She stomps toward her office, bumping into Benson on purpose and pushing past him.

What am I going to do? I can't allow this. I won't allow this.

***

12:37 a.m. She sits upright on a tiny vinyl sofa in the lobby of her office. She peers out her office door. The hallway is dim and quiet. She slips into the hallway and closes the door to her office. She slinks along the walls and shadows and enters the lab. Travis lies suspended in catatonic animation. His skin is bluish with patches of pink. Her heart sinks. Memories of pulling his frozen body from the ocean flash through her mind. She sighs.

Emily initiates the data screen to his neuropod. It has been over six and a half hours since they suspended him. She initiates the resuscitation process. *Thirty minutes, Travis, and I'll have you out of here.* She paces and peers out the door, scanning the hallways for any sign of movement.

"Time." Emily opens the neuropod with a whoosh, releasing frosty steam into the air. She transfers his body to a gurney and covers him with a sheet. She takes hold of his right arm and injects him with a hypodermic needle.

"Sleep tight, Travis. This will all be over soon."

Emily pushes him along a desolate hallway and rolls him into an elevator. She taps the button for the surgical floor and holds her breath while closing her eyes. She cradles his hand inside hers. *I wish you could talk me through this, Travis. Or maybe hold me like one of your goats.*

The gurney arrives at Operating Room number three.

***

Four hours of surgery was exhausting. Emily's brilliant mind and her delicate hand removed every bit of shrapnel from Travis's brain. She reconstructed his face back together and there is a good chance his scar won't be as prominent as she remembers. His leg couldn't be saved, but he'll do just fine with a prosthetic. He's been resting well and recovering fast.

"Master Sergeant McCallister? Can you hear me? My name is Dr. Emily Grace. You can call me *Doc*. I'm your surgeon. You're going to be fine, Travis. Your surgery was a success. You'll be going home very soon to your family."

Travis glances at her with glossy eyes and grins. *Oh, God.* There are those dimples she fell in love with. His eyes crisscross and close. "Thank you, Doc."

The sound of his voice grips her heart with a bittersweet twinge. She wants to hug his neck and crawl into his bed with him. This new gift she has acquired has given him his life back instead of sentencing him to a distant and lonely future. Soon he will go home to Cheyenne and Sage. He'll never know the love they shared or the trials they endured together. She can never tell him their story—not that he'd believe her, anyway. She isn't convinced any of it happened herself. Time is a paradox and reality an enigma. We may never resolve or comprehend either concept. We can only reconcile them through faith.

Emily wheels him into her office. "I'm going to dress you, Travis. Then I'm going to take you home. Do you understand?"

He nods. His eyes focus, then close.

She helps him into a wheelchair and wheels him into the main elevator. Her toe taps the floor while she mutters a random '80s tune, waiting for the ding to signal the end of the ride.

She heaves a breath and pushes his wheelchair out of the elevator door into the lobby.

"Dr. Grace? You working late again?"

"Uh...yeah, Lawrence. I have to take this poor guy across the street for some testing. He came out of his sleep prematurely. I'll be right back. Leave the light on for me, will ya?"

"You're one crazy doctor. Don't you ever sleep?"

"No. I try not to. Too much to do, Lawrence. Way too much to do."

She moves with purpose, wheeling Travis into the parking garage and parking his wheelchair next to her car.

"Okay, Travis. I need your help here, buddy. Get in there. My God, you're heavy. That's good. I'm going to fasten you in, okay? Nod if you understand what I'm saying. Good man."

Her tires screech exiting the garage. She speeds off into the night, headed for home.

***

"Good morning, Master Sergeant McCallister. Can I call you Travis? Do you remember who I am?"

"Hey...yeah, Doc. Where am I?"

"Here, I made you an omelet. Mushrooms, green peppers, anchovies, and jack cheese."

"Huh? Now, how did you know this is how I eat my omelets? Are you a psycho fortune teller or something? What kind of doctor did you say you were?"

"Did you mean to say *psychic*? I'm probably more of a psycho, but... just a lucky guess. I'm a neurosurgeon, Travis. Eat up. As soon as you're finished, we need to have a serious talk."

"This is damn good, Doc. Thank you. Go ahead and talk. I'm listening. I'd love to know what the hell is going on...I-I don't recall much of anything."

"Travis, it's kind of a long story. Well, it's a very long story. But I'm going to give you the shortened version and explain the reason you are here, your condition, the surgery I performed to save your life, and the insane bull crap the United States Army is trying to pull. More specifically, a certain major named Benson."

***

"Hey, Dr. Grace. Dr. Diaz is requesting your presence in a meeting with that scary Army major who was here the other day. He wants to see you in his office right away. He sounded a little agitated."

She sighs. "Thank you, Samantha. Whew. Not looking forward to this. Wish me luck. I'm going to need it."

Eduardo's face is flushed; his eyes are wide and blinking. Major Benson rises the moment she enters the office. A cocky smirk forms across his face. An MP stands stone-faced and at attention in the back corner of the room. *Probably here to arrest somebody. Gee, I wonder who?*

"Have a seat, Emily. Please. Major Benson has informed me that Master Sergeant McCallister is missing. Would you happen to know his whereabouts? Please tell me you're not involved."

"I'm afraid I *am* involved, Eduardo. I'm guilty of wheeling Master Sergeant McCallister into the O.R. and saving his life just the way I said I would. He's safe and recovering well. He sends his regards, Major."

"Aye, Emily. Why? Why would you do that?"

Benson grins and folds his arms. "Sergeant. Take Dr. Grace into custody, please."

She glances at Eduardo. "Can he do that? Arrest me? I'm a civilian."

"Yes, Emily. This is technically a military-run operation now, and you are on government property."

"Okay. Hold on a minute, Sergeant. I'm allowed one phone call, correct?"

"What are you trying to pull, Dr. Grace? Detain her, Sergeant. That's an order."

She peeks her head out of Eduardo's office.

"Has my guest arrived yet, Samantha?"

"Yes, Dr. Grace. He certainly has. Should I send him in?"

"Oh, please do."

"Eduardo. Major Benson. Sarge. Please allow me to introduce you to General Richard McCallister. I'm pretty sure he has a few questions for you regarding his nephew. General? You have the floor, sir."

Major Benson and the sergeant stand at attention.

"At ease, Major. Sergeant. Please, sit. It's come to my attention that my nephew, Master Sergeant Travis McCallister was being held against his will, Major. The Master Sergeant is a disabled vet and is scheduled for an honorable discharge at the end of the month. I would appreciate you explaining to me why he is being processed into a cryonics program here at this institute without his consent or my knowledge. I would have appreciated a simple phone call."

Eduardo beams. He glances at Emily and shakes his head, then shoos her away. "Yes. Please explain everything to the general, Major Benson. I never quite understood the details myself. I recall you mentioning to me it was *top secret* and that I didn't have a *need to know*."

Emily smirks at Major Benson. "Well, I can see you all have a lot to talk about and catch up on. I'm just going to meander back down the hallway here...and go back to work if that's okay with everyone. Major? Have a great day."

Eduardo chuckles and nods. "Mujer loca."

***

Emily taps on the doorjamb to Eduardo's office.

"The door is open, chica. Come on in. Sit. We have much to discuss."

"Eduardo, I just want to thank you for everything. For rescuing me from myself and for always helping me."

"Why do I feel like you're trying to say adios to me, Mija? Don't tell me you're leaving us."

Warm tears well and trickle along her cheeks.

"I am, mi amigo. You've been like a papa to me at times. A loyal friend to me at other times. Sometimes a real pain in my ass. I have a feeling if I ever needed you to secure my future, you would take great care in setting me up with everything I could ever need. Except for your taste in apartments, maybe.

"I am going to leave the Promise of Lazarus program and the Institute. I'm going to devote my time and energy to my private practice and to finding cures for the incurable—to allow people to live their lives in the present with their families. Not lost in some future reality all by themselves."

"Without you, there is no Promise of Lazarus program. We'd have to shut it down. Is this what you want?"

She wipes away her tears and laughs. "Yes. It's what I want."

36

THE HOMECOMING

Travis is being released today. His surgery and discharge are confidential, and his family believes he is still serving in Syria on a top-secret mission. The honorable discharge came through last week, and the Institute is releasing him to Emily's care today. She will brief him, out-process him from the Institute, and drive him home. The biggest test of unconditional love is the ability to sacrifice your own heart and desires for the heart and desires of another. She isn't sure how she will measure up to the *biggest test*.

"Master Sergeant McCallister? May I call you, Travis, sir?"

"Yes, ma'am. You can call me anything you like. Call me Travis. Call me Mac."

"I'm not calling you Mac. Sounds too much like *Big Mac Daddy*. I'll stick with Travis."

"*Big Mac Daddy*. Now that's clever. You come up with that yourself? I like it. Has a nice feel to it."

She pauses and blinks. "Well...apparently, I must have." She shakes her head and sighs.

"Suit yourself, Doc. Call me whatever blows your skirt up. I want to thank you for patching me up. I am forever in your debt, and if there is anything I can do to repay you..."

"You already have, Travis. Many times, over. You'll just have to trust me on that. Are you ready to go home to your family?"

He squints and cocks his head, then presses his tongue against his cheek.

"Are you sure we've never met before, Doc?"

Her heart flutters. An ache hovers at the base of her throat. Her mind screams to tell him everything.

"No. No, Travis. We've never met. I don't think I'd forget a character like you anytime soon. Or a cowboy like you."

"Cowboy? What makes ya think I'm a cowboy?"

"Intuition. Your John Wayne strut. Or maybe that raspy Sam Elliott drawl that gives you away. I have to confess that I've been riding horses out at your ranch, and I've met your wife, Cheyenne, and your son, Sage. I wanted to meet them before I brought you home. You have a beautiful ranch and an amazing family. A wonderful life to go back to. You're a very lucky man. Well, Mr. McCallister, let's take you home. I'll drive."

***

"I'm beginning to like you more and more, Doc. You drive a Chevy pickup. You ride horses. Hey, I gotta ask, are ya single?"

"You just hold that thought there, Cupid. I'm not ready to meet anybody right now if that's where this conversation is headed. Let's just say I'm not in a good place at the moment."

"Ah. An old love still gotta grip on your heart, huh? Well, he must be one special kind of hombre."

"Oh, he is. One of the kindest, most considerate, and bravest men I've ever known. Also, the biggest pain in my ass. He taught me about life, Travis, and gave me something more precious than diamonds. He taught me that sometimes a person has to do the wrong thing to make a difference in the world. And he opened my eyes to what is important in life and love. I know it sounds trite, and maybe a bit corny but..."

"Hm. This *is* a man we're talking about, right?"

She scoffs and slaps his shoulder. "You have no idea."

***

Emily's tummy flutters, and the tips of her fingers tingle as they roll to a stop in front of the driveway of his ranch house.

Her breathing turns shallow, and her heart is pounding into her throat. Her arms want to hold him and never let go. *I don't think I can do this. I'm going to throw up.*

"Doc? You, okay? The air is a bit thin up here. Breathe deep and slow. That's it. Here, let me try something..."

"No. I'm not a goat. I'm all right. I'm ready now. Let's go."

Emily trails behind him as he lumbers and limps towards the front door. She pauses and lingers in the yard, her arms crossed. She bites into her lower lip, anticipating her heartbreak and her elation at Travis's reunion with his family.

The curtains flutter. Cheyenne's face peeks through the glass window. The front door flies open, slamming against the porch wall. Cheyenne cries out and jumps off the porch, and dashes towards him. She leaps into his arms, wrapping her legs around his waist and burying her face into his chest.

"Daddy!" Sage sprints from the stables. Emily's tears blur the endearing scene. It plays out before her like a homemade movie reel. Her heart thumps in rhythm with her sobs. This is real. She has reunited a family. Not with promises of hope, but with unselfish, unconditional love. Love in its purest form. This isn't *playing* God. This is *understanding* the true nature of God.

Travis turns and points at her. Cheyenne's eyes meet hers. She mouths, "Thank you. Thank you so much."

Bo rides up and dismounts his horse. The two brothers embrace with a powerful hug, slapping each other on the back and roaring with laughter. Travis glances her way and waves.

"Doc! I want you to meet my little bro, Bo. Come on over here and say hi."

She wipes moisture from her eyes then folds her arms as she strolls towards the two brothers. The family resemblance is uncanny. They even speak with the same inflection and tone.

"Hey, Bo. Nice to see you again."

She glances at Travis. "We've already met."

"Well, shit. That's great. Doc, can ya stay for supper?"

"As long as you're not cooking and we're not having mac 'n' cheese. Sure. I'd love to."

"Damn, Travis. She knows you pretty dang good. Ha-ha."

"Call me, Emily, Bo. And *you* may escort me inside, cowboy."

***

Eighteen-Months Later

"Are ya ready, babe?"

She punches his arm. "Don't call me that. You know how I hate it. Call me sweetheart, sweet cheeks, anything but *babe*. Got it?"

"Alright, darlin'. Are ya ready, Mrs. McCallister?"

He takes her by the hand and escorts her as she waddles up the sidewalk towards a weathered red-brick building. They walk hand-in-hand through a glass doorway. The words *Camelback Motherhood Center and Obstetrics* are written across the front of the door.

"I don't know, sweetheart. I-I'm not sure I can do this."

"How about you cowboy up, or something? Don't be such a wuss, Bo. I'm the one doing this, not you. Just keep me company and hold my hand. And tell me how much you love me and how beautiful I am every single day. That's your job. If you want to keep me happy, that is. You do want to keep me happy, right?" She chuckles and punches his arm.

He wraps his arm around her shoulders and rubs her belly.

"I'll love ya every single day for the rest of my life, darlin'. You are the most beautiful gal I've ever laid eyes on. And I'm going to love our son, Kyler McCallister, with all my heart...whenever that boy decides it's time to meet his parents. I know my nephew, Sage, is gonna love having a cousin. And Travis is going to be a darn good uncle."

Emily buries her face into Bo's chest and wraps her arms around his torso.

"Now you're doing everything perfectly. You're going to be an awesome daddy, Bo. And I guess...you're my horse, not Jasper. Or better yet, you're my stallion."

He crinkles his nose and furrows his brow. "What?"

She giggles. "Never mind. Just something a little angel once said to me."

If this is a dream, I never want to awaken from it. If this is my reality, I never want to question it.

Dear diary,

The Theory of Relativity came to Albert Einstein in a dream. Who's to say the world in which we live isn't all just an elaborate illusion of what we decide it should be? Have you ever had a dream that came true? Precognition, it's called. A glimpse into the future, perhaps? Or maybe the result of the mind experiencing time travel while engaged in deep REM sleep. Who can say for sure?

I retained all the knowledge and experiences of my life-changing journey. It turns out my patients didn't dream while under cryonic sleep after all. Instead, they traveled beyond the boundaries of time and space and into an infinite number of possible futures. The secret to time travel isn't a machine or a wormhole. It is the human mind.

The End.